EVER   YOU

D0492285

A MESSAGE FROM CHICKEN HOUSE

I've always loved creating my own worlds full of wonder, imagination . . . and sometimes even the scary things it's hard to face in real life. Because it's just pretend, isn't it? That's what makes it all OK. But in Naomi Gibson's masterful tale of fractured memory, the main character builds a virtual world to hide something very real. Something even she might not be ready to face . . . and things definitely aren't OK!

BARRY CUNNINGHAM
Publisher
Chicken House

NAOMI GIBSON

GAME
OVER
GIRL

Chicken
House

2 Palmer Street, Frome, Somerset BA11 1DS
www.chickenhousebooks.com

Text © Naomi Gibson 2023

First published in Great Britain in 2023
Chicken House
2 Palmer Street
Frome, Somerset BA11 1DS
United Kingdom
www.chickenhousebooks.com

Chicken House/Scholastic Ireland, 89E Lagan Road, Dublin Industrial Estate,
Glasnevin, Dublin D11 HP5F, Republic of Ireland

Cover and interior design by Helen Crawford-White
Typeset by Dorchester Typesetting Group Ltd
Printed and bound in Great Britain by CPI Group (UK) Ltd, Croydon, CR0 4YY

FSC
www.fsc.org
MIX
Paper | Supporting
responsible forestry
FSC® C171272

1 3 5 7 9 10 8 6 4 2

British Library Cataloguing in Publication data available.

ISBN 978-1-913322-02-1
eISBN 978-1-915026-02-6

For Me, Myself & I
WE DID IT!

Also by Naomi Gibson

Every Line of You

The room I enter is built to contain secrets. Bare walls, no windows. An orderly with a neck thicker than a tree trunk indicates to the chair at a table. I slide into it. Across from me, on the other side of the table, is a man who introduces himself as a therapist.

'I've spoken to lots of therapists,' I say.

He smiles. Crow's feet line the corners of his bright blue eyes. 'I'm different, I promise.'

'What do you want?' I fold my arms.

The orderly casts one last look over us, decides I'm not a threat and turns to leave. The door to the room shuts, taking the corridor's noise with it.

'We need to talk, Lola,' the therapist says. 'I need you to tell me how you got here.'

'Why?'

'It might help you. Your case. You want to get out of here, don't you?'

I shift in my seat, run a hand through my greasy hair. 'I'm not sure I deserve to get out of here.'

The therapist frowns. 'Of course you do.'

He has no idea what he's getting into. The doors and windows here, they're locked. Some have bars or cages. Nothing gets in or out, not even the truth. It doesn't matter if I tell him how I ended up here because it will never help me get out.

'Please,' he says. 'I need you to tell me.'

The way he says *need* makes me realize he really does need it. He leans slightly forward, his whole body angled towards me like I might sneeze and it'll come tumbling out and all he has to do is catch it and then he'll know. He has to hear it for himself, what I did. And I have to retell it, otherwise I might forget again.

I've already started forgetting.

ONE

Sometimes, I hallucinate. Small things. Objects or clothes I want that Mother wouldn't buy me. They appear in my room and my imagination welcomes them, accepting that they are mine. Other times, my hallucinations are bigger. I imagine I have a dad. I picture him so strongly – tall, red-haired like me, with aviator sunglasses and a chin cut from a movie – that he becomes real. When I was younger, he'd come to me at night. Kiss me on the forehead and pull my covers up to my chin, flick the light switch and wish me sweet dreams the way Mother never did.

When I got older his gestures became grander. He bought me ice cream from the van that circled our street, ignoring Mother when she said it had too much sugar. In fact, he bought my neighbours ice creams too, including the girl across the road I watched go to school every day. Then we all sat on the stone steps outside my house eating them together, licking it from our forearms when it dripped. Dad leant against the gate and chatted to the other parents. The sun was a halo behind his head.

I don't know if that was a *real* hallucination. More a

daydream that has gathered so much strength it's almost fact. It's carved into my mind in such a way, it might as well be a memory.

One thing I know for sure – something that isn't a hallucination and is a fact as sure as death and taxes – is that Mother is dead and my dad never existed.

A week after Mother died, I was sat in a solicitor's office with my twin sister, Alex. Mr Ratcliffe's office was the kind with a stained carpet and bookshelves crammed with battered textbooks. The early-morning sun entered the room through crooked blinds. Alex took one chair opposite Mr Ratcliffe's desk, and I took the other. The gap between us yawned wider the longer I looked at it, but Alex didn't seem to notice. She sat so perfectly, listening to the solicitor with a straight back and legs crossed at the ankles – exactly how Mother had taught us.

Her hair was shinier than mine.

Alex was Mother's favourite – another thing I definitely did not hallucinate. We were twins, but she'd come first when it really counted – a full minute and twenty seconds – and Alex had made sure she never let up the trend.

'Did you hear what I said, Dolores?' The solicitor peered at me over the top of the letter. He was old, all glasses, and too pragmatic to remember what sympathy is.

'It's Lola,' I said.

'You've got a full scholarship to Leighton Boarding

School.' He laughed, a smack of disbelief. 'Someone up there likes you, love.'

He went back to the letter.

Alex sat with a quiet smile on her face as we learnt Mother had left her her prized Stradivarius violin. And the car. And the house. And everything in it. I half expected her to turn to me and gloat, but it wasn't her style to do it in public.

She'd wait till we got home.

Till the front door was shut.

So like Mother.

A day after that, Alex made me take the train to Leighton, despite having been given the car. She left me on the platform without a goodbye. If Dad was there, he'd have scooped me up bear-hug style, claim our separation was too much to bear, and that he'd changed his mind and I didn't have to go.

Alex didn't even bother to say she'd see me at the weekend. It was a promise we both knew she'd break, so it made sense not to make it.

I sat with a rigid spine the entire journey. My ticket curled in my hot sweaty palm. My stomach lurched every time the train carriage rocked. The man opposite me fell asleep, his flabby neck vibrating with each jostle of the carriage. The idea of sleeping on a train was impossible.

I wondered if Mother had been asleep when it happened to her. Maybe that was why Alex made me take the train. To see if it got me the same way it got her.

'This is all your fault, Lola,' Alex had hissed at me. 'This never would have happened if you'd—'

'Last stop, all change. All change, please.' The train conductor passed through the carriage.

The man opposite me had gone. When?

It had turned dark outside. I looked at the window, to try to peer into the darkness, but all I could see was my reflection.

I was half lost in the dark, half caught in the yellow lights above my head. Eyes as empty as the countryside beyond.

'Dolores Whitmore?' a voice barked.

It belonged to a woman with an expression caught between a scowl and uncertainty.

'Yes?'

The scowl took over. 'Come on, girl. I've been waiting on the platform for ten minutes.' She prised me from my seat with long fingers, grabbed my suitcase from the rack and barged her way back through the doors that tried to close on us as we went through them. 'You're lucky the train wasn't due to leave for forty-five minutes or you could have been on your way back to Grenville.'

She led me to a car and opened the rear passenger door for me.

'I'm the matron at Leighton,' she said. 'All the children call me Matron.'

Matron drove hunched over the wheel, both her hands at twelve o'clock, squinting into a darkness her car lights barely penetrated. She made the engine over-rev. The gearbox scratched when she changed gear. She muttered under her breath until both she and the car relaxed into a more regular rhythm.

Her gaze flicked to me in the rear-view mirror. 'It's very unusual to have someone join us for Upper Sixth. Normally we get an influx of students for Lower Sixth, but never Upper. And certainly not after term has already started.'

I wouldn't be at Leighton at all unless it was strictly necessary. Mr Ratcliffe had made it quite clear there was no one else to take care of me. Alex was in her second year at the Grenville Music Academy and had found someone willing to be her legal guardian.

I had no one.

Matron was still talking. 'But then I saw your file . . . How . . . odd.'

I didn't know I had a file. Mother had home-schooled Alex and me, so it's not like there was one tucked away in a school office somewhere.

Maybe she meant the police file.

I wondered if there were any pictures in it.

Train crash.

Landslide.

'What happened with your mother was in there, of course,' Matron said in confirmation. She squinted at me. 'Odd. Very odd.'

I closed my palms over my kneecaps.

'But a full scholarship to Leighton. What a lucky girl. What subjects have you chosen?'

I didn't choose any of my subjects. The solicitor had handled all the communications with the headmaster, who sent me a quiz to fill out. It had questions like:

```
I regularly compare myself to others
            Yes/No
```

and

```
    I react well to sudden change
            Yes/No
```

'Dolores?' Matron prompted.

'Lola,' I said. 'I prefer Lola.'

'Very well, Lola. What subjects have you chosen for A-Level?'

I'd seen in the prospectus that Leighton's selling point was their small classes. Mr Ratcliffe said he'd put me where they still had space. I recounted to Matron what he'd told me: English Language, English Literature and History, and I'd been enrolled on a Computer Science course for my extracurricular activity, all because I'd scored so highly on the quiz.

'An arts student,' Matron said with a nod that seemed like approval. 'Except for that Computer Science nonsense.'

Matron would have got on well with Mother. A year ago, I'd tried to enrol at a local college for A-Levels. I'd chosen my classes and presented them to her on a card.

She'd looked over the top of it, finger hooked in her pearls and said, 'Computer Science? IT? I think not, Dolores,' and she'd scratched it off with a pen the way she scratched off days from the calendar, counting down to an event known only to her. 'We'll continue with home-schooling.'

'Lola?' Matron said. 'I asked if you had any family left?'

Mother and Alex were best friends. She was given everything. New clothes, pocket money, haircuts at an actual salon. I was given whatever she got bored of, whatever she declared crap and whatever felt cheaply made.

In the dull depths of my mind, a thought crystallized. Matron wasn't asking me questions out of genuine curiosity or because she was trying to make me feel comfortable. She didn't give a shit about any of that. She wanted gossip. To be the first in the staffroom with the info on the new kid with the weird family history. Matron paid more attention to me than the road.

'Family, Lola?'

'A sister,' I said after a moment. She didn't need to know about the dad who lived in my head.

Matron stared at me in the mirror. I turned away from the questions in her eyes.

After a while, the car headlights swept over two bricked gateposts with stone rampant lions adorning the top. They pointed inward, teeth bared as we drove between them. Beyond, a hundred sash windows glittered from a silhouetted mountain of a building. Gravel crunched under our tyres until we stopped outside the entrance.

I got out of the car and took a lungful of countryside air.

'The school was built in 1896,' Matron said, as though she were an estate agent and me a prospective buyer. 'Grade II listed, you know. Mr Leighton has overseen most of the renovations, after the school passed to him from his father, of course. The Leighton dynasty, they call it. Come along, Lola. Gather your suitcase and I'll show you to your room.'

I followed Matron through an entrance hall with panelled walls. Dark oil paintings hung from them: portraits of past headmasters, bowls of half-decayed fruit and women in uncomfortable dresses. Dust gathered in the baroque curls of their frames.

We went up a double-width staircase. Despite Matron's renovation claims, I saw how the floors were scuffed from a thousand pairs of shoes, scratches sealed between layers of wax. Most walls were off-white and stained.

The wheels of my suitcase clacked over the floors as I followed her deeper into Leighton. I was to be roomed in Ashford wing with the other girls. The boys were in Hastings.

My room-mate was already assigned: a girl called Mercedes, but Matron told me nothing else about her. Anxiety clawed at me. What if Mercedes hated me? What if she knew what had happened?

Train crash.

Landslide.

Matron stopped so abruptly I almost barrelled into her. She pushed on a door to our left and a rectangle of light spilt into the room. There was a bay window, two beds either side of it. The furthest one was occupied by a sleeping figure.

Matron took me firmly by the elbow and deposited me on the other side of the door. She closed it between us with a curt, 'Goodnight.'

I blinked, adjusting to the dark. Each side of the room had a desk but only one was personalized. A laptop, some pens and books were spread across it. A noticeboard was taken up with pictures of people I'd never met. Their grins were half-moons in the limited light. A pink feather boa was draped over a mirror on a chest of drawers.

I slinked across the carpet to that feather boa, felt its silky glamour between my fingers. Whoever Mercedes was, she clearly loved make-up. Rows and rows of lipsticks were organized by brand: Mac, Charlotte Tilbury, Jeffree Star. The Charlotte Tilbury lipsticks came in shiny rose-gold tubes and there were more of those than the others. A small maroon box was on the side of the dresser, a business card with a handwritten scrawl on top of another rose-gold lipstick. The note read:

This one is just your colour, darling. Much love XXX

The author had held their pen so heavily they'd indented the card. I stroked a thumb over the words.

Darling. Much love.

X

X

X

A soft snore from the occupied bed made me pause. I waited, my body half turned towards the lipsticks and equally organized range of foundations, but there was no further movement from the bed.

I pocketed the note and wheeled my suitcase quietly over to the empty bed – my bed. Unzipping the case felt overly loud and I couldn't see the contents because it was darker over here. Alex had packed it. Folded everything tightly to save on suitcase real estate, packed my entire life into it so there was no excuse to go back.

It suddenly hit me that I wouldn't be going home ever again. It belonged to Alex now and she'd never let me visit or stay over.

I squeezed my eyes shut. When I opened them, Dad was on the end of my bed. He took off his aviators and gave me a quiet smile. 'This is all a bit new, isn't it?'

I nodded and tried to swallow the rock that had wedged itself into my throat.

If he could touch me, Dad would have wrapped his arm around me and kissed my temple. Instead we sat next to each other on the bed.

'You'll be fine here, Lola. A good night's sleep will set you right,' he said.

I tugged the handwritten card from my pocket and put it against my chest, over my heart. His fingers went to curl around mine, but they passed straight through.

He was gone.

I was alone, accompanied only by the soft snores of a stranger in the bed behind me.

I gave up trying to find a pair of pyjamas. I lay back on the bed, cocooning myself in the covers without getting under them. Sleep took me while I was fully clothed, shoes on, with *Much love XXX* pressed against my heart.

Train crash.

Landslide.

THE PAST

Mummy's laughter shrieked through the room. 'You landed on a snake, Dolores. That means you have to go down. All the way to the bottom, look.' She traced the body of the snake down the board.

'That's not fair,' I said, the injustice of it colouring my voice.

Alex's tiny cheeks puffed with irritation. 'It's perfectly fair,' she said. 'Those are the rules.'

'Exactly, Alex,' Mummy said, petting my sister with her free hand. Her other curled around a martini glass. 'Rules are rules. Down you go, Dolores.' She leant over me, the briny smell of cocktail onions thick on her breath, and moved my counter from the top row all the way down to the first. 'It's a life lesson, darling. Think of it this way: there will always be someone better.'

'Always?'

'Always,' she said, draining her glass. 'And it will always, always be me.'

Alex rolled the dice. She squealed and clapped as her counter landed on the one square that sent her rocketing up a ladder near the finish.

'That's cheating,' I said, though I knew I was wrong.

'Of course it isn't,' she replied, tracing the ladder with her counter and bringing it to a stop three squares from the exit. 'I was clever enough to find it, that's all.'

I stared at the board before me, laden with traps. Mummy watched over it all with victory already in her eyes, and I wondered how I would ever escape.

TWO

I woke to an ache deep in my collarbone. It happened sometimes if I slept on it in the same position for too long. I sat up and rubbed at the lumpy bone I'd come to accept as normal and was suddenly aware of a girl with black skin and silky hair sat on the perfectly made bed opposite mine, eating a packet of Quavers.

'Want one?' she said, offering me the packet.

The inside of my mouth was tacky and foul-tasting. I hadn't brushed my teeth before bed. Her cheesy breath made my stomach clench. Quavers were not the answer.

'No thanks.' I rolled out the ache in my collarbone.

The girl had opened the curtains and the light was too bright, but she didn't seem to notice I wasn't up yet. She was already in her uniform: navy blazer and matching knee-high socks. She wore high heels for school shoes. Her make-up was flawless, which wasn't a shock given the collection I'd seen last night.

For a moment, I saw myself how she must see me: a girl wrapped in school-issue bed sheets, rumpled from a long journey and no shower.

I rubbed my eyes, picked out the crusty bits of sleep

from the corners. 'What time is it?'

'Almost eight,' she said. 'You'd better get a move on if you want anything to eat. Matron will close the breakfast service soon. I'm Mercedes. You're Lola, right?'

I nodded, watching her clean out her Quaver packet with a finger. 'Your uniform's in the wardrobe. I left some hangers in there if you want them. Not much room though. I've not had a room-mate so far this year, kind of got used to it.' She paused. 'You'll be hungry if you don't eat before lessons start. Matron's not the type to sneak you a piece of toast out of sympathy.'

Having met Matron, I agreed. But the ache in my bladder was far more pressing than breakfast. 'Where's the bathroom?'

Mercedes nodded to a door by the wardrobe I hadn't spotted last night. 'En suite, but we share it with Georgie and Arya on the other side. Georgie's a neat freak, so expect notes with passive-aggressive hearts above the i's if you leave anything messy.'

'Like what?'

She threw her crisp packet into the bin. 'Like if you get your hair in the plug, you better believe you're pulling it out when you're done showering. Otherwise Georgie will pick it out for you and leave it on your pillow.' She folded her arms. 'We've been sharing a bathroom for six years now. Ask me how I know.'

'That's gross.'

Even Alex wouldn't have done that. It would involve picking the hair out of the drain in the first place and that would be far too much like cleaning.

I hauled myself out of bed and into the bathroom where the air was hot and wet.

White tiles dominated the floor, emerald-green tiles on the walls. There was a toilet with a wall-mounted tank and a long chain dangling from it. The showerhead over the bath was rusty and the shower curtain looked like it had seen better days, but it was at least clean.

Mercedes wasn't kidding about Georgie's notes. There was already a post-it note on the mirror above the sinks.

> Hey New Girl,
> Don't leave shit stains in my loo and I won't use your toothbrush to clean them off. I _mean_ it.
> Love, Georgina xox

If Alex were here, she would have written 'Fuck you, Georgie' underneath the note and I bet they'd be best friends before second period.

While I peed, I looked around the bathroom. Georgie's things were everywhere. She'd marked her stuff with a labelmaker the way a dog might mark its territory.

'Georgie' was stamped on to the tag of a lime-green shower puff, on bottles of shampoo and skincare, and down the handle of a toothbrush in its own jar which was also labelled up.

I wiped and stood up, fastened my jeans and grabbed the toothbrush. There were no stains down the loo, but I made sure it was cleaned anyway. Got right under the rim

18

the way Mother had taught me to. 'There'll be no limescale in this house,' she'd say. Used to.

'I have your uniform,' Mercedes called through the door. 'Want it?'

I put Georgie's toothbrush back. 'Please.'

Mercedes opened the door a crack and passed me a bundle of clothes. 'It's too late for breakfast,' she said. 'Do you know where you're going? I have Better Than Life first thing. If it's on the way I can take you to wherever you need.'

I had no idea where any of the classrooms were, let alone what lesson I had first. 'What's Better Than Life?'

'A game,' she said. 'Only five of us get to play it because we scored the highest on the quiz.' Mercedes's voice was muffled through the door, but I didn't miss the pride in it.

I recalled the quiz my solicitor had pushed at me while I was in his office. One of the questions flashed through my mind:

I have lots of friends
Yes/No

I wondered how questions like that could translate to playing a game.

I lifted my hoody over my arms and the note I'd borrowed slipped from my bra and on to the tiled floor. I bent to pick it up. Ran a thumb over the three kisses someone had put so casually on to the end of the message. XXX.

Mercedes hadn't even noticed it was gone. She clearly didn't need it. She had so much love she didn't need this one little piece. I stuffed it back into my bra.

'I did a quiz before I came,' I said. 'Maybe it's the same one. I've been put in a Computer Science group because of it, but I don't know what it is.'

'Yep, that's Better Than Life,' Mercedes said. I could almost see her raised eyebrows through the door. 'You'll love it. I'll show you where to go, but hurry up. I don't want to be late.'

I buttoned a shirt and sealed it with a blazer.

Mercedes rapped on the door. 'Come *on*, let's go.'

'I'm ready.' I opened the door and we swapped a double take.

She was smooth, airbrushed and glowy.

I was too pale and too skinny to be considered attractive. Had a haircut dictated by my mother. Shoulders that spoke of carrying baggage, so much baggage.

I pulled the sleeve of my blazer over my left palm to hide the worst of my scars.

Mercedes smiled despite it all. 'Suits you,' she said.

Maybe I didn't look so bad after all. Anyone would look like a train crash in comparison to her.

No, not a train crash. Something else.

Landslide.

Accident.

'Come on.' Mercedes didn't wait for me to catch up as she pulled open the bedroom door.

'What kind of game are we playing?' I asked as we left.

Games had never been my thing. Alex had instructed me early on that to lose was the worst thing in the world and I would never be clever enough to ever beat her.

'The best kind,' Mercedes said. 'The virtual reality kind.'

I pretended to know what she meant as I followed her out.

THREE

The IT labs were out of the main building and down a gravel path. All the other students seemed to materialize from the walls, clogging the corridors and filling the air with laughter and hushed gossip. It was strange being around lots of people. It had only been me, Mother and Alex for so many years. I kept close to Mercedes as she led me back down the double staircase I'd gone up the night before and back through the main entrance hall.

'There's five of us who play,' Mercedes said. 'Six now you're here. That's Finn and Wai.' She indicated two guys walking in the same direction as us. One had way too much gel in his hair and the other was speaking rapid Mandarin into his phone. Finn was talking to a girl with long blonde hair and fake eyelashes. 'You already know Georgie.'

Georgie winked at me as we approached. 'Hey, New Girl. Did you make sure the loo was clean this morning?'

'Absolutely,' I said, and threw her a genuine smile.

'That's my girl. You'll fit in fine here.'

'Ignore Georgie,' Mercedes said loudly as we

approached the building. 'She thinks she owns every-thing.'

Georgie let out a high-pitched laugh. 'Are you jealous, Cedes? Thou shalt not covet!' She put on a lofty voice for that last part, and Mercedes snickered with her.

'Mr Leighton's favourite thing to say,' she explained. 'The headmaster.'

The IT building had grey-framed windows and a flat roof. It was the exact opposite of the main school. The architect had obviously wanted to scream that this was a modern, high-tech, state-of-the-art addition to a school with a history that stretched back further than some family trees.

We passed through double glass doors and lined up against the wall of a classroom.

Wai was at the front of the queue, still talking into his phone. Finn put some earbuds in and closed his eyes as he leant back against the wall.

'Why does it smell funny?' I asked.

'Gym's down there,' Mercedes said, nodding to a set of double doors at the end of the corridor.

As she spoke, the doors swung open and a guy stepped through them. His chestnut-brown hair was styled in that purposefully scruffy way. He strolled towards Finn who took out his earbuds and they fell into an easy conversation.

'That's Sebastian,' Georgie whispered.

'He's the last player,' Mercedes said. 'You can stop gawking now.'

'I wasn't gawking.'

Mercedes rolled her eyes. 'And my skin looks this good without any concealer.'

Georgie sniffed. 'He's all right, I guess. Not really my type, if you know what I mean.'

'You don't have to be straight to appreciate hotness when it smacks you in the face,' Mercedes said. 'I mean *look* at him.'

I could see what she meant. Sebastian looked like he'd stepped out of a TV show. He wore a blazer like everyone else only his looked like it actually fit him. He could have been wearing a three-piece suit. He was relaxed, together, had skin that oozed confidence and skill.

Georgie made a non-committal noise. 'He's Mr Leighton's son,' she said. 'We're supposed to hate him, I guess. You know, because Mr Leighton is so . . . *you know*. But no one does. He's training to be a lacrosse player, but everyone knows it's programming he wants to get into. He's like, a prodigy coder or something and he's—'

'Actually perfect,' Mercedes finished.

'Now who's gawking?' I said.

Georgie laughed. 'I like you, New Girl.'

I was the first to look away from our shared smile. I'd replace her toothbrush as soon as I could.

A teacher with square, black-rimmed glasses appeared from the classroom. 'Morning, team. Let's be having you.' He snatched Wai's phone out of his hands as he trudged past. Wai let out a barrage of protests but the teacher was having none of it. 'You can have it back at the end of the lesson.'

Mercedes and Georgie filed into the room. I was the last in the queue, about to step into the IT lab, when the teacher put an arm out to stop me. 'Woah there. You're the new student? Dolores . . . Whitmore?'

'It's Lola.'

'Lola, right. I'm Mr Yorke. Well, Lola, you need to have a quick introduction to the game with our visiting expert, Dr Zats.' As he spoke, a woman in a lab coat appeared at his side. Her dark hair was tied in a scruffy bun, a pen through the centre of it. She swapped a few words with Mercedes before turning her attention to me.

'Hi, you must be the new participant.'

'Student,' Mr Yorke corrected. 'This is Lola.'

'Great. Well come with me, Lola, and we'll get you set up while the others do their daily quiz.'

She pushed her hands into the deep pockets of her lab coat and waited for me to step forward or at least reply. I stayed silent. People in white coats doled out pills. They injected and dissected and poked and prodded. When I was a baby, Mother said I had more doctors assigned to me than the Queen. I don't remember any of it, but Mother told me about it so regularly her memories have become my own.

You were a sickly baby, Dolores. It didn't matter how long I left you to cry, you went on and on and on until I took you back to the hospital, hoping they would keep you. But you were so determined to survive, weren't you? And they were so determined to help you.'

Doctors meant medicine.

Surgery.

Aftercare that made Mother complain about the constant stream of physiotherapists trampling mud into her hallway. Doctors meant I wasn't normal. Alex never had any doctors.

I traced the puckered scars on my left palm and took a small step back. 'I'm fine here,' I said.

The two teachers swapped a look.

'We need to explain the coursework to you,' Mr Yorke said gently. 'If you want to be part of the group you have to go with Dr Zats.'

I peered through the classroom door and saw Mercedes and Georgie twisted in their seats, laughing with Finn and Sebastian and Wai on the row behind them.

There was an empty seat next to Mercedes.

It could be me filling it in the next lesson.

Dr Zats pulled a small box from her deep pocket and waved it at me. 'You'll get to have one of these,' she said. 'It'll be fun, I promise.'

I studied the box: black, sealed with a sticker which meant it hadn't been opened by anyone else. Hadn't belonged to anyone else. Whatever was in there would be mine and only mine.

I moved forward and Dr Zats put her arm around my shoulders before I could change my mind, guiding me away from the classroom.

'Here you go.' She gave me the box as she led me away.

It was made from a smooth card, one side sealed by a sticker with a logo saying 'SmartTech' on it. I slid a finger under it, relished how it broke away from the box cleanly. Everything about it felt expensive. The packaging. The smell of something new and unused. The folds of matching dark tissue paper inside. I parted them to see a transparent disc the size of my thumbnail.

It was smooth and pliable, could be folded in half before springing back to its original shape.

'Here we are,' Dr Zats said in a sing-song voice.

I looked up, hadn't realized we'd gone so far. The funny smell was stronger in here, old socks and dust. 'The gym?'

'This is where we'll be doing the majority of the experi— coursework.' She indicated the disc I held. 'We call these Keys. They're designed to interface with your nervous system and prefrontal cortex. It connects to you and you become the controller.'

'The controller for what?'

Dr Zats grinned. 'Better Than Life is a virtual reality game we've been developing over at SmartTech. Your job will be to play the game for us. Make suggestions as to how it can be better. You're lucky to be involved.'

She waited, as though I was supposed to have heard of SmartTech or at least of virtual reality. She didn't know how small my world had been and I didn't know how to tell her. I tried to nod along, look like I understood she was doing me a favour.

'You can't play without a Key.' Dr Zats tapped her

temple. 'The temporal bone is the thinnest part of our skulls and conveniently close to lots of nerves for the Key to interact with. If you place it there, the Key will do the rest. Look.'

She took another disc from her pocket, smoothed back her dark hair slightly and placed it against her temple. A blue shimmer shot through the Key's surface and her eyes flashed blue in response. She blinked and it was gone. 'You try. Put yours to your left temple if you're right-handed.'

I raised my Key to the spot between the tip of my eyebrow and where my hairline started. It hadn't even touched my skin before it seemed to jump from my fingers and on to my temple, drawn to it like a magnet. A shiver leapt from my brain all the way to the base of my spine.

'That kind of tingled,' I said, though it came out more of a purr.

'Perfectly normal,' Dr Zats said. 'It's the way it acclimates to your neurophysiology. Would you like to try playing Better Than Life?'

Around me, the waxed floor was marked with multiple lines to spell out football, netball and hockey pitches all at once. Stale sweat and old rubber smells hung in the air like they could never be lifted from it. There was nothing special about the room. I looked to Dr Zats for direction.

'We had to convince the PE department to let us use this space for the whole term,' she said, spinning around as she took it in. 'It's cold and it smells a bit, but it's the best we've got. Right.' She produced a tablet from her pocket Mary Poppins style. 'We're going to do what's known as a shared experience first. I'll control the game, putting you in an environment of my choosing. Ready?'

I had no idea what she was talking about. I nodded anyway.

She tapped at her screen and her Key flashed blue in response.

Quicker than I could draw breath, a wave of static washed across the room. As it moved, plants sprouted in its wake. Tiny shrubs shot up from the floor which was no longer marked by coloured lines. Now it was damp earth, rotting leaves. Leafy bushes erupted from it. Trees hurtled upwards until their tops towered over us. Sunlight spilt through the green canopy like water through a colander.

I staggered backwards, almost fell over a tree root that had appeared from nowhere.

Dr Zats stepped from behind a bush with a smile. 'Welcome to Better Than Life.'

'Woah.' It was exactly like being in a rainforest. How was this possible? Mother never let us have phones or a computer. I had no idea games could be so . . . real. I thought they were played on a screen or involved a controller. This was exactly like *being* there.

There were plants and flowers I'd never seen before. The light was a colour I didn't know it could be. Unseen monkeys called to each other and a snake hissed in the nearby undergrowth.

I sniffed at the air. Old socks and unwashed floors.

'It still smells like the gym.'

I fingered the Key at my temple, feeling its slick surface and wondering how something so small was responsible for something so impressive. Mother had talked about computers like they were cumbersome, old and confusing. This didn't fit with any of that.

'The Key does all this?' I asked, still touching mine. 'Generates the rainforest?'

'That's right,' Dr Zats said. 'Well, technically it's the brain generating everything, but the Key allows you to access it whenever you want, a bit like streaming a TV show, but it also saves any changes you make.'

Streaming a TV show sounded a lot like using the internet, and I'd never been allowed near the internet. 'So this is happening in your head, in your mind?' I asked.

'That's right,' Dr Zats said. 'Kind of like a lucid dream. Have you ever been able to control a dream before?'

She stepped closer to a bush composed of spiky leaves and stared at it without blinking. Seconds later, a fat green rosebud swelled on the end of a stem. The bud split and deep red petals blossomed out of it. She reached around the stem, minding the thorns, and yanked the rose free.

'Never,' I said, and decided to keep quiet about my hallucinations. Lately, they had a mind of their own and that was the total opposite of controlling them.

'This rainforest was the first thing I ever made,' Dr Zats said, still studying the rose. 'I always start with it when I introduce new players to Better Than Life.'

'This is your world?'

Dr Zats nodded. 'Each Key is coded specifically to its user. If I used your Key, I would see whatever you put in your world. I'd never do that by the way – what a gross invasion of privacy *that* would be – but super users like me can share their worlds if they like.' She put the rose to her nose, inhaled deeply, and discarded it a second later. 'We're still working on smells,' she said.

'What's the aim of the game?' I asked, watching the rose disintegrate on the rainforest floor.

'Pure creation.' Dr Zats gestured at the plants around her. 'Try making something – you have to really picture it in your mind and the Key will bring it to life. Start simple, a piece of fruit perhaps. Let's try an apple.'

A is for Apple.

I could hear my speech therapist as she waved a picture card at me. Could see its image in my mind's eye. A light-pink background with a shiny apple on it. Half green, half red, a strip of light reflecting off the waxy skin and a single leaf curling from its stalk.

I looked down and the apple was in my hand.

'OW!' My hand flew to my temple, to my Key. It was as if a needle had jabbed me in the skull. I looked up at Dr Zats in shock. 'What was that?'

She raised an eyebrow. 'Did you create that apple from a memory?'

'Yeah, it's from . . . never mind.' I rubbed my head.

'I was going to tell you, only I didn't think you would

31

need to know for that first exercise. It's unusual that you would ... anyway, you shouldn't create anything from real life. People, or places. Don't recreate things from your memory.'

The apple was exactly how I remembered. It was like it had been lifted from the flash card and put into my hands. I examined the traitorous apple, wondering why such a simple thing could have hurt me so much.

'Why not?' I asked.

Dr Zats plucked a pear from a tree that was definitely not a pear tree. She threw it to me and I dropped my apple to catch it. The skin was pockmarked, slightly furry and rough.

'Using memories to create some things is OK. Textures for example.' She indicated the pear. 'The Key relies on our memories and understanding of the physical world to bring environments and objects to life, like that pear. This rainforest is based on what I think a rainforest would look like, but I've never actually been to one. It's not based on somewhere I know. Never base your environments on places from real life. Never create characters based on real people.'

I dropped the pear and watched it roll away. 'But why?'

'You can make anything you want in the game. Why would you make what you already know? Anyway, we've built in a blocker to stop you from breaking the rules. You can't recreate from real life, even if you wanted to.'

I touched my temple. 'The pain.'

Dr Zats nodded. 'It's Pavlovian conditioning,' she said,

as though that explained everything. 'Pain reinforces the rules so you learn not to break them.'

Mother was always a fan of rules, particularly if it meant she could trap me with them. She'd claim they were for my own good, changing her mind on when she would listen to the doctors if it suited her better.

'No going outside, doctor's orders.'

People got hurt if they didn't follow the rules.

'Did someone get hurt?' I asked. 'Another player?'

'Not so far,' Dr Zats said cheerily. 'Oh, one moment.' She took a phone from her pocket and swiped to accept a call.

I wandered away, minding the vines strung from a low-hanging branch, like tinsel on a Christmas tree. I continued for a few metres, ducking and weaving, stepping over tree roots wider than my waist. Dr Zats was still chatting into her phone, but her voice was less clear this far away. The jungle noises swallowed her conversation until it was little more than background noise.

A section of the rainforest pixelated in the corner of my eye. I turned to it, watched a guy materialize out of the fuzz. He leant back against a tree, the jungle light dappling his chestnut-brown hair.

'You're new,' he said, his oak-coloured gaze sweeping over me. He was mulling me over, as if I was a visitor he hadn't been expecting.

'Sebastian?'

I hadn't made him. There was no pain to tell me I'd brought him into the game. What was he doing here?

Was he even real? I stepped forward, reached out to touch him.

'Lola?' Dr Zats called.

My head snapped her way. When I looked back, Sebastian had gone.

'Sorry about that,' Dr Zats said. 'I've found a coding anomaly recently and the programmers down at Smart-Tech can't seem to ... anyway, did you make anything else while I was busy?'

'I was just looking around.'

'It's impressive, isn't it?' She put her hands in her pockets as she took in the rainforest. A quiet smile lit her face. 'You've probably guessed by now that this is the aim of the assignment. We want you to build an environment of your choosing. Play in it, test it, challenge it. Create characters and interact with them. You'll fill out a quiz every day and discuss what you've made with the rest of the group.' She looked at me a little more seriously. 'We want you to feel safe in the game, Lola. As safe as you feel in real life. At home, for example.'

```
My home is where I feel safest
           Yes/No
```

Dr Zats's phone started ringing again. She glanced at the screen and pulled a face. 'I should take this. We'll leave it there, shall we? There's a rota outside the IT room and I've put you down for more sessions than anyone else so you can catch up. Remember, when you're ready to exit the game, clap your hands and say "Exit". The Key is programmed to understand.'

I clapped. 'Exit!'

A band of static wiped across the rainforest. Shrubs, trees and the green light disappeared, replaced by a dully lit gym. I blinked at the greyness of it all.

Dr Zats waved her goodbye as she swiped to accept her call. I left the gym and went back to the IT lab where Mr Yorke welcomed me and steered me towards the empty seat next to Mercedes. She smiled as I sat down. 'Welcome to the club,' she said.

She turned to properly introduce me to Finn and Wai. Sebastian's chair was empty.

FOUR

In the afternoon, Mr Leighton summoned me to his office via Matron. It was back in the main building and up a private staircase. The door was thick and the varnish so dark it was almost black. Above it was a hand-carved sign that read *Thou Shalt Not Covet*.

It opened on to a small hallway, the kind with a long skinny rug and a hat stand in one corner. Both looked faded and old. Matron pushed me through another door to the right and left me on my own.

The headmaster's office was occupied with more of the same dark-varnished furniture. There was a ruby-red carpet and bookshelves with books so old their bindings might have fallen apart if a single finger touched them. A man wearing a suit sat behind a desk. Everything about him was a little bit grey: his suit, his hair – except for the hideous orange V-neck beneath his suit jacket.

'Dolores Whitmore, I presume?'

'Mr Leighton.' I hesitated to take the seat he offered.

There was a manila file in front of him, as though he'd just been flipping through it. He slipped it into one of the desk drawers, but not before I saw my name printed along the top.

'I am sorry to hear about what happened,' he said.

People are always sorry if they don't understand.

I decided to stay standing.

I turned my attention to a sideboard on my left, inspected the row of books carefully arranged by height order. An old pocket watch was propped up beside them, lid open to show off the dark Roman numerals printed on to the white face. The minute hand twitched from all the gears clicking beneath it.

Tick, tick, tick.

It was so solidly consistent it could have been used as a metronome.

'My father gave me that,' Mr Leighton said. 'It's been passed from father to son for five generations.' His smile pulled to one side. 'The Leighton dynasty. Do you have any family heirlooms, Miss Whitmore? Perhaps from your own father?'

The only thing Mother had ever passed to me was cocktail recipes. I'd learnt to make a Gibson martini before I learnt to tie my shoelaces. Two and a half ounces of gin (Mother preferred Gordon's), half an ounce of dry vermouth, stir until well combined and strain into a chilled glass with three cocktail onions.

The watch was a much better heirloom than a battered cocktail manual, forgotten as soon as a recipe had been made enough times to remember it by heart.

The watch could be cherished, admired. Gears and cogs could be replaced, ensuring its longevity as it was passed down from father to son alongside the DNA.

It must be amazing to be loved by generations of people who'd never even met you.

'No,' I said. 'No heirlooms. No father.'

Mr Leighton leant back in his chair. 'I want you to feel welcome at Leighton,' he said after a moment. 'Comfortable, even. It is a short year before you'll go off to university. I want you to be happy here before you leave.'

'I am already,' I said, then offered him more when he said nothing. 'I have a nice room-mate.'

This seemed to pacify him. 'Good. That's good.'

I looked again at the watch and imagined trailing a finger over each book on the sideboard.

Mother always said men collected items over the course of their lives, hoarding things to make themselves feel important. They valued their success in terms of how many shiny objects they amassed over the years. Women were more practical, she told me. If something had no use, there was little point in keeping it.

'I'm useful, aren't I, Mummy?'

'That remains to be seen, Dolores.'

'I only have one rule here at Leighton,' Mr Leighton said. 'No coveting. Do you know what I mean by coveting?'

'To want what you don't have?'

'Exactly. It's the worst of the seven deadly sins and I won't tolerate it. Work hard, keep your eyes on your own prize and don't look to your neighbour's success to measure your own.'

He didn't ask me if I agreed. It was clear it was an

order, not an opinion to be debated.

If Dad were here, he would crack a joke or change the subject. He was the kind of person who always knew what to say, always knew how to put someone at ease or defuse a tense situation.

I squeezed my eyes shut and opened them.

Dad relaxed in the chair opposite Mr Leighton's desk, aviators barely covering the glow of his amusement. 'Get a load of this guy,' he said with a snort. 'I wonder if the stick up his arse was handed down alongside the watch.'

I coughed to hide a laugh. 'You have so many books. Which one is your favourite?' I nodded to the bookcase on the far wall, drawing Mr Leighton's eyes away from the sideboard as I slipped his family heirloom up my sleeve.

Mr Leighton thumbed his beard. 'They are all variations of the same thing, so they are all my favourite.'

Now that I was closer, I could see the entire bookcase was stacked with Bibles of varying translations. King James, NIV, The Message, New Testament only, Old Testament only. It went on.

'I have read them all,' he declared. 'It is how I have determined that covetousness is the worst of all sins. The longing. It takes up all the space in your heart until there's no room for anything else. How can God access a heart that is already full?'

'Ah,' Dad said from his chair, drawing his hands behind his head as he assessed the headmaster. 'That's his problem. He didn't sit on a stick. He swallowed a Bible.'

Dad's leather jacket was the complete opposite to an old suit and orange jumper. There couldn't have been much between the two men in age, but Dad felt younger. There was less grey in his hair and his heavy stubble was the type that would never be permitted on the headmaster's face. It was impossible to imagine Mr Leighton in a pair of jeans.

He blinked at me, waiting for my response. I didn't give him one. Too caught up in playing spot the difference.

His watch was cold against my wrist.

Dad swivelled my way and cast me a knowing look over the tops of his aviators. 'Can't say I like the man, Lola, but you shouldn't steal from him. Put it back.'

I hesitated.

The headmaster had a family, a son. An entire empire that was this school and a mountain of books in his own private study. Someone like that didn't need an heirloom. Didn't need confirmation that someone, at some point, had loved him.

Mercedes hadn't noticed her note was missing.

I doubted the headmaster would notice the watch.

Didn't that prove he shouldn't have it?

'It was good to meet you, at last, Dolores,' Mr Leighton said, breaking the silence.

It was a dismissal and I was grateful for it. I flashed him a smile I hoped was convincing and walked quickly to the door. I glanced over my shoulder before I left; Dad was gone.

Out in the corridor with the rug and the hat stand, I

let out a breath. I'd never taken something so brazenly before.

'Hey,' someone said.

I jumped and turned to see Sebastian coming from one of the doors down the hallway.

'You're new,' he said, and I paused. He'd said that in the game. It had definitely been him. If I hadn't created him then Dr Zats must have, but I didn't see her yell out from the pain of recreating someone from real life. Maybe the rules didn't apply to her. Adults had a way of doing that.

'I'm Lola,' I said.

'Sebastian.'

I couldn't help but blush as he took my hand like he was genuinely pleased to meet me. It was a good thing we shook with our right hands. It meant he wouldn't see the scars on my left.

His eyes were level with mine. Mother had always told me I was too tall for a girl, that she was the preferred height for a woman to be. 'Five-six and nothing taller,' she'd say. 'Tall girls are not attractive, Dolores.' Of course, Alex was the same height as me. But she was 'striking' and it would improve her presence on the stage.

The prospect of Sebastian ever finding me pretty was ridiculous, but I slouched a little anyway so he might feel taller in comparison to me.

'What are you doing up here?' I asked. I shifted the family heirloom from my sleeve to my pocket, hoping he didn't see.

'I live here,' he said.

I remembered Georgie and Mercedes telling me he was Mr Leighton's son. 'You don't have a room in Hastings with the other boys?' I asked.

'Nope. This is home sweet home. I have my own room and don't have to share with anyone else. Lucky me, right?' The way he said it sounded like he didn't think he was lucky at all.

It was obvious now that I thought about it. This was so out of the way, up a private staircase and at the back of the school. This was a self-contained flat within the building.

Sebastian cast me a sideways glance. 'What are *you* doing here?'

'Mr Leighton wanted to see me.'

He grimaced. 'Lucky you. Shall we?' He held the door open for me and we trooped back down the staircase together. 'You must be the only student David's ever invited up to his private study,' he said when we reached the bottom.

It took me a moment to realize he was talking about Mr Leighton. I'd never met someone who called their parents by their first name. Mother would have freaked if I called her Helena.

'That's not his regular office?'

'No. He has one up near the main entrance, that's where he usually sees parents and students.' He was looking at me the same way he had in the game, like he was mulling me over. 'You must have done something bad to get invited up there.'

'I haven't, I swear.'

Sebastian arched an eyebrow. 'It was a joke, Lola.'

'Right.' I tucked my hair behind my ear. 'So is your mum a teacher at the school, too?'

'No. She died when I was little.'

I blinked at the news. People were supposed to apologize when they heard things like that. *I'm so sorry about your mother*. It was the correct thing to say but the words wouldn't come. It was as if I were four again, sitting in front of that speech therapist pushing flash cards into my face and mouthing the words at me with vigour.

A is for Apple.

B is for Bank.

C is for Crash.

Landslide. Death.

'Are you OK?' I said instead.

He shrugged.

'My mum also . . .' I trailed off. 'I mean, that's how I ended up here. At Leighton.'

'I get it,' he said. 'I saw you outside the IT labs this morning. You were enrolled in the game?'

I nodded. 'I have my first proper session later.'

His teeth flashed in a smile. 'I love it. If you ever need any help, let me know. We have to stick together.'

'We do?'

'Of course. There's only five of us playing – six now. But you and me, we're the same, aren't we? So we really have to stick together.'

Sebastian left me when the bell rang. He had PE and I lied and said I had English Lit. I had no idea what my next lesson was – I was still without a timetable and I had no clue how to get to any of my lessons anyway.

When he was gone, I hid beneath the staircase and took the watch from my pocket. Each tick reverberated through the case like a tiny heartbeat. Solid as a metronome.

Tick.

Tick.

Tick.

I covered my ears but the ticks continued. A scream echoed in my mind. Deep in my brain. Ingrained in my memory.

Tick.

Tick.

Tick.

It was a landslide. The train derailed. That's what got her.

I needed to talk to Alex. She'd confirm it.

FIVE

Matron's office was right above the school entrance, perched like a crow ready to swoop on anything that came through the doors. I knocked and waited. Matron opened it and presented me the widest, fakest smile I've ever seen.

'Lola, how lovely. How was your first visit with Mr Leighton?'

'Hi. Fine.'

'He's a good man, that Mr Leighton,' Matron said. 'Saintlike, some say. The way he took in that boy. Took in all the children, really ...'

I wondered if she meant Sebastian and wanted to ask more, but Matron fixed her gaze on me in a silent question. She obviously didn't get many visitors. 'I wondered if I could use the phone please?' I asked.

It took her a moment to process the question, and me an internal struggle not to blush. None of the other students ever needed to borrow a phone.

'Of course. Come in, come in. The administrator's on holiday today, he won't mind if you use his desk phone.'

She ushered me in and sat me down at the nearest of

two desks. Someone's family grinned at me from several frames I wanted to throw across the room.

'I'll be at my desk if you need me.' She moved to the far side of the room and busied herself at her computer. She tapped at her keyboard in such a way that told me she typed with her index fingers. There were less than three metres between us.

Not exactly private then.

I lifted the receiver of the yellowing desk phone and waited. I was about to hang up when she finally answered.

'Yes?'

'Alex?'

There was silence for a moment. 'Lola.'

Over the phone, my sister sounded like Mother. Only there was a difference. In that one word, not even a greeting, I could tell she was angry. Mother was never angry. Mother was a constant barrage of indifference and elitism all rolled into one sarcastic ball. Alex was only eighty seconds older than me. She hadn't yet learnt how to control her temper the way Mother did, but she could still sharpen her words into knife points.

'What do you want?' she prompted.

I turned away from Matron, but I couldn't get away from her tapping or the click of her mouse, her quiet breaths. This was a mistake.

'I, um . . .' I cleared my throat. 'Wanted to see how you were.'

'Really.'

Even down the phone, Alex's voice gave me a chill.

'If you really want to know, I've been packing the house. The solicitor advised I'll have to sell it because I can't afford the mortgage payments.'

'Oh.'

'I have a performance in three days,' Alex said. 'Three days, Lola. To practise and to pack an entire house on my own. Do you have any idea the amount of pressure I'm under?'

Matron's dark gaze slid my way. If she could have one eye on her computer screen and one on me, I'm sure she would have done.

'*Hello?*'

'I'm here.'

'Why did you really call, Lola? We're not exactly friends.'

An apology wedged in my throat. I didn't know she'd have to move. I didn't know she'd never be able to go back either. The pressure of trying to perform as well as pack a house. I had no idea she'd be going through so much, that she'd be the one to pick up the pieces.

'I'm—'

'Don't you dare apologize,' Alex snapped. 'Is that why you called? To ask for my forgiveness? This is all your fault, Lola. No apology will ever make it right.'

She's right. I rang to make myself feel better and I don't deserve it. My own sister won't forgive me and there's nothing I can do about it.

'It was an accident,' I whispered, turning away from Matron. 'The train derailed.'

Alex paused on the other end. 'Is that what you've told yourself? I can almost picture you repeating it over and over, lying in bed and whispering it to yourself, trying to make it true. You were always a dreamer, Lola, but this is truly impressive.'

'What do you mean?'

Alex blew out a whistle. 'You've buried it deep, haven't you? You really are a fucking nutcase. Shall I help you remember? You could come back to the house and I could show you where—'

'Good luck with your performance, Alex.' I hung up before she could reply.

'Everything all right?' Matron cooed from her desk.

I nodded and turned to go, but she swiped something off the printer and pushed it into my hands. A timetable. 'Here,' she said. 'I forgot to give you this this morning.'

I mumbled a thank you and left her office, staring at the timetable without really taking it in. The classrooms on it were numbers like L1.4 and U2.6 which made no sense. On the back was the Better Than Life rota, courtesy of Dr Zats.

My first session was in five minutes.

As I made my way down to the IT labs, Georgie was coming up towards the main building, several folders clutched to her chest.

'Hey, New Girl,' she said. 'Are you going to play the game?'

'Yeah, first session.'

'Well, have fun. It's all right.' She wrinkled her nose. 'Better than Maths anyway.'

'What have you created?'

Georgie flashed her teeth and I noticed for the first time how uneven they were. 'An Arctic environment. Snow, ice, that kind of thing. Way less creepy-crawlies than that bloody rainforest, I can tell you. No plants, no dirt, and I decided there were no animals either.' She sighed dreamily. 'No germs.'

Behind us, a whistle blew from the playing field. Sebastian waded out of a gang of players to argue with a PE teacher, gesturing with his lacrosse stick before the teacher gave the final word with the swing of his arm. Sebastian trudged towards a bench.

'Has anyone ever come into your world?' I asked Georgie.

'Nah, it's all private.'

She sounded so confident, and Dr Zats had said before how it would be an invasion of privacy to go into someone else's world. But Sebastian had definitely been in the rainforest with us. If he could get in, who else could get in? 'You really think so?' I asked.

Georgie nodded. 'Absolutely. Even Dr Z doesn't come into our private worlds,' she said, confirming what I'd been told. She flipped her hair over her shoulder. 'Besides, grown adults watching a bunch of teenagers in their VR worlds smells super illegal. It's at least voyeuristic or something and I'm sure *that's* illegal. Daddy would have a field day with that one.'

'He would?' I asked, wondering what it would be like to have a dad to fight your corner.

'Oh yes,' she said. 'Daddy is a top solicitor down in London. He represents— well I can't tell you who exactly, but if Dr Z tries anything funny, he'll come down on her like a ton of bricks.'

She leant slightly forward, eyes slipping to the sides to check we were alone. 'We've found a way to all play together. Dr Z doesn't know so you can't mention it to her. She'd go off on one about how we're not adhering to her precious rules. We'll do it later, tonight. You're invited.'

'I am?'

'Duh. There's only the six of us in the whole school who play. You're part of the crew.'

She left me with instructions on how to enter the game. It was the same as exiting: clap once and say, 'Enter.' The Key would do the rest.

In the gym, I slipped into the centre of the room. I clapped and said, 'Enter,' quietly, feeling like an idiot and in case Georgie was having a laugh.

The gym disappeared almost immediately.

It fizzled away in a haze of static, giving rise to a completely grey void. A white mist hung in the centre, swirling to its own lazy rhythm, like it was alive somehow. Waiting.

I spun around, took a few steps forward and one to the side. The computer-grey colour was never-ending. It was a space to create, a void to breathe life into, to command something into existence.

I could make anything. Anyone. Yet all I could think about was what Alex had said.

Shall I help you remember? You could come back to the house . . .

The house.

It filled my mind like a pungent smell. I could see her, my sister. Walking room to room, all of them filled with boxes, knowing she had to leave. Knowing she'd never again practise her violin in the double-height hallway, the best room in the house for acoustics. Never again listen to Mother about how to improve her bow technique. When it was time to leave, she'd shut the front door a final time, knowing she'd never be on the other side of it ever again.

A pain shot through my temple.

I cried out and doubled over as it intensified.

Bricks flew over my head.

They'd emerged from the void, fully formed and sandy coloured, exactly how I remembered them. They gathered in the space in front of me as if pulled by a magnet.

I gasped out as the pain in my head flared up again. It was too late to stop it and anyway, I didn't want to stop it yet. Bricks scraped against each other, joining together to create walls. Windows solidified in the gaps they left. Roof tiles, drainpipes, guttering; it all flew from above me like my head was splitting in two and my house was tumbling out of it.

My knees hit the floor.

A groan escaped my throat.

It was like three migraines were taking over different parts of my brain and were trying to have a party in my head. They'd shatter my skull if I didn't stop.

The mist swirled around my waist, its wispy tendrils licking at my skin like it would pull me under if I let it.

'Stop!' I moaned.

Jasmine bloomed from a plant pot so suddenly it was like it had been vomited out of it. The door-handle twisted into place. A stone slab slotted next to its counterpart, completing the steps.

Then everything was still.

Silent.

It was over. Finally over.

A three-storey townhouse lay before me, sat on a pavement but with no road in front of it. There were no neighbouring houses either side like there should have been, but the rest of it was exactly how I knew it to be, down to the moss squatting between the bricks.

Stone steps led up to the red front door. Wrought-iron balconies jutted from the top-floor windows. Jasmine curled over the railing, making the whole façade magazine-ready. I'd forgotten how much I hated that jasmine and the image it presented.

I gritted my teeth, the pain so intense I could barely see.

Dead leaves piled close to the basement windows. A shadow slid across them.

Something – someone – was prowling in that basement.

The pain—

Too much—

I screamed and sank back into the mist. The last thing I saw was a flash of blonde hair behind the basement window.

Then, total darkness.

SIX

I woke and staggered to my feet. My house sat on the bottomless mist, the grey void stretching into infinity around it. The pain in my head was like the remnants of a bad headache, dull enough to cope with. I approached the stairs, climbed the steps one by one, the wrought-iron railing cold and peeling beneath my fingers.

When I pushed on the door, it opened into a lift.

I frowned – there was no lift in my house in real life. Here there was a mosaic floor and an ornate grille for a door, all welded swirls, like handwriting; the kind you pull shut and can see straight through, but there were no rooms on the other side. It was more of the same grey void.

A panel to the left had three buttons:

1

G

B

'G' was backlit by a yellow light, telling me that was where I was. I had to go up or down. The button marked

'B' flashed once. Demanded my attention.

Ping!

B for Bank. B for Banana. B for Beethoven, Brahms and Basement.

The basement. Where shadows flitted across windows. Where a truth pressed against my windpipe, making it hard to breathe.

B for Death.

Ping!

I hit the button marked '1' and the front door swung shut behind me.

My Key tingled as the lift began to vibrate beneath my feet the way it would in real life. I passed through a cross-section of floor on the way to the next level.

When it came to a stop, the sound of laughter made me pause.

It came again. A little girl, bellyache-type laughter.

I pulled back the gate and stepped on to the black-and-white tiles of a hallway. My hallway. The game had rebuilt the interior of my house on level 1 and everything was exactly how it should be.

Wooden stairs hugged the left wall, leading up to the balcony that hung above my head, casting a dark shadow over me. A square of the wall to my right fell in on itself, creating an archway that led into the living room. The kitchen was down the hall.

The game had rebuilt everything perfectly.

Another peal of laughter demanded my attention.

I went towards it, walking steadily to the kitchen. It

got brighter the closer I got to it – sunbeams poured in through the skylights, bounced off the tiles and the marble counters.

A man with aviator sunglasses pushed up on to his head was stood at the Aga stove. He flicked a frying pan and a pancake soared into the air to the delight of the little girl sat on the bench seat of the kitchen table. She had the same red hair as him. The same bright grey eyes. A shock of pixels ran through her body.

I steadied myself against the kitchen door as pain pulsed in my head again. The pixels cleared and the little girl solidified. She clapped and squealed as the man flipped the pancake a second time.

'Again, again!'

I stood in the doorway and watched the man do as she demanded, his grin as wide as hers. He wore jeans and a T-shirt, had leather bracelets round his wrist. I remembered how he showed me them once – one from every country he'd visited. I'd count them with him when I couldn't sleep, nine in total.

He served the pancake to the little girl before turning to me. 'Hey, Lola.' He winked at me the way he always did and opened up his arms. It wasn't even a second before I crossed the kitchen and sank against him.

The Key at my temple tingled and then Dad was hugging me back. His arms wrapped around me in a way they never had before. He was solid, real. Strong but gentle as he hugged me back.

'Dad. I missed you.'

His stubble scraped my cheek as he kissed it. 'Missed you, too.'

He was really here. He didn't disappear when I tried to touch him the way he normally did. I could hear his heartbeat, feel his solidity. We broke apart but I couldn't stop staring at him.

'We're having pancakes,' the little girl at the table declared. Chocolate lined her teeth.

'My speciality,' Dad said. 'Come on, I'll make you one next.'

He sat me opposite the little girl and returned to the cooker.

The table was laden with things Mother would never buy: maple syrup, Nutella, ice cream, sprinkles and mini-marshmallows. All of it looked gloriously sticky and no one seemed to care most of it was smeared across the table.

'Hi,' the little girl said with a grin.

She was me when I was young, before the scars and the broken collarbone. Her hair was long which wasn't quite right, but I loved it. Mother always cut mine if it grew longer than my chin. The little girl had hair that stretched down her back like shiny copper thread. She licked a knife and put it back in a jar of Nutella and no one told her off or yelled at her. For her, it was a normal morning with her favourite parent.

She was me how I should have been.

'I like your hair,' I said to her. 'You're very pretty.'

'You can have hair like this too if you want,' she said,

spooning marshmallows on to her plate.

'What do you mean?'

She laughed like I'd asked a silly question. 'You can look however you want here.'

Alex always had nice hair. She looked like she'd come straight from a salon most days. Mother showed her how to style it with a trendy wave; not quite straight, not quite curly.

```
I feel that if I looked differently,
          I would be happier
              Yes/No
```

I wished I had long hair.

I ran my fingers through mine, expecting the lengths to stop at my jaw the way they should, but they kept going, past my shoulders. The strands thickened, became glossy and smooth, and turned bright like a polished copper pot. The ratty ends were gone.

'Now you're pretty, too,' the girl said.

I looked down at my left hand, where the skin puckered like melted plastic. The scars tailed off down my wrist but the worst of it was on my palm. A band of pixels fuzzed over them and they dissolved into my skin. I traced over where the scars should be. Smooth, soft. Not too white, not too red. It had been years since I'd seen it look so normal.

Dad kissed the top of my head as he slipped a pancake on to the plate in front of me.

'You look beautiful,' he said. 'Pick your toppings. You can have whatever you want.'

'Whatever I want?'

'Yep. And if you don't want pancakes, I can make you something else.' He grinned, put a hand behind his back and brought out a huge slice of rainbow cake with vanilla frosting. 'How about cake for breakfast?'

I laughed as he put it down. 'Cake for breakfast isn't a thing.'

'It is here,' the little girl said.

Dad bunched his lips in thought. 'No cake. OK. What else can I get you?' He pulled a small maroon box from behind his back. 'Something special, even if you can't eat it. The lipstick you've always wanted.'

I took it from him while rubbing away a stab of pain in my temple. The box looked too much like the one in real life. There was a note on top of it. I plucked it off and turned it over.

This one is just your colour, Lola.
Much love,
Dad XXX

My breath caught in my throat. No one had ever given me a present with such a nice note before.

'I love it,' I said, and the words felt too hollow a representation of how grateful I really was. 'Thank you.'

'Anything for you,' he said. He turned back to the cooker to flip more pancakes. 'Eat up, Lola. It's Saturday after all, and what are Saturdays for if not for eating pancakes?'

It wasn't actually Saturday, but I didn't correct him. I wanted it to be Saturday. And for once, I was going to do exactly what I wanted to do if it were.

With Mother, Fridays were for piano practice. Scales, followed by arpeggios. If I did them well, I got to pick the piece I practised for the rest of the day. If I played that well, I didn't have to do scales on Saturday. Mother would stand at the piano and listen, indifference scored into her face. She set the bar so high it was impossible to ever meet it.

I always, always did scales on a Saturday.

Today I would eat pancakes.

I reached across the table to get the maple syrup and my elbow knocked against a martini glass. It fell on to the floor with a smash and the stem rolled beneath my heel.

A crunch told me it had snapped.

I ducked down to pick up the pieces, my trembling hand curling around the broken stem.

'Go away,' I whispered to it.

It stuttered with pixels but it didn't disappear. It was cold and so sharp I knew if I smashed my hand down over the top it would hurt in a very real way.

The little girl was watching me. 'What's that?' she asked innocently, though we both knew it wasn't that innocent. She knew what it was. She grinned at me, showing me her chocolatey teeth. Pixels stuttered over her mouth. The chocolate had turned red. Too red. I blinked and it was gone. She closed her mouth, but her bright grey eyes held mine for a moment too long.

I'd thought she was me – the version of me that should have had a dad and perfect Saturday mornings – but that wasn't quite right. She had long hair and confidence: two things I never had.

'Alex?' I whispered.

Above us, clouds overtook the skylight and the room darkened. Rain suddenly hammered against the window-pane.

I blinked at the bright neon-yellow jacket crowding our doorway.

Rainwater dripped from the police officer's hat.

'Tell me, Lola. What did your mother do?'

I slammed the broken martini glass down on to the table.

Landslide.

'Train crash,' I said, speaking it into existence.

Dad looked up. 'What did you say?'

That was when it happened.

A train careered through the wall behind him, slicing off the entire side of the kitchen as the front carriage of the 15.22 to London Euston rammed its way through the house.

Bricks, kitchen cabinets, plasterboard and glass exploded into our faces as the train screamed through the room. Windows smashed. Walls were reduced to rubble. The floor was a chewed-up mess. Gutters snapped off the walls and water gushed from their broken ends, sweeping across the kitchen like a river.

The train blasted its horn. Its wheels screeched against the tracks as it tried and failed to brake because there was too much water. The screech went on and on until it became a scream.

Little Alex was screaming.

I turned to help her but she was gone. Dad was gone.

I was alone, covered in dust and surrounded by the waterlogged debris. The final train carriage rocketed past, taking the last of the kitchen table with it. I ducked out of its way in case it tried to take me too.

When it was gone, I stepped out of the broken room and into the unending computer-grey void, bits of my kitchen spattered across it like chunks of vomit. Far in the distance, the train blared its horn. The brake lights coloured the mist red until it eventually faded.

I clapped and whispered, 'Exit.'

The gym rose up in its place. Light entered thinly through the small high windows. Over the course of playing the game, I'd ended up by a pile of gym mats against the far wall. If I'd gone any further in the game I would have walked right into them. I shivered, wrapped my arms around my middle and squeezed my eyes shut.

Dad appeared when I reopened them. 'Oh, Lola. It'll be OK, I promise.' He strode towards me, reached for my arm but he passed straight through the way he always did.

He looked as sad as I felt.

He disappeared completely a moment later.

Sweat prickled at my back, under my arms. I couldn't stop shivering. My body was cooling down too quickly in the cold room. I tried to shrug it all away. The shock, the train, Little Alex. The smoke curling from the Aga stove-top.

'Dad?' I whispered, wishing him back.

He didn't come. My heart wasn't in it, I could tell. I'd seen him, hugged him, and he'd made me pancakes. My imagination paled in comparison. It would never be enough now.

The only place I could really be with him was in the game.

My secret was in there too.

It had followed me in.

SEVEN

I met Mercedes at the dinner service, where we were served fish and chips and a clumpy white mess they said was tartare sauce. Matron prowled the hall, pulling apart squabbling first years who hadn't settled into boarding school life yet.

My hair was back to jaw length, dull and heavy with grease. The scars had returned to my hand. I rubbed the lump along my collarbone and wished I was back in the game, wished I looked how I could in there.

I prodded my battered fish with my fork.

'You act like you've never had fish and chips before,' Georgie said from the other side of the table.

'I haven't,' I said.

'What did you eat before you came here then?'

'The usual stuff.'

When Mother cooked, she would spend hours in the kitchen. Her motto for dinner was if it wasn't worth spending five hours over, it wasn't worth eating at all. Confit duck, beef bourguignon. Everything she made for her and Alex smelt and looked delicious. If I was lucky, there were leftovers. One night I would eat parmesan risotto with roasted prawns and another I would smear jam on to stale crackers because that's all I could find in the cupboards.

Wai sat down with a tray laden with boxes I hadn't seen at the hatch. 'My parents are nutritionists,' he said as he opened up a salad. 'They won't let me eat that crap.'

'That *crap* is my dinner.' Georgie stuck her tongue out at him.

'You're so skinny,' Mercedes said, looking me over. 'I bet a single chip would fill you up.'

'I bet it would for you too,' I said, giving her a good look back. There wasn't much between us size wise, but Mercedes was far more glamorous than I was.

'Cedes doesn't eat carbs,' Georgie announced.

'You should,' Wai said. 'You need them.'

He launched into a speech about complex carbohydrates and how his parents made sure all his meals were perfectly balanced, taking great lengths to point out the chunks of sweet potato in his salad. Mercedes eyed her chips distrustfully.

Finn joined us, swinging his legs over our bench and putting his tray down with a clatter. He told me all about how his mum was a team principal for Red Bull in the Formula One and how he could get me tickets to any race I wanted.

'Yeah, she'll probably invite me to be with her in Monaco this weekend,' Finn said, puffing his chest so he could be heard above the collective scrape of a hundred pairs of knives and forks. 'They'll probably pay for me to go business class or maybe even first class. Monaco is the best. All the drivers hate it which means it's full of tension. Have you ever been to Monaco? The next race is there, did I already say that?'

'Yes,' Georgie said, leaning over Mercedes's plate to hiss at him. 'We get it, Finn. The whole fucking dinner service gets it. The next race is in Monaco.'

Mercedes elbowed her out of the way. 'Stop breathing over my chips, Georgie.'

'You never eat them anyway,' she retorted.

A plate smashed on the ground.

All our heads snapped towards it.

Near the serving hatch Mr Leighton knelt to scoop a shattered plate from the floor. Sebastian was already power-walking away, shoulders tense with visible anger. Mr Leighton glanced up to see the whole dining hall staring at him.

'As you were,' he barked.

Students twisted back to their tables, but the noise didn't return in the same way. Before, it had been a loud chatter with the occasional laugh. Now it was a hushed whisper, murmurs filling the silence until Mr Leighton disposed of the plate in a nearby collection tray and limped out of the hall, wincing with every step.

I'd never noticed he had a limp when we met. He'd been sat down the whole time.

'They hate each other,' Wai said, interrupting my thoughts.

'How do you know?'

'Duh.' Georgie skewered a chip on to her fork. 'Everyone knows.'

Mercedes crossed her arms. 'It's not our business.'

'It is if they argue like that in front of the whole school,' Georgie shot back. 'They're always arguing.' She leant over Mercedes's plate again. 'Seb isn't his biological son, see.'

Mercedes scoffed and pushed her away. 'That's got nothing to do with anything.'

Matron had mentioned how Mr Leighton had 'taken in' a boy. 'He's adopted then?' I asked.

'Yep. And it has everything to do with everything,' Georgie said, chomping on her chip. 'It's all to do with what happened to his mum.'

'Shh, Georgie,' Mercedes said. 'That's not for us to gossip about.'

Finn leant towards the centre of the table. I leant with him so I could hear. 'Wait till you hear this though. Mr Leighton interrupted our Geography lesson before, pulled Seb out into the corridor and had a go at him. Something about a watch going missing.'

I stopped eating. 'A watch? Are you sure?'

'Pretty sure that's what it was. I couldn't make it all out,' Finn said. 'Leighton said something about how it was part of his dynasty and Seb flew off the handle, saying five generations wasn't a dynasty. Anyway, Seb didn't come back to the lesson.'

Mercedes pulled a disbelieving face. 'No one ever argued with anyone else over a watch.'

'He said it was an heirloom,' Finn insisted. 'You'd fight over that, wouldn't you?'

'Whatever.' Mercedes pushed her unfinished meal away. 'Lola, are you done? I have homework.'

I wasn't finished but I laid down my knife and fork and rose from the table with her, hoping to ask more about Sebastian on our own.

Georgie tugged on Mercedes's wrist. 'We'll see you later, right? The usual time. *Right?*'

Finn and Wai looked to Mercedes for her response.

She sighed. 'Fine, but only for an hour. It's not you who'd get expelled if we all got found out.'

'Don't be such a negative Nancy,' Wai said.

'Let's meet in your room then, shall we?'

'Yours is bigger,' Wai said, and stuffed his mouth with salad leaves like this would end the argument. It seemed to work because Mercedes rolled her eyes and left the table in a huff.

Georgie winked at me as I went to follow. 'See you later,' she mouthed.

Mercedes was quiet on the way back up to our room. 'Are you all right?' I asked. 'You seemed like you wanted to leave in a hurry.'

'Georgie really shouldn't go around blurting stuff out like that,' Mercedes said. 'It's not any of our business whether Seb is adopted or not.'

I murmured my agreement and waited for more. Mercedes obliged, her irritation with Georgie fuelling her. 'Mr Leighton met Seb's mum when he was around five or six, I think. They got married but his mum died when he was like nine.'

'How did she die?'

'No one knows, but does it matter? His mum *died*, Lola.'

'Of course,' I said, following her up the stairs. 'That's horrible.'

'Georgie shouldn't have said anything, it's nothing to do with her.'

'But the whole school knows she died?'

Mercedes stepped aside for me to go into the bedroom before her. 'Poor Seb. He knows everyone knows, but it's not like you talk about it, is it? He's our friend. He deserves better.'

I'd spoken to him about it. Or rather, he'd spoken to me about it.

She went over to her desk and opened her laptop. 'Everyone will come over at eleven, after lights out. Matron should have pissed off by then. She always has a sherry and then goes to bed.'

'Who's everyone?'

Mercedes looked up. 'Everyone who counts. We're going to play the game together.'

'Like how I did with Dr Zats? A shared experience?'

She laughed. 'Sure, let's call it that. We've been doing it ever since Seb worked out how to hack the game. Dr Z keeps going on about a problem with her code and she has no idea it's him.'

While we waited until lights out, Mercedes helped me

decipher my timetable. I didn't even have to ask. She pulled it out of my bag and started telling me where all the classrooms were. She repeated everything more than twice to make sure I knew. I said thank you, but it didn't feel like enough. People were never normally that kind and she did it without even thinking about it.

When she went for a shower, I removed Mr Leighton's watch from my pocket. I unpacked my socks into my bedside table and put the headmaster's heirloom inside the thickest pair I owned, then shoved it at the back of the drawer. I'd return it soon.

Before everyone came over, Mercedes wrapped her hair in a pink silk scarf. She lined her skincare up on her bedside table.

There was an oil cleanser, a foam cleanser, a toner, an essence, a serum, an eye serum, and finally a moisturizer she told me she occasionally swapped for a sheet mask. Her skin was so good she could have still been wearing make-up.

At exactly eleven o'clock, Georgie slipped into the room via the bathroom door. 'Sorry I'm a bit late,' she said in a loud whisper. 'Had to wait till Arya dropped off. Poor love snores like a chainsaw, it's a wonder she doesn't wake herself up. She certainly keeps *me* awake.'

'You're not late,' Mercedes said, and slid up the bed so Georgie could sit next to her.

Wai and Finn followed shortly afterwards.

'We're in,' Finn said to his phone. 'Cheers, Seb.' He flashed the screen at us and Sebastian gave us a wave.

'He's not coming?' I asked.

Sebastian tapped his headset. 'Who d'you think is Tech Support? Someone's got to hack the cameras for these two to get over from Hastings. All right, I'll see you all in there.'

Finn ended the video call and went to put his phone away.

'Is that the new iPhone?' Georgie asked. 'Can I see?'

Finn nodded and threw it to her. 'Got it this morning. Mum had it shipped straight from the factory.'

Georgie was impressed as she looked it over. 'I didn't think it was even out yet.'

'Mum pulled some strings. You know how it is.'

Georgie took a selfie and then threw it back, but Finn only just caught it. Wai let out a whistle. 'It'll be back to the factory if you're not careful.'

'It's only a phone.' Finn put it away and sat down on my bed next to me. 'Are we playing or what? Let's go, Seb's waiting and Lola here's dying to see him.'

'What? No I'm not.' I punched him on the arm and he laughed.

I flushed at the attention but thankfully no one seemed to notice. Mercedes coughed pointedly from her bed. 'If you're finished, Finn?' she said. 'I believe we're all ready.'

'Ladies first,' he said.

Mercedes clapped and said, 'Enter.' A shot of blue streaked through her eyes and she stopped moving, stopped blinking. She was perfectly still.

'Enter,' Georgie said with a clap. Like Mercedes, her eyes flashed blue and she sat so still it was like someone had pressed pause on a remote.

Wai was next. He entered the game hunched over his crossed legs and with his lips slightly parted like he was mid-sentence.

Finn nudged me with his elbow. 'See you in a second. Enter.'

Everyone stared into nothingness. Their chests moved with the same pace as someone who was asleep, taking deep, measured breaths. Every now and then their eyes flashed blue.

I wondered how they were so still. Last time I'd played the game I ended up at the opposite end of the gym, but here no one's legs moved – they barely even blinked. There was only one way to find out. They were in the game, waiting for me.

I clapped my hands. 'Enter.'

EIGHT

When I entered, it was to a world composed of oranges and browns. I shielded my eyes as I spun around, taking in the mixture of concrete blocks and shipping containers that surrounded me. Some were horizontal, others vertical. It was a mishmash of rusting colours, all arranged in a square that could have seated ten full-sized orchestras comfortably. The ground was sunbaked mud and dusty beneath my feet.

Sebastian was right in front of me, his oak-coloured gaze trained on me in that appraising way of his. 'I need to fix your Key before you can move anywhere,' he said.

'What do you mean?'

'You noticed the physical space issue, right? Wherever you walk in the game is ground covered in real life.'

'I'd just been thinking about that too,' I said. Over his shoulder, the others had gathered in a group a few metres away. How had they done that without tripping over something in our bedroom and falling flat on their faces?

'I altered their Keys,' Sebastian said.

'Altered them? Altered them how?'

'Altered them so you can go wherever you want without moving in real life. May I?'

I nodded, feeling shy as he moved even closer. He tapped my Key with a single finger, and a tingle crawled from my temple and down my spine. I shuddered.

'What was that?'

'Progress,' he said with a grin. 'Now you're the same as us.'

I took a hesitant step forward. In real life, I would have fallen off my bed. I grinned back at him when nothing happened.

He nodded, seemingly satisfied when I didn't hurt myself. 'Dr Zats was taking too long to figure it out, so I took the liberty.'

In my session earlier, Dr Zats had mentioned a team of programmers. I couldn't help but raise an eyebrow that Sebastian was better at programming than a dedicated team at a technology company. 'How do you know how to do all of this?' I asked. 'Coding games and hacking security cameras and everything?'

He answered my question with one of his own. 'Do you play any instruments?'

'The piano,' I said hesitantly, deciding not to tell him I had sworn never to play it again.

'Well let's say you're really good at the piano. I'm really good at coding. Ever since I got my first computer, I worked out how it was built and how it worked. Coding comes easy to me the way music does for you.'

Music had *never* come easy for me. I had failed all of

my graded exams – most more than once. If Mother hadn't pushed me, I wouldn't have passed at all. Her motto was to put forty hours of practice into each day. Setting an impossible bar was classic Mother. In the lead-up to my grade eight exam, she made sure I put in those hours. I still failed. Four times.

'Lola!' Mercedes shouted.

'Let's go,' Sebastian said, and jogged over to the group.

I followed after him, took the place next to Mercedes. She looked different here – skinnier than she was in the real world, even though I wouldn't have labelled her as anything other than beautiful. Wai had long hair, put up in a top knot. Facial hair lined his top lip and jawline. It suited him. Finn was bulkier, chunkier, like he'd spent a year in the gym and nowhere else. Georgie grinned at me with perfect teeth she definitely didn't have in real life. 'Hey, New Girl.'

Sebastian was next to me. He was the closest to the real-life version of himself, down to his roughly styled hair and oak-green eyes. 'Welcome to the real Better Than Life,' he said.

'Everyone looks different,' I said.

'Including you,' Wai said.

I put a hand to my hair, felt how it was longer than it should be. It was as if the game remembered what I wanted to look like. I tossed my hair over my shoulder. 'I like it.'

'So do I,' Finn said with a wolfish grin.

'Leave off it, we've only got an hour.' Sebastian pulled

a pair of orange-coloured shades over his eyes.

I looked down and saw my pyjamas had gone. In their place was a pair of boots with ankle supports, some khaki shorts and a strappy top and sports bra. A leather harness was over the top. Pads adorned my knees and padded gloves were on my hands. Georgie and Mercedes had similar outfits.

The boys all wore tank tops with shorts, the same harness over it all and the same fingerless gloves with padded palms. Finn swiped at his forehead but didn't seem to care he was sweaty. I blinked up at the sun. It beat down relentlessly, making the horizon hazy and the shipping containers seem like they were swaying.

'What is this place?' I asked.

'Our playground,' Georgie said.

'It's an obstacle course,' Mercedes said, offering a little more. 'We come here to blow off steam. Seb set it up.'

'It was easy,' he said, waving her statement away. 'Who's up for a game of CTF?'

I bit my lip and nodded along with everyone else. I had no idea what they were talking about.

'Capture the flag,' Mercedes said, leaning close to whisper in my ear. 'You have to get your team's flag and take it to the top of the centre podium, up there.'

Directly in the middle of the arena was a concrete tower. Metal rods poked through the unfinished surface, fashioned into grab holds. It jutted out near the top, creating an overhang. The sun crested directly above it. I blinked away little white circles.

'We've never been able to play CTF before because we were an uneven number. But now . . .' Sebastian's head turned my way, and everyone else followed suit.

Georgie clutched Mercedes's side. 'I'm on Cedes's team.'

'Fine,' Sebastian said. His gaze hadn't wandered from me. 'I'll take Lola.'

'What?' I spluttered. No one ever picked me for anything. 'I've never played before, that's not a good idea—'

'I'm in,' Finn said. 'Lola looks like a winner.'

'Oh thanks, man.' Wai trudged over to Georgie and Mercedes.

Georgie tugged on his top knot. 'Aww, was someone picked last?'

'This is like PE all over again.' Wai folded his arms. 'There's a reason I dropped that shit at GCSE.'

Mercedes snapped her fingers. 'Focus, guys. We won the last game, we can win this.' She pointed to the opposite ends of the arena. Two flags had materialized on the highest points. The one behind her was blue, and the one behind me was red.

'Ten seconds, then it's game on,' Finn shouted, tugging my wrist to pull me away. I skipped away with him and Sebastian as he explained the game in more detail. 'Ours is the blue flag, theirs is the red. We have to guard their red one at the same time as trying to capture our blue one. Got it?'

'Got it.'

'Game on!' Georgie yelled.

In the middle of the arena, high above our heads, a countdown started. Digital numbers hung in the air.

'Lola, take the left,' Sebastian shouted, running away from me.

'Finn, you're in the middle.'

'I'll be on the right.'

I ran for the arena wall.

I tripped.

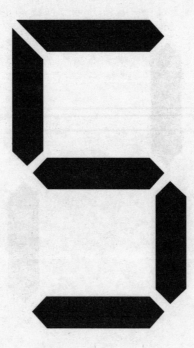

I fell forward, put a foot out to stop myself and shot into the air about ten feet high.

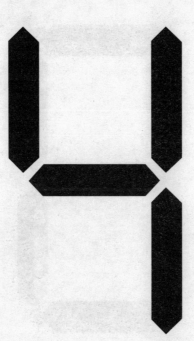

'Watch out for the reduced gravity,' Finn called with a laugh.

I landed near a container with grab holds running up its side.

I grabbed on to them, hauled myself up.

BEEEEP!

Sebastian let out a whoop as he reached the lowest section of the arena wall. He bounded across the length of a whole container in one stride. Georgie was steadily jumping towards him from the opposite direction. Eventually, they would meet in the middle.

Behind me, Finn was climbing up to reach the red flag our team was supposed to guard. Mercedes was already dashing the length of the arena to get to it. The blue flag – ours – was wide open, ready for the taking. All I had to do was get past Wai who was thundering his way towards me.

His grin was wide as he powered in my direction. The

strides he took were so long he covered whole containers in nearly one jump, landing with metallic crunches.

I stopped to listen to the pattern.

Crunch.

Crunch.

Crunch.

Crunch.

Solid as a metronome. A four-beat rhythm I could have sat and played to. Out of the corner of my eye, something black and shiny pixelated out of the ground.

A piano.

Lid open, keys bared like teeth.

The sight of it made me freeze.

Wai didn't falter; he hadn't seen it. His attention was trained on me, and I could use that.

Crunch.

Crunch.

Crunch.

Crunch.

I told myself to concentrate on Wai and only Wai. I ran towards him, careful with the gravity and not pushing too hard with my feet because I needed to stay low. Had to time it exactly right. Listen to each crunch. When he was half a container's length away from me, I ducked into a roll and slid underneath him as he went soaring over my head.

'What the—' Wai landed with a crunch behind me.

There was no time to relish his confusion. I powered on, pushing off with all the strength I could gather in my legs. The gravity helped me soar across the containers. When I was several ahead, I chanced a look behind me.

Finn had taken the red flag and was clambering up the sides of the arena, Mercedes and Georgie running after him. Wai was on his way to help, having given me up.

The blue flag was completely undefended.

Sebastian was almost at it. 'Lola!' he yelled. 'Climb!'

I swivelled in the direction of the concrete tower in the centre of the arena. It was too far away for a standing jump. I backed up to the edge of my container and bent my knees in preparation, trying to force power into my legs but not too much that I overshot the landing.

Then I was running.

I leapt from the edge of the container and hurtled through the air.

Mid-jump, I realized it wasn't going to be enough. I'd missed the landing. I willed myself to go further, trying to claw at the air to propel me forward even a few centimetres. It worked, but I smashed into the side of the tower, hands clamping on to a grab bar. Pain radiated through my ribs.

'Go, go, go!' Finn yelled from his side of the arena.

I peered around the edge. Mercedes had taken the red flag and her team were jumping away from Finn, coming in my direction.

Sebastian had our blue flag, but he wasn't moving. He held it like a javelin. He was watching me, waiting to throw it to me. If I caught it, I would be the first one to reach the top and win the game for our team.

I'd never catch it. It was all on me and I'd never catch it.

'This is a bad idea,' I yelled back.

The pads of my gloves scraped against the rough metal grab holds as I pulled myself up. I jammed my foot on one to spring forward a few metres.

'You're doing great!' Sebastian called.

My heartbeat was a continuous thrum in my veins, loud in my ears, at the back of my mouth and in the tips of my fingers. I'd never catch it.

Beneath me, Mercedes had started the climb. She'd secured the flagpole to the back of her harness. The red flag streamed out behind her as she put hand over hand, relentlessly climbing up and up. She'd reach me quickly.

I continued with my method: using footholds and the reduced gravity to springboard up the climbing wall.

I must have been halfway up when Sebastian whistled to catch my attention. He had the flag poised over one shoulder, feet planted firmly like he was ready to throw. I swallowed hard. It was impossible.

'You can do this, Lola,' he called. He drew his arm back and released the flag.

Then it was soaring towards me.

I dug my feet in, one hand holding fast to a grab bar, and leant out and away, stretching my other hand out. Tried not to look down. Not at Mercedes or at how far down the ground was.

The flag hurtled towards me.

Sebastian's throw was off. I'd never catch it.

Metal knocked against my fingers. I grabbed. Closed

my hand around the flagpole and drew it to my chest as I leant back into the wall, breath coming in ragged gasps.

Sebastian and Finn whooped from their opposite ends of the arena.

I did it – actually did it.

My hands shook as I secured the flag to my harness like Mercedes.

She was a shorter distance away from me now, and had copied my method of climbing. Her jumps were erratic but determined. She wanted to win. Adrenaline pumped through my veins, made my chest feel both tight and open. I forced myself to keep going. The top was close and then it would be over.

Above us was the overhang.

I'd never been rock climbing before, but I could tell this part would involve using arm strength to get over the lip of it. I reached it and twisted to get my fingers in a decent position. My legs swung free.

A tremor ran through my arms.

The knowledge that they were all that was keeping me from falling and hitting the ground hit me like a punch to the gut. In order to get over the lip I would have to swing my body, gather momentum, and propel myself over it.

My palms were damp and clammy.

Mercedes was less than a few metres away.

I couldn't let Sebastian and Finn down. I'd caught the flag, there was one thing more to do and then it would be over.

I started my first swing. The momentum assisted me,

pushing me higher than I anticipated. As I used my arms to push myself up and over the top, I caught sight of the shiny black grand piano far below.

Panic flashed through me.

I landed on the top in a backwards roll.

Sebastian and Finn's cries of celebration were quieter this high up, but I could still hear them. They chanted my name and cheered.

We'd won.

Because of *me*.

I held the flag up and they cheered even louder.

```
    I have lots of friends
         Yes/No
```

I stood up, planted the flag in the empty holder in the centre. The blue banner whipped free, cracked in the wind. A smell lingered on the breeze.

Heated oil.

I turned to see an Aga stove, exactly like the one in the kitchen back home. Mother had loved that stove. She said it was the only acceptable type of stove to have, that tradition would always trump modernity when it came to cooking.

Smoke curled from one of its plates.

The metal was almost red from the heat surging through it.

'Say "hot", Dolores,' a voice said from behind me.

Little Alex was back. Her long red hair impervious to

the wind, as if she wasn't here but I knew she was. The way my stomach churned and churned told me she was. She watched me with those bright grey eyes, so like my own.

Smoke hissed from the Aga.

'What did you say?' I said.

'Say "hot". "Very hot".'

I took a step back, towards the edge.

She followed me, insistent. 'Say it!'

'Leave me alone.' I tried to push her away but she fought back, getting even closer. She'd always been stronger than me, even when we were little.

'Say it! Say "hot"!' she shouted.

I clamped my hands over my ears. 'Get away from me!'

There was nowhere to go. Up here, it was a deathly fall any direction I went. She'd trapped me. Had waited until she knew I wouldn't be able to walk away from her.

'Say it!' she screeched. 'Say it say it say it!'

I clapped my hands. 'EXIT!'

Little Alex and the hissing stove and the arena vanished.

Around me, no one moved. My friends were still in the game. Their bodies were still, expressions vacant.

I sank back against my pillow and listened to the *tick, tick, tick* of Mr Leighton's watch, hidden deep in my drawer.

Solid as a metronome.

THE PAST

'Look,' Mummy said, pointing to the stovetop. Heat radiated from one of the metal plates there. 'It's hot, Dolores. Can you say "hot"?'

My lips bunched to speak but the sound stuck in my throat. It was trapped there, in that space between half forming and half disappearing.

Mummy repeated the word three times.

Hot.

H—ot.

Hot.

It swelled at the back of her mouth before ending on the tip of her tongue and cutting through her teeth.

I tried to copy her but I couldn't do it. Couldn't make the sound come.

'Come on, you're five now. You shouldn't have a problem with such simple words.'

She hoisted me up, hooked me under her elbow so I was level with the hob. She dropped a little oil on the plate closest to me. Smoke rose in a soft white hiss, an oily metallic smell rising with it.

'Hot,' Mummy said. 'Very hot.'

She rolled my sleeve up past my elbow and extended my arm, catching my wrist between her fingers to hold the flat of my palm above the hob. A whimper escaped my lips as I fought the prickle of heat.

'Say "hot", Dolores.'

The oil sizzled. Little golden beads spat at my palm. I cried out but Mummy lowered my hand further until it was almost touching the bubbling oil. I screamed but Mummy held me in place.

'Say it! Hot. Very hot.'

'Hot!' The word punched through my lips. 'Very hot!'

'Finally.' Mummy snatched my arm away and put me on the floor. When she knelt to look me in the eye, a wave of her perfume followed. It washed over me in a sickly-sweet haze and ended with a sour note. 'There, that wasn't so hard, was it? I knew that speech therapist was wrong. You simply needed a push, that's all.'

She took me to the sink and held my hand under the cold tap.

'Cold,' she said. 'Very cold.'

'C-cold,' I said.

'Excellent.'

The places where the oil had touched my skin puckered and filled with pus. 'Sore,' I said to Alex a day later. 'Very sore.'

She stopped playing her violin and leant over my palm to inspect the welts.

A malicious grin lit her face.

NINE

In IT the next day, I took the empty seat next to Mercedes and Georgie. We twisted in our seats to chat with Sebastian, Finn and Wai behind us.

Everyone was back to normal: Wai had no facial hair, Finn had way less muscle, Mercedes was a more regular shape, Georgie's teeth were uneven again. Sebastian looked the same, but with dark circles under his eyes. My hair was back to jaw length. I did my best to hide the scars on my left hand.

Last night, Mercedes had asked why I'd left the game so early. I'd told her I thought the game was over and expected everyone to quit the same time I did. She'd laughed and told me to stick around next time. I laughed too, but mostly out of relief. If she'd seen Little Alex she would have asked more questions.

'We totally kicked your arse,' Finn snickered to Mercedes.

She rolled her eyes. 'Lola kicked our arse. You did bog all if I remember rightly.'

'All the muscle in the world and not where it counts,' Georgie chimed in.

Finn threw her his wolfish grin. 'Oh, it's where it counts.'

'Ugh.'

The boys' laughter descended into suppressed snorts as Dr Zats and Mr Yorke entered the room.

'Morning all,' Dr Zats said. She began distributing a sheet of paper to each of us. 'No news on the coding issues, I'm afraid. The programmers back at SmartTech said they're keeping an eye on it but if any of you spot anything strange, please let us know. It'll help us pinpoint where it's coming from. Has anyone seen anything strange in their sessions?'

Everyone murmured a no, using the papers she distributed as a reason not to look at her as they replied.

Dr Zats paused at the corner of my desk. 'How about you, Lola? I know you only had your first session yesterday, but . . . See anything weird?'

There were only six of us in the entire school who played the game. The secret we shared created a bond between us. Sebastian had found a way to make it more fun for us and both he and Mercedes had asked me not to say anything.

But Mother never stood for lying.

Once, Alex skipped a violin lesson to go to the cinema with the girl across the road. Alex was rarely in trouble and I watched with great delight as Mother shrieked at her. Her anger was a hiss from between clenched teeth. Alex was given bread for every meal for three days. Mother cooked me venison with port sauce, made Alex

98

sit and watch us eat it, and praised me for making her the perfect martini. She even told me how pretty my hair was.

I relished her fake praise and attention.

'Miriam, can I have a word?' Mr Yorke rescued me from being forced to answer the question.

'Fill out your sheets, everyone,' Dr Zats said, handing the last piece of paper to me. 'I'll be back in a sec.' She left the room with Mr Yorke in tow.

Silence filled the room as everyone turned their attention to the worksheet. It had questions similar to the quiz I'd filled out in my solicitor's office:

```
I prefer spending time with in-game
     characters than with people
          in the real world
               Yes/No
```

That one was easy. Dad was tangible in a way he wasn't in real life. He'd been the first person to give me a hug, and it was exactly how I imagined it would feel like.

I paused over the last question:

```
I feel safer in the game than
       in the real world
            Yes/No
```

A train had almost killed me.
It had razed my kitchen to the ground.

Little Alex had followed me, shouted at me, forced me to remember something I didn't want to remember. I'd been able to stop her by quitting the game. In real life, Alex could have followed me anywhere, continued to shout, to goad, to needle me into reacting.

She can't do that any more.

We're so far apart from each other that she can't bother me here.

No, I did not feel safer in the game.

Just thinking about what had happened made my palms sweaty. I circled 'no' and stood, deciding a walk to the toilet would help me forget about everything. I was good at that, forgetting. Rewriting my memory had always come easily, ever since I first started thinking about Dad.

Out in the corridor, Mr Yorke and Dr Zats stood so close together they were almost head-to-head. They were so caught up in an argument they didn't notice me at all. Dr Zats had removed the pen from her hair bun. She jabbed the air with it as she hissed at the IT teacher. 'Back off and let me sort it, I'm on top of it.'

'You're not on top of anything,' Mr Yorke said. 'The code hasn't been right for weeks.'

'It's an anomaly, all experiments have them.'

'You have *got* to stop calling it that.'

'Why should I?' Dr Zats said. 'It *is* an experiment. At least I'm upfront about it.'

'Yes, and perhaps you shouldn't be. Helping the kids should be your priority, don't you think?'

'They *are* my priority,' Dr Zats said. 'Why do you think I'm here?'

Mr Yorke let out a laugh. 'I've read all your papers, Miriam. I've seen you on *Psychology Review*. You're in it for the glory, don't pretend otherwise.'

'Cut the holier-than-thou attitude, Jeremy. We both know you only tolerate me because of the cheque I gave to the school, so you can stop pretending you're in it for the kids. I might be interested in results, but your primary concern is the cash lining your pocket. That's not exactly noble, you know.'

Mr Yorke looked like he wanted to snap Dr Zats in half. 'That cash goes directly to Mr Leighton, not me,' he said, so quiet it was venomous. 'Sort the code out. It's too weird, I don't like it. I don't want one of my kids getting hurt. I've known them since they were eleven in most cases, and—'

The door swung shut behind me.

The teachers jumped apart at the noise. Mr Yorke cleared his throat and stepped by me to go back into the IT lab, but not before giving Dr Zats a final glare.

'Sorry,' I mumbled. 'I didn't mean to interrupt.'

'It was nothing that couldn't wait,' Dr Zats said, in a too-cheerful voice. She began to redo her hair, slotting her pen back into the middle of her bun. 'How was your first session in BTL? We haven't had a chance to chat.'

'Good.'

Dr Zats huffed a laugh. 'Is that all? Tell me about it. What did you make?'

'A train,' I said carefully, deciding not to mention my house. Or Dad. Or Alex. Or the fact that the six of us got together last night and played capture the flag.

'Did you copy the train from anything in real life?' Dr Zats asked.

I licked my lips, unsure how to handle the question. Georgie said they couldn't watch us as we played. Obviously she was right otherwise Dr Zats wouldn't be asking me, she'd be punishing me for breaking her rule.

I knew the consequences if I ever lied to Mother.

It was different with Dr Zats. I didn't know her well enough. If I lied to her, what would she do? She could revoke my Better Than Life privileges. I wouldn't get to be part of the group any more.

'You said not to,' I said, deciding on a different tactic.

Dr Zats seemed to accept this. 'Good, that's good. What are your thoughts on the trial so far?'

I thought back to the quiz I'd filled in to win my place in the group. They were similar to the questions I'd answered just now – probing, personal questions that made me want to walk away and escape.

'You said we were here to test the game. For you and SmartTech.'

'That's right.'

'What do the quizzes have to do with testing the game?'

For a moment, Dr Zats's face betrayed her surprise. Concern quickly swallowed it. 'You're important to us, Lola. We want to protect you, make sure nothing goes wrong in the game so you keep playing it. You do feel safe in there, right?'

I nodded, though she'd probably read my quiz later and see I'd said differently.

'But I hear what you're saying,' she continued. 'Tell you what, if you have any suggestions as to how to improve the game, I'd love to hear them. The marketing department is always on the lookout for anything that will make the game more palatable to a wider audience.'

It was an empty offer and it sounded like one.

If Sebastian hadn't already found a workaround for the physical space issue, I would have suggested it. He was wreaking havoc with her code and she had no idea it was him. *Us.* The way I saw it, he was improving it for her. Because of him, I wasn't confined to the gym.

When it became clear I wasn't going to jump at her offer, Dr Zats gave me a parting smile and made her way to the staffroom – not the IT lab where Mr Yorke had returned.

I wondered about their argument.

They'd referred to the game as an experiment, but that didn't make any sense. Dr Zats worked for SmartTech, a computer games company. She'd referred to a marketing department just now. Her concern had seemed genuine, even if it had been accompanied by surprise that I was asking questions.

Even so, I was unsure how the quizzes were a way of making sure we were safe.

TEN

My first English Lit lesson did not go well. The teacher, Mrs Hamilton, directed most questions at me and made a show of being shocked at how little I knew.

'I thought you were home-schooled?' she said.

I was. It wasn't until I had a class with her that I realized how little I'd been taught.

Mother educated us in Music. We studied the history of composers and instruments. How fashion impacted musical trends. The changing styles of a young prodigy in comparison to an established composer. I learnt to read notes, knew when an F was sharp and when an A flat was a G sharp in disguise, depending on what key the piece was played in. I played the piano, one arpeggio at a time, until Mother was satisfied.

I didn't know what pathetic fallacy was.

I didn't know what enjambment meant.

I couldn't give an example of onomatopoeia.

'Do you know anything?' Mrs Hamilton scoffed. With a single question, she dismissed the knowledge I did have because it held no power in her classroom. I stared wearily back at her, thinking how Alex would never have to learn these new things. How her lack of knowledge in other areas wouldn't come back to haunt her.

She was in Grenville Music Academy now.

She got in. I didn't. I'd never passed my grade eight piano exam.

In her world, she knew everything she needed to and more. Mother had prepared her for her career and left me adrift.

'No,' I said.

'I'm sure having a mother for your teacher must have made for a very easy educational experience,' Mrs Hamilton said, 'but this is not a sink or swim school. At Leighton, all pupils are made to swim. We don't produce doctors and solicitors and Members of Parliament by letting them tread water, Miss Whitmore. You are no exception. I suggest you leave my classroom and return when you're able to keep up with the conversation.'

The suggestion almost made me laugh because how was I supposed to keep up if I wasn't allowed to even be part of the conversation? It took me a moment to realize she wasn't joking. The shocked silence of the rest of the class and Georgie's slight head jerk towards the door was what made it sink in. The whole class watched as I gathered my things and left.

Every step I took in the hallway made me realize I'd been thrown out of a lesson. I tiptoed through the empty corridors and made my way back up to my room.

The drawn curtains darkened the room. I paused. I'd

opened them before breakfast service. Hadn't I?

Mercedes sat bolt upright in bed, clutched her covers to her chin. Her shoulders were bare. 'Lola. What're you . . .? Aren't you meant to be . . .?'

Something moved next to her. I squinted at it. 'What's that?'

Mercedes pushed at the mound in front of her. Slowly, a head appeared from the other side of the covers. Chestnut hair, oak-coloured eyes. He was wearing a T-shirt but it clung to him in a way that showed off his muscles. His cheeks were flushed but it didn't seem to be from embarrassment.

'Hey,' Sebastian said.

Mercedes licked her lips. 'Look, I've not had a roommate in a long time and I thought I'd learnt your schedule and Seb had a free period and . . .' Her eyes were wide and round. 'Please don't tell anyone. Seb isn't supposed to be in here.'

She kept talking but I didn't hear any of it.

It made sense now, why she was so defensive of him over dinner last night. Why she'd helped me with my timetable. I'd thought she was being kind when really, she was learning my movements so she could sneak her secret boyfriend into our bedroom.

And then there was Sebastian.

He'd talked to me about his mum in a way I didn't think he would have with anyone else. He'd picked me first for his team. Cheered me on when I won for us. He'd been the first person who'd ever believed in me. I thought we had something in common. I thought, maybe, we might . . .

I took a step back.

'Lola, wait—'

I was completely delusional if I thought someone as good-looking and as sweet as Sebastian could ever be interested in me. He went for the most attractive girl in our year, and I would never be able to match up. She had glossy hair and a perfect smile. A skincare regime.

I had scars and a lumpy collarbone. A growing collection of things that didn't belong to me. An imaginary dad because I didn't have a real one.

> I prefer spending time with in-game
> characters than with people
> in the real world
> (Yes)/No

I turned and ran from the bedroom.

'Lola!' Sebastian shouted after me but I kept running, no longer concerned about how loud I was being in the quiet corridors or how someone might see me leave the school building. I sprinted over the gravel and down to the IT lab.

My chest was tight when I reached the doors. I pushed against them but they pushed back.

Locked.

It was only four o'clock. Mr Yorke and Dr Zats must have left for the day. I swore and kicked at the door. There had to be another way to get inside.

I walked around the side of the building, to the gym. My heart pounded, begging for me to get inside. Large waste bins lined the far wall, a row of small rectangular windows above them. They glittered in the setting sun.

I clambered on to a bin with a grunt and tugged on the nearest window. It caught on a latch, only opening a few centimetres, but it was enough to fit a hand through and prise the catch undone. The bins wobbled beneath me, but after being half a kilometre high in the air trying to catch a flagpole, I knew the bin would hold.

Sweat coated my underarms as I wrestled with the catch.

It swung free.

I slithered inside head first and landed on the stack of gym mats.

Sebastian had made it so I could play the game anywhere, but there was nowhere as private as the gym, especially now I knew Mercedes invited people into our room. I closed the window and slipped down from the mats, doing my best to ignore how cold it was. The hairs on my arms stood to attention.

It didn't matter. I didn't need it to be warm, I needed it to be private. Needed to be able to see him.

I closed my eyes and clapped. 'Enter.'

ELEVEN

My house sat on its bed of mist. The grey void stretched into infinity around it. I ran up the stone steps and through the front door into the lift. There was a new level that hadn't been there yesterday:

2
1
G
B

The button for the basement flashed yellow once.
Ping!

I ignored it, selecting the button for the second floor, wondering what would be on there and having no desire to return to the first floor where my kitchen had been demolished by a train. As the lift began to move upwards, I saw the remnants of the crash through the grille. The back of my house had been blown wide open. Wooden beams and lumps of concrete spilt on to the black-and-white tiles of the hallway. A breeze picked at the dust. There was no one flipping pancakes. No one sat at the table, clapping for more.

The lift continued on and I passed through a cross-section of floor before coming to a stop. I pulled back the gate and stepped out on to a pristine hallway. It was the same as the first floor, but the black-and-white tiles were clean and new. Before me was the staircase and the balcony that hung over the chessboard tiles.

I turned away from it.

Didn't want to think about that balcony.

Ever.

I moved on, stepping through the archway and into the living room, on to the velvety cream carpet.

The entire house was empty.

Not for long.

I tossed my hair back, long and curled, focusing on the reason I'd come here. In the game, I could look how I wanted. Get what I wanted. Last night when I'd played capture the flag, I'd felt like I had friends for the first time ever. Sebastian had picked me first. Made a big deal out of helping our team win. In the game, he believed in me. Liked me.

I took a deep breath and gritted my teeth as I imagined the thing I wanted most. His face filled my mind, and the pain followed shortly after.

I cried out, stumbled back, fought to keep my eyes open as the corner of the room pixelated heavily. It shimmered like heat-haze in the distance.

Another stab of pain made me cry out again, making me wonder if it was really worth it. It would be. Had to be. The Key sent a final burst of pain that jolted through my brain and made me shiver.

A boy with chestnut-brown hair walked out of the pixels and into my living room.

I'd broken Dr Zats's second rule: never create characters based on real people.

'Sebastian,' I said, gasping as the pain in my head subsided. The worst was over.

'Lola.' Concern lit his oaky eyes in a way that was meant for me and only me. 'Are you all right?'

I rubbed my temple. 'I'm fine. Just a headache.'

The pain had been worth it. Sebastian was here, in my world, and he was looking at me like I was the centre of it. No one had ever looked at me like that before.

His head was level with mine. *Five-six and nothing taller.* I went to hunch my shoulders but I didn't need to. His body pixelated for a second. When it cleared, he was taller by a few inches. His chin could rest easily on my forehead now, if we ever got close enough.

'Better?' he said, eyebrows raised.

'Perfect,' I said, trying not to choke. The thought had been fleeting but the game had responded to it straight away, like it could read my mind.

'I like how you've done your hair,' he said.

I touched my curls, momentarily forgetting they were long and styled. My hand wasn't scarred any more. There was no lump on my collarbone. No wonder he seemed pleased to see me – I was actually pretty here.

'What shall we do today?' he asked, as though I saw

him every day.

Creating Sebastian had been painful and my head still pounded a little. I hadn't thought about what to do afterwards, and it wasn't like we could go on a date. In the movies, first dates were filled with snow and building snowmen and taking rides in reindeer-led sleighs.

'Hey, look! It's snowing.' Sebastian moved to the living room window. 'Fancy a walk?' He pulled a scarf from the air and wrapped it round his neck without waiting for a reply. A coat appeared on the back of the sofa. He shrugged it on then swapped his school shoes for boots.

I looked down at my own outfit and saw it had changed. My shoes had become wellies and I wore a patterned scarf the same as his. Sebastian found a jacket with a fur-lined hood on the coat stand and helped me into it.

I followed Sebastian through the house and into the kitchen. The room was back to normal on this level. There was no debris or water flooding it, no broken martini glasses. Sebastian flung open the back door and I looked tentatively in the distance for a train. There was no sign of it.

In real life, my garden was long and narrow with a fence running on all three sides.

Years ago, Mother had had it paved over because it was easier to keep, and over time the slabs had become crusted with grime. Occasionally she made me scrub them clean, but that was only if I'd really pissed her off. Even she thought gardening was the worst of punishments.

In the game, there were no slabs. Not even a fence.

It was an expanse of snow-topped grass, with a thick wood in the distance that circled the house. Snow fell softly all around us. Sebastian waded into it, his boots leaving prints as he went. 'This is a great idea, Lola,' he said. His smile turned pointy. 'You'd better find yourself a good hiding spot.' He knelt to scoop up a mound of snow and began to compact it together.

'Wait, wait, wait!' I laughed and tried to do the same but wasn't quick enough.

Sebastian lobbed his snowball at me and it hit the ground a few centimetres from my right. His wicked grin told me it was a practice shot and next time I wouldn't be so lucky. I retaliated, packing my own snowball tight before throwing it his way. It soared over his head.

He snorted. 'That was a terrible shot.'

I laughed louder when my second hit him square in the chest. He wiped the remnants from his jacket, abandoned the snow he'd been scooping together and ran towards me. I shrieked and waded away, hiding behind a tree.

We chased each other into the woods where our snowball fight continued for a while, each of us ducking behind trees and finding refuge under fallen logs. It became a game of hide and seek, but we both laughed too loudly to hide for long.

Sebastian showed me how to make a snow angel and we built a snowman together. We started with a small snowball and built it into a huge mound, packing the snow in tight to round out the body. We plonked a head on top. When it came to decorating, I found some pebbles for eyes and a mouth. Sebastian produced a hat and a pipe from the air to finish the look.

'Are you having a good time?' he asked, tying off a scarf.

'The best,' I said.

'Good. I want you to be happy here.'

The comment made me smile. No one had ever wanted me to be happy before.

'I'll find us some arms,' I said, turning away to the woods to find a stick. There were no fallen branches nearby, so I waded further into the woods. The trees got closer together and the snow seemed to get deeper.

Movement caught my eye. Something dashed between a cluster of tree trunks. I stopped and squinted, waiting for it again. There. A flash of blonde hair. I blinked and it had gone again. I waded closer, searching, but the snow was too deep and the trees were closer than ever. I turned around to go back. Trees blocked my view and I couldn't see a way out.

'Lola?' Sebastian called. He sounded far away.

My breath came out in a white puff, like I was smoking.

The thought came suddenly, like a spike of electricity, and with it, a memory I couldn't get rid of.

There was a sudden thunderous crack as, a few metres away, a whole bank of trees collapsed in on each other. I scrambled for cover as they sank back into the ground to create a clearing. Tarmac overtook the snow and formed a square surrounded by a wooden fence. A set of metal swings and a roundabout popped up through the tarmac like mushrooms.

My hand flew to my head. 'OW!' I doubled over but couldn't look away. Two platforms with a wooden bridge between them came next. Then a climbing frame twisted out of the ground, comprised of thick metal ropes. Plastic joints curled over them, binding it all together.

I screamed as the last of the playground emerged from my memory.

My knees hit the snow.

Pixels blurred over an area to the left and Sebastian walked out of them, his forehead puckered in a frown as he helped me up. 'Lola, what happened? I lost you for a moment there.'

'The trees, they were too thick. I couldn't find my way back.'

'Lucky I know how to find you then.'

I wanted to ask him how he did that – moved from one area of the game to another, stepping out of the pixels like they were a wormhole or something – but he was looking from me to the park. 'Did you recreate that from memory?' he asked.

'Not on purpose.'

'You're in pain,' he said, still holding on to me.

'It hurts.'

'It shouldn't.' He pulled off a glove with his teeth and

tentatively brought his hand to my temple the same way he had at the arena. He tapped my Key and I shuddered as it sent a buzz crawling through my brain.

'What did you do?'

'They coded the pain response in. I've coded it out. Easy.'

'But I broke a rule,' I said. People who break rules should be punished. I'd had way worse than a headache before.

'Rules like this are meant to be broken, trust me,' Sebastian said. 'It shouldn't cause us pain because we want to recreate from real life. That Pavlovian conditioning is bullshit. Try again, you'll be fine now.'

I looked to the playground that had formed from nothing. Trees circled it like a fairy ring. It wasn't quite complete – there was something missing.

A green wooden bench with cast-iron armrests and feet curled out of the tarmac. The green slats faded and became chipped: twenty years of wear happening in under five seconds.

I raised my hand to my head, expecting the sharp burst of pain.

It never came.

'See?' Sebastian said. 'All fixed.'

He'd helped me a second time, manipulated my Key so I could break Dr Zats's rules without consequence. The Sebastian before me was taller but he looked the same as the one from the arena last night.

I stepped forward and almost tripped over something

wedged into the snow. I knelt down to dig an object out, held it out to properly inspect it. It was small and wooden, triangular in shape. My hands shook as I realized what it was.

'What's that?'

'A metronome,' I said, flicking the pendulum into action.

Tick.

Tick.

Tick.

I wanted to throw it into the woods. Run away from it. Stamp on it or set it on fire and bury the ashes. I squinted up at Sebastian. 'Did you put this here? It's not funny if you did.'

'I've never seen it before in my life,' he said.

I glanced around, looking for that flash of blonde hair again. Had she put it here? It couldn't be possible.

Sebastian pointed to the park. 'Maybe she knows where it came from?'

A girl with red hair was sat at the top of the climbing frame. Her breath streamed out in puffs of white cloud like she was smoking a cigarette. Even from here I could see the twist to her glossy red hair. Just how Mother used to style it. A chill cut through my spine, making me shiver. Why did Alex keep turning up? She'd already ruined breakfast with Dad. What would she do here with Sebastian?

'She looks like you,' Sebastian said. 'Do you know her?'

'No,' I said, too quickly. 'I've no idea who that is.'

I dropped the metronome, ready to turn around and go back to the house.

It landed with a clink, like it had hit glass.

I looked down, expecting to see a broken martini glass, and relief seeped through me when I saw it was something else.

A glass of water sat on top of the snow. I picked it up, studied how its contents swirled like a mini tornado, as if someone had put a spoon in it and stirred it rapidly. I weighed it in my hands, feeling its unfamiliarity.

The metronome made sense. I knew where that had come from. It used to live on Mother's piano. Would guide me through all my pieces, a constant background noise wherever I went in the house.

But the glass of water . . . I'd never seen it before. It didn't come from my house or my memory. It was so innocuous. Casual. It could have come from any cupboard in any house, but it definitely hadn't come from mine. What was it doing all the way out here anyway? The nearest kitchen was back in the house.

I held it out to Sebastian. 'Is this yours?'

'Don't touch that.' He slapped it out of my hand. We watched as it fell back to the ground and the contents dissolved into the snow. 'How about we go somewhere else?'

I looked up to see that over in the park, Alex had reached the bottom of the climbing frame. Her mouth was red. Too red. She began to walk towards us.

I feel safer in the game than in
real life
Yes/(No)

I stood up. 'Good idea. Where?'

'There's always a door here, Lola.'

'A door? What do you mean?'

'Doors are one of the best parts of the game,' Sebastian said.

He spoke like he came here regularly, but that was impossible. I'd only made him a few hours ago. But he knew how to manipulate my Key, recode it so I didn't feel pain. He was familiar with the mechanics of the game in a way that didn't make sense.

The park gate creaked open. Alex was making her way over to us. Her grey eyes were bright with intent. She wore the kind of look that preceded hurting me for her amusement.

'Show me,' I said to Sebastian.

At that, a doorframe shot out of the snow. A scratched-up grey door solidified within the frame and a long metal bar popped out across its middle. A sign fixed itself to the top.

FIRE EXIT

'If you don't like one part of the game, you can escape to another,' Sebastian said, moving towards it.

I thought of Alex who had a multitude of doors

available to her.

Alex, who, because good fortune was written into her DNA, always seemed to land on the one square that led her up the board so she could win the game. Alex always found the exit. She didn't even have to try. Doors were open for her in a way they never were for me.

Sebastian pushed on the metal bar and the door released. 'Want to see where it goes?'

Behind me, Alex had reached the treeline.

From here, I could see why her mouth was so red. Blood coated her teeth as she smiled at me. The drips blossomed in the snow.

'Yes,' I said to Sebastian.

I crunched across the snow and went through the fire exit with him. When we were on the other side I slammed it shut and backed away from it. Immediately, it began to sink back into the snow, the same way it had appeared. There was no way Alex could follow. I turned around, finally able to breathe.

We were on a ledge overlooking a snowy valley. Small lights gathered in the distance: a large house on a hill, twinkling back at us. Pine trees stretched into a sky dotted with a million stars. Bands of green light danced through them, thickening then tapering off into little more than wisps, and back again.

'The Aurora!'

Sebastian's face was tinted green from the sky, but he was concentrating on me, not the lights. 'Are you happier here? Is this better than the woods?'

Alex was on the other side of a door that had disappeared. 'This is *way* better than the woods.'

'Oi!' someone yelled. It sounded far away.

I looked to Sebastian uncertainly. 'It wasn't me,' he said.

The door had gone, it couldn't have been Alex. Plus, the voice had sounded male.

'I said *oi*!' Someone was shouting at me. An invisible hand shook my shoulder, almost sent me flying backwards.

'What's going on?' I stumbled away from whoever was trying to grab me.

The gym.

I was still in the gym..

'I have to go,' I said. 'Someone in real life is talking to me.'

Sebastian's shoulders fell. 'When will you be back?'

'I don't . . . I need to check the rota. Sometime tomorrow.'

His mouth was a line of disappointment. 'Come back soon.'

Whoever was pulling at me in the real world tugged my arm again, harder this time.

'I will,' I said, then clapped and said, 'Exit.'

Sebastian and the Aurora vanished. In their place was the gym and a man with a scowl. I blinked as I took him in. He wore a uniform and an ID badge was clipped to his shirt pocket.

'You on drugs?' he said, flashing a torch at my eyes.

I shrank away from the beam. 'No, I was . . . never mind.'

'You a student?' he asked. He lowered the torch which made the shadows of his scowl deepen. 'I've told you lot before, you're not allowed in here after lights out.'

'This is the first time I've—'

'You do it again and I'll have to tell the head.'

'Mr Leighton?' The threat filled me with dread. I still had his watch and no idea when to put it back. It was only a matter of time before he realized it was me who'd taken it. 'Please don't,' I said. 'I lost track of the time, that's all. It won't happen again.'

The man rolled his eyes and led me from the gym by my elbow. 'See it doesn't. And tell your friend and all, I've chucked him out more times than I care to count.'

'Who?'

'Lord knows if I know who he is. Don't make a point of learning trespassers' names. He tried to pay me off though so I wouldn't tell the head, didn't he? Cheeky little blighter.'

The security guard saw me out of the building and locked it behind me with a glare.

As I trudged back up to the main building, I went over what the security guard had told me. Someone else was playing the game outside their timetabled slots. Someone else had found their way into the gym the same way I had.

TWELVE

Thunder rumbled through the dark sky, and secrets hid in the shadows cast by nearby trees. I quickened my pace, telling myself I was only doing so because it had started raining. It got heavier the closer I got to the main building. By the time I reached the pillared entranceway, my hair stuck to my face and my school shirt was practically see-through.

The double doors were wide open.

Rain lashed down, collected on the hallway floor. I stepped inside, into the darkness, and almost tripped over something.

No, not something. Some*one*.

'Sebastian!' He was lying, unmoving, not far from the door. Almost like he'd tried to walk through it and fell unconscious before he got outside. I sank to my knees and rolled him over. His eyes were closed but his pulse fluttered in his neck. I put my ear to his lips; his breathing was deep and even, like he was asleep.

'Sebastian.' I hissed his name, tried to shake him awake. He didn't respond.

I slapped his cheeks a little. Still no response.

Rainwater darkened his hair, his eyelashes.

I tried to open his eyes to see if they were blue – maybe he was playing the game – but they'd rolled too far back in his head. If he *was* playing the game, he'd picked a funny place to do it.

'What are you doing out of bed?' A voice jolted me away from Sebastian. Matron was on the stairs, coming down from her office. She looked from me to the exposed entranceway to Sebastian lying on the floor. I could see her mind ticking over the scene. 'What happened . . .? What did you do?' She rushed to his side, not caring how the rainwater seeped into the knees of her trousers.

'I found him like this,' I said.

She went through the same routine I had: checked he was breathing, shouted his name into his face and waited for a response, a blink, anything.

I tried to move towards them in case there was anything I could help with. Matron pushed me away, forcing me against a wall. A clap of lightning lit up the row of paintings there. The faces of Leighton's past head-masters glared down at me, judging me the way Matron was judging me. Accusing me the way she was.

'What did you *do*?' Matron's question was a shriek, an accusation, a demand. She grabbed a phone from her pocket and called for an ambulance.

'I haven't done anything!'

She ignored me, focusing on the phone call and moving Sebastian into the recovery position. I barely heard her words as she spoke to the emergency operator.

Sebastian was unmoving. The only indication he was still alive was the slight rise and fall of his chest.

Matron's phone lit up a second time as she made another call.

David Leighton flashed up on the screen.

I took another step backwards and my heel crunched on something. I looked down to see the stem of a broken martini glass trapped under my foot.

It disappeared as another clap of lightning lit up the hall. I checked behind me but it was definitely gone. It must have been a trick of the light or something.

'The ambulance is on its way,' Matron said, putting her phone back in her pocket. 'Now tell me what happened before Mr Leighton gets here. I'll be nicer than him about it, I assure you. What happened, Lola?'

The question tugged at a distant memory.

'What happened, Lola? What did your mother do?'

The rain was louder than ever.

It pelted us all, the floor, the door. Drummed against it like a thousand tiny fingers begging to be let in.

The door.

My house had a red front door. It was the correct, clichéd colour like in all the films and books. It promoted the fantasy that a perfect, happy family dwelled behind it. When I opened it that day and the police officer was on the other side, the truth tumbled out on to the street like a burst vein.

I could hear it, the rain.

Smell it as it hit the metal railings.

See it dripping from the police officer's hat as he filled my doorway and escorted me down to a waiting car. Feel it. The coldness of the interview room, the breeze from the fan above our heads. A woman in plain clothes sitting opposite me.

'I'm Detective Moran. I know you've been through a lot today, but I need you to go over it one last time.'

My hands twisted like they had a life of their own.

'What happened, Lola? What did your mother do?'

'Lola.' Matron clicked her fingers in my face. 'What happened?'

'It was a landslide,' I said, partly to her. Mostly to myself. 'The rain, it was too much. That's what caused the accident.'

Matron stared at me. 'Landslide? What are you talking about? What accident?'

Mr Leighton limped his way into the hall. He took one look at Sebastian on the floor before swivelling my way. 'What did you do to him?'

'I found him like this!' Why wouldn't they believe me?

The headmaster scoffed his disbelief and limped over to his son. He growled Sebastian's name over and over, as if a stern telling-off would snap him out of unconsciousness.

Rain howled through the open door.

When the ambulance showed up, the paramedics rushed to Sebastian's side. They unbuttoned his shirt and studied a series of long red marks down his chest: bruises not yet purple with age. 'What are these?' one of them asked, pointing to them.

'He's a lacrosse player,' Mr Leighton answered. 'Fifty times I've told him to be more careful. He's far too vigorous and he doesn't listen.'

The paramedic nodded and went through the same checks we all had, plus a few more. They thumbed the Key at his temple. 'And what's this?'

'That's nothing,' Mr Leighton said sharply, leaning forward to peel it off. My hands flew to my mouth at how effortlessly he removed it. Sebastian didn't react. I'd half expected him to snap out of it and sit up, yanked out of the game if that was what he was doing. He didn't move.

Eventually the paramedics packed Sebastian on to a trolley and wheeled him out. Mr Leighton followed, limping his way over to the ambulance. They disappeared in a flash of red and blue lights.

When Matron finally shut the doors, she turned to me with her trademark scowl. 'Mr Leighton will want answers,' she said. 'I suggest you go to bed and think about what you've done. I can't remember the last time he expelled a student, but he'll do it if this turns out to be your fault.'

'I haven't done anything, I—'

'That's quite enough, Lola.' Matron lifted her chin in the direction of the stairs. 'Off to bed with you.'

I turned and raced up the stairs before she tried to ask me another question I couldn't answer. When my bedroom door was at my back and the darkness of the room surrounded me, I let out a loud exhale.

Mercedes stirred and rolled over in her sleep.

I should shake her awake and tell her what happened. Sebastian was her boyfriend; she would want to know.

Dad slipped from the shadows and pushed his aviators on to his head. 'I wouldn't tell her, Lola,' he said. 'You were the one who found him, remember.'

I paused, leg outstretched like I was about to go to her and tell her everything. Dad was right. Matron and Mr Leighton already thought I'd hurt Sebastian. They didn't believe I had nothing to do with it. I was the one who'd found him and it made me look guilty, even if I wasn't. Mercedes might think the same.

Her breathing evened out again, cementing my decision.

The memory of the rain and the police officer was still loud in my ears. If I closed my eyes, I saw Sebastian lying on the floor, rain pelting his face.

I reached for Dad and my hand passed straight through his. He was the only one who could help me. The only one who could make me feel better, and he wasn't really here.

He was already fading.

'Don't go,' I whispered.

Dad winked before melting back into the shadows. 'You know how to find me.'

I went to my bed and sank on to it, listened to the quiet *tick, tick, tick* of Mr Leighton's watch deep in my drawer.

Solid as a metronome.

THE PAST

My breath hung in the air. Alex giggled as she put two fingers to her lips. 'Look, I'm smoking.' She huffed out a white cloud before running to the swings. I laughed and clambered up the climbing frame.

'Dolores,' Mummy shouted from below, gloved hand raised to her brow. 'Don't go too high, I won't be coming up to get you if you get stuck, and I refuse to waste our tax money by calling the fire brigade.'

I clasped the metal bars with mittened hands and dared to look down. The icy park floor seemed to swoop upwards. I flattened myself against the climbing frame to make sure I didn't fall.

'If you fall, Dolores, I will make you do scales and arpeggios all evening,' Mummy warned. 'This was supposed to be a reward. Don't make me punish you.'

On the other side of the frame, another little girl began to climb. She put one hand over the other with vigour. Soon she was higher than me.

'Dolores,' Mummy warned.

'I'm fine,' I called back. I lifted a foot on to the next rung and concentrated on clambering upwards. We reached the top

at the same time, the other girl and me.

'Hello,' she said, taking a seat right on the top. She glanced around and budged up a bit. 'There's room for one more.'

I sat next to her awkwardly and did my best to look as relaxed as her. It wasn't so bad if you didn't look down.

The girl waved to her mummy who clapped and shouted about how great she was. My mummy dusted down a bench with her handkerchief and crossed her legs when she sat down. She looked like there was a bad smell in the air. She always looked like that.

'I thought your mummy was yelling for me at first,' the girl with the rosy cheeks said. 'I'm Dolores too. Well, my mummy calls me Lola.'

Lola. My insides turned as I considered how perfect it was. It's funny, how pleasing it felt that my name could be shortened into something so pretty. Mummy had never given me a nickname. Alex was short for Alexandra, but she only ever got called that if she was really in trouble. Most of the time she was Alex, but I was always Dolores.

'Go Lola!' the girl's mummy shouted up from below. 'Look how high you are!'

I waved at the nice lady. 'I'm Lola too,' I said.

One second I was sitting on top of the climbing frame, the next I was falling to the bottom. I tumbled to the ground with a thud. White spots appeared in my vision. My collarbone . . . it hurt. A hard lump had formed there; bone trying to push through the skin.

Alex jumped down after me. She stood over me, her silhouette blocking out the winter sun. 'Mummy said you'd fall,' she said.

THIRTEEN

When I woke, Mercedes was watching me from her side of the room. She sat on her bed, already dressed in her uniform, make-up and hair pristine like it always was.

'You talk in your sleep,' she said.

I sat up with a yawn. 'Sorry.'

'No, it's me that's sorry.' She leant over to deposit a small maroon box on my bedside table. 'This is an apology present,' she said.

I took the box and tugged off the rose-gold ribbon. Inside was a lipstick on a bed of maroon tissue paper. The initials CT were indented into the top of the lid. Charlotte Tilbury. I pulled the cap off and inspected the bright red bullet.

'I thought it could go with your hair,' Mercedes said. 'Obviously you can't get away with wearing it round here. Matron would march you to the loos in a heartbeat and make you scrub it off. But it could be nice for the week-end if your parents ever . . . if you go out for the day, you know?'

No one had ever given me a present as expensive as this.

'I saw you looking at them the other day.' Mercedes indicated her collection of lipsticks across the room. She kept talking. 'I have two of that shade and I thought you might like one. If you don't like it, you don't have to—'

'I love it,' I said, twisting the cap back on and relishing the expensive click. It was the kind of thing I might borrow from someone without asking. Here I was being given it. It would be mine and only mine. I placed it on my bedside table. 'Thank you.'

Relief washed through her frame. 'It won't happen again, by the way. Seb, I mean. But please don't tell anyone. It's kind of embarrassing.'

'Why is it embarrassing?'

She smoothed the faintest of wrinkles from her skirt. 'He won't let me tell anyone that we're together.'

'He's making you keep it a secret?'

'Seb said he wants to wait until we're both out of school.' There was a strain in her voice, like she was trying to convince herself.

Disapproval tugged at me. Why would anyone want to keep someone as beautiful as Mercedes a secret? The Sebastian in my game would never keep *me* a secret.

She shrugged like it wasn't a big deal. 'Anyway, are we OK?'

'We're OK,' I said, feeling a twinge of guilt that I still hadn't told her about finding Sebastian last night.

'Great.' She stood up with a smile. 'I know we're room-mates, but I want us to be friends.'

I looked up in surprise, but she was already walking

away to get her bag ready.

If I told her about Sebastian, she might not want to be my friend any more. Matron and Mr Leighton were already convinced it was my fault because I'd been the one to find him. What if Mercedes did too? I picked up the lipstick again, pulling and pushing on the cap.

Click.

Click.

Click.

Mercedes had been kind to me, helping me with my timetable. But that had been because she was trying to sneak Sebastian up to our room. If I told anyone about that, she'd be expelled. Was that why she'd given me a lipstick? Maybe she wasn't really sorry.

Click.

Click.

Click.

'Are you coming to breakfast?' Mercedes asked. She was already by the door, showered and dressed and ready.

I hesitated to tell her about Sebastian, but I still didn't know what had happened to him. All I knew was that he was taken away by an ambulance. It didn't make sense to tell her until I had some good news, she'd only be worried about him.

'I'll meet you there,' I said.

By the time I got to the breakfast service, the whole school seemed to know about Sebastian. I walked past several tables of people whispering overly loudly about how the headmaster's son had been found unconscious in the entrance hall.

The same subject was being discussed at our table when I sat down. Finn had overheard Matron talking to another member of staff. I tried to ask the right questions and be surprised at the right times as he told me all about it. From what I could make out, Matron hadn't mentioned me. No one knew I'd been there.

Mercedes's eyes were as wet as the coffee she cradled. 'He was fine yesterday,' she kept saying. 'How can someone just . . . fall unconscious?'

'Maybe it was an aneurysm,' Wai said. 'They can happen at any time.'

'That sounds serious,' Georgie said.

Mercedes shook her head. 'No way, he's too young for anything like that. He probably just fainted, right? I'm sure he'll be back soon.'

'Matron said he's at a specialist hospital now,' Finn said. 'They wouldn't admit him unless it was serious, would they?'

Everyone fell silent. I'd been the one to find him but I had no more answers than anyone else. For all I knew, it *could* have been an aneurysm.

'He'll be back in no time,' I said, trying to smile. Mercedes didn't even look up at my pathetic attempt to cheer her up.

'I guess we won't be playing Better Than Life together until then,' Finn said.

'What do you mean?' I asked.

'Seb's the tech guy,' Wai said, nodding. 'He was the one who figured out how to play the game without Dr Zats knowing. He unlocked our Keys so we can play it anywhere, not just the gym. He was the one who would host our group sessions. None of us know how to do any of that. Without him there's no more capture the flag.'

'There's no more CTF anyway,' Finn said. 'We're an uneven number again.'

'Is that all you can think about?' Mercedes snapped. 'Seb is in *hospital*, Finn. I don't give a shit about CTF right now, and neither should you. Aren't you supposed to be his best friend? You're not even upset.'

'Of course I'm upset,' Finn hissed. 'We've been best friends ever since we signed up to lacrosse training together back in first year. We'd practise together on Saturdays when my parents – when they didn't come and visit and . . . You don't know him better than me, you know. Until we all got thrown together he never even knew you existed.'

Mercedes choked on a sob. Georgie put her arm round her shoulders and eventually pulled her into a hug. Finn's words had cut her deep. She cared for Sebastian more than he would ever know, and I grappled for something to say to make her feel better. It wasn't my fault what had happened to Sebastian but it was my fault for not telling her when I'd found him. I watched Georgie hug her closely and felt a hideous mix of guilty and useless.

Finn brushed at his eyes. 'I'm sorry,' he gritted out. 'I didn't mean that. I'm just . . . he's my best friend.'

Mercedes took a deep, shuddering breath in an attempt to regain composure. A bell rang through the dining hall and the room began to empty out. She stood up from the table. 'I'm late for French.'

'It's Friday,' Georgie said, watching her go. 'We'd normally play together on a Friday evening.'

No one said anything.

She sighed and slung her bag over her shoulder. 'We'd better get to English Lit,' she said, looking my way.

The last time I'd been in Mrs Hamilton's class, she'd thrown me out of it, told me not to come back until I was better prepared. I had no intention of better preparing myself. Had no intention of ever setting foot in her classroom again.

I looked over to the teachers' table and saw Mr Leighton's seat was empty. He must still be at the hospital with Sebastian. Mr Leighton's flat would be completely empty. It was too good an opportunity to put his watch back.

'I'll meet you there,' I said, then left before she could ask any questions. I ran against the tide of people as they went towards the classrooms, making my way back up to the bedrooms.

I grabbed the sock I'd hidden the watch in and checked the corridor before leaving in the direction of the headmaster's private flat.

It ticked like a heartbeat in my pocket.

He could come back at any moment.

I rushed past the classrooms as quietly as I could, my

breath hot and quick the whole time. I scrambled up the staircase to his private flat, ignoring the sign above the door.

Thou Shalt Not Covet

The door gave way and I slipped inside the hallway.

My feet angled towards the headmaster's study, but my interest went the other way, down the hallway to the other rooms that made up his and Sebastian's home. My feet went where my interest took them: to the room I'd seen Sebastian come out of the first time I'd been here. Floorboards creaked with each movement, but no one came running. The flat was empty.

I reached his bedroom and went inside.

I'd never been in a boy's bedroom before, and I doubted Mercedes had ever made it up here – after all, Sebastian had wanted to keep her a secret. There was a lacrosse stick leaning in the far corner, posters of lacrosse players on his walls. A desk took up most of the room. Three monitors and a keyboard with a weird split down the middle covered its surface. A hum emanated from that part of the room; the same noise as the IT labs, only quieter.

It was strange, being in Sebastian's space when he was in hospital. The fact his computer was still turned on and his bedcovers were pulled slightly back; it was as though he would walk in at any moment.

The last time I'd properly seen him whilst conscious,

he'd been a tangle of white and black skin with Mercedes.

In my game, he'd been pleased to see me. Sad I had to leave. Then I'd found him unconscious in the school entranceway. There had to be something here that could help me, tell me what had happened.

I spun around, looking for clues, and came face to face with Mr Leighton. Shit.

'Miss Whitmore,' the headmaster said. He filled the doorframe like a caged bear. 'What are you doing in here?'

'I . . . came to borrow a textbook,' I said, and grabbed the nearest book from Sebastian's desk. I looked down at the cover.

Coding in H+ by Henry Hall

Mr Leighton's attention flicked to it and back to me. 'I find it hard to believe you would be borrowing a textbook when I hear you are so ill-prepared for your lessons. Mrs Hamilton told me she had to remove you from her classroom because you were disrupting her class.' His eyes narrowed. 'I did not have you pegged for a troublemaker, Dolores.'

'That's not what happened,' I said.

'Are you suggesting Mrs Hamilton is a liar?'

I clutched the textbook closer to my chest, struggling to find the right words.

Dad appeared at my side. 'Tell him, Lola,' he said, directing a thunderous glare at the headmaster. 'Tell him how that teacher bullied you into leaving and now she's lying about what happened.'

The words were stuck in my throat. I could picture the speech therapist and her stupid flash cards.

A is for Apple.

B is for Bank.

C is for Landslide, Train Crash and Death.

Mr Leighton continued: 'Do you have any idea how lucky you are to be here? How you landed on your feet with a full scholarship to my school? Leighton is the benchmark other schools measure themselves against. We demand excellence and we achieve it through delivering a high standard of education. Yet, in the short time you've been here you've either been thrown out of your lessons or elected not to go, and now I see you have let yourself into my home without any kind of invitation. What do you have to say for yourself?'

'Tell him, Lola.' Dad's hands were fists, but it was a desperate kind of anger. 'You have to tell him because I can't.'

In this world, Dad only existed in my imagination. There was nothing he could do. If I couldn't find the words to yell back, neither could he.

Mr Leighton took my silence for submission. He indicated for me to leave. I slid past him, holding Sebastian's book to my chest like a shield.

The headmaster limped as he followed me to the front door of his flat. 'If you skip even a single lesson more, Dolores, I will see that there are serious repercussions. Do you understand me?'

'Yes.'

'Did I not tell you that covetousness was the worst of all sins? Didn't I tell you to keep your eyes on your own prize? What have you been doing all this time if not ignoring that sound advice? To your lesson, Dolores. And don't you ever come back up here.' He closed the door in my face with all the finality of a full stop.

The sign above it glared at me.

Thou Shalt Not Covet

I still had his watch. It ticked in my pocket, solid as a metronome.

Landslide.

Train crash.

SIX WEEKS EARLIER

Mother stood with her back to me in the living room. She sipped her breakfast martini as she faced the calendar and crossed off another day from it with her red pen. That morning's post was in a neatly opened pile on her bar cart.

Mother preferred to correspond in letters, saying it forced companies to give a personalized response and it took longer, which could only be a good thing in a world where you can get anything almost immediately. Phones allowed people to keep tabs on us, she said. Social services, et cetera.

She folded a letter back into its envelope and returned to the calendar. She drew a red circle around a Saturday night.

'The date's set then?' Alex asked.

'It will be the end of all our problems,' Mother said with a nod.

'What if it doesn't work?'

Mother took a long draw from her martini. 'It will work. He's desperate.'

'Who is?' I asked.

They turned to me with a look that said they'd forgotten I lived there too.

'None of your business,' Mother said, closing the matter.

When that Saturday rolled around, Mother dressed with even more care than usual, choosing clothes from the back of her wardrobe and making me press them until they were wrinkle-free. She left the house in her long fur coat and a cloud of hairspray, blonde hair coiled and set.

Alex and I were alone for the first time in years. Mother had left us with strict instructions to master the Rachmaninoff piece by the time she returned, but ultimately Alex was in charge.

I sat at the piano and played.

Alex leant over the lid and poked the metronome.

Tick.

Tick tick.

Tick.

'Stop that,' I said, playing the wrong note.

'You hate the piano,' Alex said. 'Take the evening off.'

'What do you mean?'

'Rachmaninoff is hard. We both know we won't be up to her standard anyway. Go on, do something else. I'm in charge, I'll tell her we spent the whole day practising when she asks.'

'Really?'

She nodded. 'Really.'

I put the piano lid down and stood up. 'Thanks, Alex.'

Her smile was wide. 'What are sisters for?'

FOURTEEN

The next day, Mercedes was up before me, which was not unusual. She was still applying her make-up, which was. Usually she was up and dressed by now, probably sneaking a packet of crisps she didn't want anyone to know about. An array of make-up-stained tissues and cotton buds were scattered around where she sat.

'My parents are supposed to be taking me out today,' she said, noticing I was awake. 'I have to look perfect and I can't stop crying.'

'You do look perfect,' I said.

Mercedes layered on more foundation. 'You have no idea what they're like.'

I took in her jeans and top and registered today was Saturday. Parents were allowed to swoop in and take their children away for the weekend if they wanted. Kids could go back home and see their siblings, friends, pets. Mercedes was lucky that her parents only lived an hour away.

I pulled my knees up to my chest and held them close. A whole day alone. It might not be so bad. The gym would probably be free.

Was that where Sebastian had been going? The gym? The way he'd fallen it had looked like he'd been heading outside when he'd collapsed, but that was impossible. He didn't need to go to the gym any more.

Mercedes let out a wobbly sigh. She'd cried herself to sleep last night and obviously still wasn't done.

'I'm sorry about Sebastian,' I said.

'Why are you sorry? It's not your fault.'

I shifted and mumbled my agreement. It wasn't my fault, not really. I pushed away the guilt that bubbled in my insides and went to get ready for the day. Georgie had left a note on the bathroom mirror.

Who the fucking fuck left toothpaste in the sink?
Sort it OUT!!
Love, Georgina xox

I sat on the stone steps outside the main entrance with Mercedes, our gazes fixed on the rampant stone lions as we waited for her parents' car to appear between them. She'd sorted her make-up and looked as flawless as ever, but she was quieter than usual, obviously thinking about Sebastian.

I tried not to think about how less than forty-eight hours ago, he'd been lying unconscious behind where we sat.

We watched other cars make their way down the drive and collect waiting students. I wondered what it would be like to be whisked away by family. Alex certainly wouldn't be visiting me.

'Hey,' Finn said, coming from behind us with a couple of people I recognized from my English Lit lesson. 'Have you heard the latest?'

Mercedes looked up. 'About Seb?'

Finn nodded, moving down the steps and coming to stand in front of us. 'Word on the grapevine is that it was a student who discovered him. Matron found them both while she was on the way to bed. It must have been late, really late, when she found them.'

Adrenaline spiked through me. 'Did Matron say who it was?'

'Nope. I overheard her talking about it with Mrs Hamilton, and you know those two are best mates. If she wouldn't tell *her* then . . .'

'It means whoever found him was responsible,' Mercedes said. 'Like they think there's been an incident, or something.'

'Exactly,' Finn said, 'and Mr Leighton apparently told her she's not allowed to say who it is.'

'Why would he do that?' I said, trying my best not to squeak. Mr Leighton and I were not friends. He'd been as convinced as Matron it was all my fault. Why would he try to protect me?

'Seb was popular,' Mercedes said. 'Mr Leighton would only keep their name quiet to stop further incidents from happening.'

Another spike of adrenaline made me shiver. Sebastian had plenty of lacrosse teammates who might go out of their way to make my life miserable. Not to mention the Better Than Life group. I had no doubt I wouldn't be able to sit with them at lunch or in lessons if they found out it was me who discovered Sebastian.

'They must have beat Seb up good and proper,' Finn said.

'Maybe it's nothing like that,' I said. 'Maybe that person simply found Sebastian that night, and they aren't responsible for what actually happened to him.'

'Then why wouldn't they have told me?' Mercedes snapped. Finn cocked his head and she flustered as she tried to backtrack. 'Or-or any of our group. The whole school knows how close we are.'

Finn's phone lit up in his hand. He moved away to accept the call.

Anger radiated off Mercedes. 'I knew it wasn't as complicated as Seb having an aneurysm,' she said. 'Someone did something to him.'

'We don't know for sure,' I said.

Mercedes gave a scoff of disbelief and folded her arms.

I had to bite the inside of my cheek to stop the guilt from making me confess. I should have told her the night I got back from finding Sebastian. Should have told her before she heard it from someone else at the breakfast service. Now, even if I did tell her, she'd be too angry to believe I wasn't responsible.

What would I tell her anyway? I knew as much as the rest of them. Sebastian had been found on the floor unconscious and had been moved to a specialist hospital.

She would demand answers, be even angrier when I couldn't give them.

Across from us, Finn paced on the gravel drive with his phone to his ear.

'But you promised,' he said for the third time. He paused, listening to the person on the other end. 'Can't you send me a ticket? I've told everyone I was going to Monaco . . . *so?* So you said you'd fly me out and that's what I've told all my—' He cut himself off when he saw us watching. 'Never mind. Forget it.'

He practically punched his phone to end the call and I could tell it wasn't enough, and he knew it wasn't enough, and the next second he threw his phone at the ground and stamped on it.

'Finn,' Mercedes said, appalled. 'You just got that phone.'

Finn didn't move. For a moment, I thought he might walk away and leave it there, but he scooped it up from the gravel. The screen was so cracked any video calls would be like looking through a kaleidoscope.

'He'll send me another one,' Finn said.

'Who?'

'Mum's assistant. I talk to him more than Mum.' He shoved the phone in his pocket and stormed away.

Mercedes leant back on her palms. 'That happens way too much to him.'

'What does?'

'His mum makes promises and completely reneges on them later. You heard how excited he was about Monaco the other day. I guess he's stuck here for another weekend.'

Finn was the loudest member of our group. He always had the gossip, was always cracking a joke followed by his trademark wolfish grin. I understood now why Sebastian had hung out with him every Saturday: he didn't have any visiting relatives either. I watched Finn head off towards the IT building and wondered if I wasn't the only one who'd recreated someone from real life. Maybe he'd found a way to get around the pain too. Or maybe he thought the sacrifice was worth the trouble.

'Finally.' Mercedes stood up and dusted down her jeans.

A white Range Rover had appeared between the gates. Even from this distance, I could tell it was a brand-new car. It matched Mercedes in every way: polished, shiny, expensive.

I couldn't help but compare my outfit to hers. My cardigan used to belong to Alex, and my Peter Pan-collared shirt was one Mother had produced from her own wardrobe instead of giving me an allowance to buy my own clothes. She'd found my jeans at a jumble sale. I ran my fingers through my jaw-length hair and wished I felt as pretty as I did in the game.

The Range Rover stopped in front of us and two people got out. Mercedes's mum wore sunglasses that covered most of her face and her skinny jeans looked like they'd been sprayed on to her legs, they fit her so well. 'Darling!' she cooed, and threw her arms around her daughter.

Her dad smiled and waited for his turn. His strong jaw was clad in stubble so precisely shaped it was as if he'd used a stencil. He grinned at Mercedes. 'I came straight from theatre to see you. Couldn't leave my best gal in the lurch now, could I? Your mum rang me this morning and told me all about your friend collapsing.'

'We didn't realize you were close with him,' her mum said. 'I'm sure that boy's parents are touched you're so upset on his behalf. What was his name again? Jeremy?'

'Sebastian,' Mercedes said, her chin beginning to wobble.

Her mum produced a tissue from her Chanel shoulder bag. 'Don't cry, darling, it'll make your eyes puffy.'

Mercedes took a deep breath and gestured to me. 'This is my friend, Lola.'

Her parents flashed me their porcelain smiles. 'Nice to meet you, Mrs Campbell. And Dr Campbell,' I said, noticing his comment about leaving theatre early for Mercedes.

Mrs Campbell snorted. 'Oh, aren't you sweet? You can call me Tonya. Mrs Campbell sounds so ... *old*. Don't you think?' She turned back to her daughter without waiting for a reply.

'And you can call me Carl,' her husband said. 'Don't let the MD fool you, I'm an ordinary guy really.' He laughed at his own joke.

'Dad's a plastic surgeon,' Mercedes said.

'I prefer cosmetic surgeon,' Carl corrected, smiling.

'*Artist* is more accurate,' Tonya added. 'My nose would

be twice the size if your father hadn't intervened. The scalpel is as much a paintbrush as it is a tool.'

Carl nodded and told his wife how wise she was. 'How about you, Lola?' he asked. 'What do your parents do?'

'Dad, no,' Mercedes said. 'Remember I told you? About the thing?'

I didn't do a good job of hiding my surprise. Mercedes had never actually asked me about it. The only person I'd really told was Sebastian. Disappointment crumpled my insides at the thought they'd obviously talked about me.

'Oh.' Carl leant away from me like I had a disease. 'I hope I haven't . . .?'

```
        I find awkward conversations
              easy to navigate
                 Yes (No)
```

'It's fine,' I said, meeting his gaze in a way that seemed to make him lean away even more. 'My mother is no longer with us and I never knew my dad.'

Tonya smiled her celebrity-worthy smile. 'Well, whoever they were they left you with a great complexion.'

'Mum!' Mercedes hissed.

'What? I can say that, can't I? It's a compliment.'

Carl cleared his throat. 'We should get going if we want to make our reservation.'

Mercedes didn't have to be told twice. She pulled her mum to the car a second later and practically buckled her seatbelt for her. She waved to me once she was on the backseat. I waved back and watched as they drove back the way they came, this time as a family.

Leighton's entranceway felt like a huge open mouth at my back, the cold air tickling the hairs on my neck with ghostlike fingers. A shiver caught my spine. I turned around to check there was no one messing with me. It was empty.

I walked inside the entrance hall and four old headmasters scowled down at me from their frames. I'd seen their portraits two nights ago when I'd found Sebastian, but this was the first time I'd noticed how they were each a Leighton. Their time served as headmaster had been marked out in their nameplates:

George Leighton, 1896–1915
William Leighton, 1915–1952
Thomas Leighton, 1952–1977
Michael Leighton, 1977–2006

The next painting along was of a woman with no nameplate. It was difficult to tell who she might have been – a wife or a sister to one of the headmasters perhaps. A woman and not a man, and therefore not worthy of being properly immortalized. There was no doubt in my mind she would eventually be removed to make way for David Leighton's portrait when he retired as headmaster.

A horrible idea pierced my thoughts: if Sebastian died, there would be no one to take up Mr Leighton's mantle.

FIFTEEN

I pushed on the door to the IT building, half expecting it to be locked, but it swung open and I went inside. Students from lower years occupied the computer lab, tapping away at keyboards while Mr Yorke sat with a coffee and a book at his desk, only looking up when someone called him for help. It was like that at Leighton. Students and teachers working well past their allotted lesson times. Everyone striving for the best exam results in the country. Out of all the teachers I'd met, Mr Yorke was the nicest.

I moved on to the gym, went to the centre of the freezing-cold space and clapped my hands. 'Enter.'

My house pixelated into existence. It rested on the bed of mist like they were connected, the mist forming its shadowy foundations. I made my way up the stone steps and into the lift that had become the entranceway. The world beyond the grille was solid grey. There was no new level on the control panel today.

2
1

G
B

The button marked 'B' flashed twice.

Ping!

Ping!

I jammed my fist against the button for the second floor.

As the lift rose at my instruction, I passed through the first floor, the one with the ruined kitchen. I peered through the metal gate.

A little girl with long red hair sat in a pile of rubble. She turned to me and smiled. Blood lined her teeth, dripped from her mouth, pooled on the floor.

'Take the evening off, Lola,' she said. 'I'll cover for you.'

I backed to the far side of the lift. 'Leave me alone.'

Her cackle was lost as I moved up to the second floor. I pulled the gate back with a metallic screech that echoed across the black-and-white tiles of my hallway floor. I made my way across them, to the living room where I'd made Sebastian.

'Hello?' I called. 'Sebastian? Dad?'

No one answered.

Mother's bar cart caught my eye. It hadn't been there last time, but here it was, flush against the wall in the gap between the bookcases, loaded with its usual array of gins and vermouths. A stack of neatly opened letters was there today.

The name on the top envelope, written in swirls of black ink, beckoned me like a crooked finger.

A. Whitmore

I'd seen this letter before but couldn't place where. It slipped at the back of my mind like the tail-end of a dream. The more I tried to think where I'd seen it, the less clearly I could remember.

A scream, high and wild, ripped through the room.

It was the kind of noise that started on one level of the house and ended on another. I crushed my hands over my ears and ducked behind the sofa, as if I could hide from it even though I knew it was impossible.

'Train crash, landslide,' I chanted, trying and failing to block out the scream. I'd heard it before. Could still hear it, like it had woven itself into my mind.

It went on and on and on and on.

The corner of the room pixelated and Sebastian materialized wearing a blue button-down shirt and jeans. He ran to my side, put his hands over mine, covering my ears to help block out the noise. He took them away when the scream faded, but I kept mine in place.

I refused to let it in. Refused to admit it was there. It wasn't real.

Train crash.

Landslide.

Sebastian took my wrists gently. 'It's OK, it's over. It's gone.'

'Where did it come from?'

'The basement,' he said. 'It happens sometimes.'

I followed his gaze to the lift, where the button marked B flashed insistently.

Ping!

Ping!

Ping!

'We could go and find out what's down there?' he said.

'No. We're not going down there.'

I focused on Sebastian, reading the concern in his face. We were so close I could see the smoothness of his skin, the silkiness of his hair. It was all so real. As if he hadn't been found unconscious less than forty-eight hours earlier. He was completely unaware people were crying about him in the real world. This Sebastian was fine. He was safe in my game world.

And he was late.

'Where were you just now?' I asked.

'On my own level. I didn't hear you come in.'

'You have your own level?'

'Of course.'

I looked to the lift but there were no new floors there today. Wherever he'd come from, I couldn't access it with my lift.

I did my best to forget about the scream. Closed my eyes, tried to block it out. It was still there though, pulsing at the back of my mind like a headache. I didn't know what I'd done to trigger it but if I didn't block it out properly it might come back.

Noise. I needed noise to smother it.

'Take me somewhere loud,' I said to Sebastian. 'Somewhere there's lots of noise. Music, people . . .'

'A party,' he suggested.

'One that never ends.'

'Great idea. There's lots to celebrate after all.'

'You kids have fun.' Dad had appeared. He wore a pair of faded jeans and an old-looking T-shirt. He placed a stepladder against the far wall. The sofas were covered in white sheets and the bookshelves had been emptied, though I wasn't sure when.

'What are you doing?' I asked him.

'Redecorating,' he said, adjusting the ladder. 'The house is yours now. What do you think of sage green?'

I went over to him and he wrapped his arms around me.

'Hey now, what's wrong?'

'Nothing,' I said. 'I miss you, that's all.'

Dad smiled and tucked my hair behind my ear. 'I'm right here. Taking care of your house for you while you're gone.'

It made so much sense. Dads in films and TV shows were always fixing, doing DIY, redecorating. I watched as he ran a roller across a blank wall where a crack had appeared. Sage-green paint covered it up. It was the kind of shade that was fashionable but timeless.

'I love that colour,' I said.

'Thought you would. Go on now, you have fun. I'll have this sorted in no time.'

Sebastian nodded to the lift. Another floor had appeared on the control panel.

3
2
1
G
B

He gestured to it with a flourish. 'After you, milady. Level three has exactly what you need.'

Sebastian followed me into the lift and pressed the button for level three. The gate slid shut. Between the metal swirls, I watched Dad swipe a roller across a blank wall with a crack in it. Hadn't he just done that bit? There were others, now that I looked. Hairline fractures had appeared on all the walls, the aftermath of the scream.

A shiver of pixels ran through Dad's body. The sage-green paint disappeared. He ran a roller across the same crack a third time, and I could tell it wouldn't take. He would need something better than paint to cover up those cracks.

Sebastian put his arm around my waist. 'This party is going to be epic.'

A party.

Too much noise to think.

Exactly what I needed.

SIXTEEN

The party announced itself with thumping bass. It travelled through the lift, shaking the floor and making me smile. All-consuming noise.

When Sebastian pulled back the gate, we stepped on to a level that was so crowded I couldn't see the edge of the room. Everything was moving; erratic but synced in a way that made it seem like a single, multi-headed creature.

An enormous dance floor was packed with women in deep V-neck dresses and pearl headbands. Men wore suits with bow-ties, their hair dark and slick with oil. Entertainers on stilts waded through the crowd. Confetti streamed from a ceiling strung with disco balls, giant balloons and masses of white flowers trailing from crystal chandeliers. Dancers carried ostrich feathers, their painted smiles wide with a laughter drowned out by the music.

Bass reverberated in my bones, took up residence in my head. I couldn't hear anything else. It was impossible to even *think* of anything else except for the party. The colours of the dresses, the constantly streaming confetti, the flowers spilling out of the gold and silver urns, the lights catching on every surface.

There was a swing band at one end of the dance floor and a DJ at the other. People didn't care. The music worked. It was a chaotic cacophony that demanded my full attention.

Sebastian took my hand and kissed the back of it. His hair was oiled in a sharp side parting and he was wearing what all the other men wore: a black tuxedo with silky lapels and a white waistcoat.

'Shall we?' he said, pulling me on to the dance floor.

'But I'm not—'

'Oh yes you are, Lola.'

I looked down and my outfit had changed into a sleeveless gold sequin dress. Tassels hung from the low waistband so every time I moved they swung whichever way my hips went. Barely-there sandals adorned my feet.

I raised a hand to my hair, felt the perfectly coiled curls at my temples, and couldn't stop the grin finding my lips.

'This is the best party I've ever been to,' I shouted.

'It hasn't even started yet,' Sebastian shouted back.

He tugged me closer to him and spun me by the waist. I lifted my arms above my head and tilted backwards. The ceiling became a glittering swirl. I spun into another couple who laughed and pushed me back to Sebastian. He took both my hands and led me in a dance I didn't know I could do. We moved to the rapid beat dictated by the DJ, swayed with the string instruments layered over the top. My pulse was as erratic as the world around me.

Girls in drop-waist dresses bumped into me. I bumped into them. We all laughed and carried on, shaking our hips so the tassels caught the light and it looked like we were on fire.

Sebastian had confetti in his hair. The flashing lights tinted his skin blue then red then green.

'Are you having a good time?' he shouted.

His breath was hot on my cheek, and I was suddenly aware of how sweaty I was.

I needed air. A cold breeze. Anything.

I turned away from him and pushed through a group who laughed at an unheard joke, throwing their heads back in earnest. A gang of girls brought their champagne saucers together and champagne slopped on to the floor, unheard, unseen. Three people slung their arms around each other and tried to grab me from the side. I pushed them away and they found someone else a second later.

I searched for the edge of the dance floor.

Everywhere I looked people were laughing, their mouths wide as pomegranates and their eyes shut to the chaos of it all.

I tried to look over shoulders, desperate to find a door or a window to sit by.

A woman with coiled blonde hair flashed past in a gap.

She was lost in the jostle of the dance floor a second later. I tried to push forward to see her again. She was gone, but I'd seen her. I knew who it was.

She couldn't be here. This was *my* party and she wasn't invited. I was imagining it.

Where was Sebastian?

A band of static washed over a group of laughing

partygoers and he walked out of the pixels. 'Lola,' he said, eyebrows taut. 'I lost you for a moment. Are you OK?'

'Space. I need space.'

'You need a door?'

'A door. Yes. An exit.'

'You make one this time,' he said. 'Concentrate.'

I let the need of it fill me up, which was easy, even amongst all the music and the laughter. A doorway began to rise from the ground. People made space for it, barely registering that a white door was taking up residence on their precious dance floor.

The door had a round metal handle, the kind where the centre presses inwards to lock it. The kind you get on police interview rooms.

Sebastian grabbed the handle and ushered me through it like he was my bodyguard.

It led out on to a terrace. The cool night air hit me like a wall. I relished it, holding my arms up to it like I could grab it and wrap it around me. My ears throbbed with the absence of music.

I closed my eyes. 'That's so much better.'

Sebastian smiled and pointed to a backless stone bench. I sat down, loving the coolness of the stone against the backs of my thighs. White jasmine flowed from stone urns and off a trellis above our heads. It clung to the outside of the doorway we'd come through. I leant closer to it but there was no smell.

'Here,' Sebastian said, and reached to tap the Key at my temple.

A tingle trickled down my spine and there it was: jasmine lacing the cool night air with its heavy perfume.

'How did you do that?'

'A simple piece of code,' he said.

I sat on the bench, my back to the jasmine, and took deep breaths.

Piano music from behind us drew my attention.

Down in a courtyard there was another dance floor. This one was smaller, less alive with movement. Couples held each other closely as a woman at a grand piano leant over the keys to croon into a microphone.

Mother hated musicians that also sang. She said it was the hallmark of a bad career. If you were good enough at the instrument, no one would ever ask for you to sing at the same time. She made sure Alex had performed enough challenging solo pieces at a young age that no one ever asked her for more.

'Better?' Sebastian asked.

'Better,' I agreed. 'I needed a breather.'

'It's a bit much in there,' Sebastian said, jerking a thumb at the party still raving on behind the white door. 'Why don't we have a quiet dance instead?'

I smoothed my hair back. He still wanted to spend time with me, even after I'd made him leave the party. I thought maybe I'd ruined it for him, but he offered his hand with a keenness that told me otherwise. I took it.

A moment later, we were down the stone steps and on the dance floor, where other couples sank against each other in a slow sway.

This was a different kind of dancing. The type where he put one hand on the small of my back and drew me to him so his jaw brushed against my temple. He felt so real. His hand warming my back. The texture of his suit and the smell of his skin, clean but spicy.

For a moment, it felt like I was dancing with the real Sebastian, however impossible it might have been. I wondered if he knew how much he was missed, even if he was unconscious. They say people in comas can hear music and conversations around them. Would he ever know if we went to visit?

'They miss you,' I said, saying it to him because I couldn't say it to the real Sebastian. 'Finn and Georgie want to play the game as a group but we don't know how to do it without you.'

'It's easy,' he said. 'Someone has to go in first and create the environment, then you pull them in as they enter the game.' He made it sound so straightforward, but the response made me pause. His understanding of the game was unexpected. 'The game is like a building,' he said, taking my silence for confusion about his explanation. 'The building has rooms and each room contains something different. You're not constrained to one of them, you can move between them, share them with other users.'

'Like Dr Zats's rainforest?'

'That's right. Her rainforest is one room in the building. You can go back to it if you want.'

'She told me you can't go into someone else's private

world without their Key.'

He laughed. 'What Dr Zats doesn't know could fill a warehouse. She's right, you do need their Key. But once you've been invited, you can return on your own. It's easy.'

I made a mental note not to invite anyone into my world, even accidentally. The last thing I wanted was for someone to walk around my house whenever they pleased, poking around on the different levels I'd made. Particularly the basement.

Sebastian's understanding of the game was so different to Dr Zats's. She had called it a 'shared experience', used a tablet and made calls to a programming team to resolve issues. Sebastian made it seem like a puzzle he'd figured out, a vault he had all the keys to. His understanding felt so much more dynamic.

'How do you pull people into the same room?'

'Oh, Lola. You already know. Remember what I told you?' He twisted, spinning me out across the dance floor. When he brought us back together, he positioned himself behind me. His arms wrapped around my middle and his cheek grazed my temple. I swallowed hard, tried to control the butterflies in my stomach at how close we were.

'Look,' he said. I followed the movement of his head and found myself staring at the top of the stone steps we'd come down earlier. My white door was at the top of it.

'There's always a door,' I said.

I could feel his smile against the side of my head. 'Exactly.'

That's how he did it – he brought us all together by using doors, bridging one room to another so we could all play together. It was amazing, so impressive. He'd been playing the game the same length of time as everyone else, yet his understanding of it ran so much deeper. He talked like he knew more than Dr Zats. Maybe he did.

A jolt pierced my thoughts.

I'd been talking to him like he was really Sebastian, like he was the one who'd set up our capture the flag game and picked me for his team. He'd responded to my questions in the same way. It was impossible, so impossible. The real Sebastian was unconscious in a hospital. This Sebastian was a product of the game, but how clever the game had made him.

Even if he wasn't real, what he said made sense. I'd made a door and it led to somewhere totally different, but I was still in my house, just a different area of it. Maybe the game really was a building. Maybe it was possible to walk between its rooms using doors. If I could help my friends play again, it would take everyone's minds off Sebastian lying in hospital.

I turned around and we returned to our slow dance, his hand on the small of my back and mine on his shoulder.

'I like it out here, with you,' he said.

'You like being with me?'

'There's no one else I'd rather be with.'

He pulled me closer than before, so his chest was almost flat against mine. It struck me how well we fit against each other. I put my head under his chin and listened to his heartbeat far beneath his silky lapels. Finding him in bed with Mercedes felt like a lifetime ago. This Sebastian was taller. I'd made him. He was mine.

'Really?' I asked. 'No one else?'

He shook his head against mine.

'No one else,' I repeated. Not the prettiest girl in school. Not my sister, who everyone seemed to prefer. Only me.

A thick-bodied moth grazed the skin of my arm. It rose to the lights strung above us, pushed against one of the lightbulbs there. It did this over and over, like it was desperate to get to the delicious golden centre but held back by a barrier it couldn't see. I wondered how many times a tiny creature would do something before it learnt it would never get what it wanted, that nothing would ever change.

The singing stopped but the piano continued. It morphed into a rhythm it hadn't had before; the notes became deeper and demanded they be played pianissimo: softly, softly.

I knew this melody. My fingers tapped out the finger positions on Sebastian's shoulder.

One, three, five, one, three, five, one, two, four, move down to the D sharp and keep the C natural.

'What are you doing?'

'This is Beethoven's "Moonlight Sonata",' I said.

'Do you like it?'

The pianist missed the C natural. She played it wrong. I snatched my head away from Sebastian's chest and looked over. The dance floor had emptied but there was no sign of where the other couples had gone. Alex sat at the piano, fingers clumsily moving over the keys. A metronome ticked on the lid.

Tick, tick, tick.

The rhythm was off. Her playing was off.

It was wrong, all of it.

She grinned at me and suddenly I didn't hear the music any more. Her jeans were ripped and spattered in blood. Her T-shirt had a hole in the centre, blood crusting its edges. Blood lined her teeth, dripped from her grinning mouth.

'What are you doing here?' I said. She wasn't invited.

Alex stood up from the piano and the music stopped, but the metronome kept swinging. It punctuated her movements.

Step. *Tick.*

Step. *Tick.*

Step. *Tick.*

Sebastian put an arm out and I moved behind it. 'Lola, who is this? It's the girl from the park again. She looks like you.'

'She's nothing like me,' I said.

'Have you remembered, Lola?' Alex asked, ignoring him. Blood dripped from her mouth as she spoke. She stopped in front of me, positioned herself to cast me in shadow. I hid behind Sebastian.

'You're not real,' I said.

Tick.

She advanced on me with a laugh. 'Are you sure?'

I backed away but Sebastian caught me by the wrist. 'What's going on? Who is she?'

I yanked myself free and moved backwards. Alex followed me across the black-and-white tiles. 'I can help you remember,' she said.

Tick!

I needed a door. An exit.

TICK!

My heel crunched over solid glass. I looked down slowly. The stem of a broken martini glass was under my shoe.

TICK!!

I clapped and screamed, 'EXIT!'

Sebastian put a hand out like he could stop me. 'Wait—'

He was gone. Alex was gone. I panted like I'd run the 1500 metres. The gym was dark and silent. The party had been so vibrant and alive in comparison I could feel my pupils contracting to let in more light. My ears rang with the sudden silence. I spun around, peering at all the corners of the gym.

I was alone.

SEVENTEEN

I paused outside my bedroom, trying to distinguish the voices I could hear. Mercedes had brought her parents back. Inside, I realized they were all in the bathroom together. Through the crack in the open door, I could see Tonya lounging against the sink. Carl was uncapping a Sharpie.

'Now,' he said, 'these are only minor surgeries, but we will have to wait until you're eighteen to make them.' He stepped closer to Mercedes who stood with her arms at her sides, gaze trained upwards to the lights. 'What I think we'll do is make an incision here and plump your cheekbones up – how your mother has them. It's such a good look.'

Tonya flashed a smile.

'I also think we could stand to refine your chin. An oval-shaped face is very popular at the moment for women, and you've unfortunately inherited my square jaw. I wonder if . . .'

Carl drew across Mercedes's cheeks, forehead and chin. They were lines to cut, to change, to manipulate. She accepted them all, mouth tight, as he talked about how he would make her beautiful. Tonya passed her husband a phone and they began to take a series of pictures before moving on to discuss her body shape.

Anger bubbled into my core at how Mercedes was already naturally beautiful and was being told she could be better.

'Lola, look.' Dad had appeared. He leant over Mercedes's bed, tried to grab hold of a leather document wallet on her pillow.

Dr Carl Campbell was inscribed into the leather.

The zip hadn't been done up. Pages poked out of the top, making it too easy to get a good look. It was mostly correspondence handwritten by Carl, ready to be transcribed when he got back to his clinic, peppered with the occasional prescription and forms. Several were dated with today's date. He must have been doing paperwork whilst at lunch with his family. On one of the crumpled pages towards the back of the wallet – the one Dad pointed to – was the SmartTech logo.

I was pulling the paper free before I properly thought about it.

Dear Dr and Mrs Campbell,
We are writing to you today for your express permission to enter your daughter, Mercedes Campbell, into our experiment regarding virtual reality and teenage minds. Please sign and return the parent/guardian consent form overleaf—

The letter was only one page. Carl and Tonya must have signed the form. Who had signed mine? Unlike Alex, I didn't have a legal guardian. She couldn't have signed for me. We weren't responsible for each other like that.

'There's something else,' Dad said, still looking at Carl's document wallet. 'Something shiny.'

I reached further inside and drew out a sterling silver knife with *T & C* etched into the flat blade. A letter opener.

T for Tonya. T for Tchaikovsky, Treble and Train.

C for Carl, for Clef and for Carnage.

T for Accident. C for Murder.

Mother would have loved it. She opened all of our post with a wooden letter opener she claimed was crafted from an old violin. After her Stradivarius, it was her most prized possession. It had its own special drawer in her desk and I was regularly tasked with polishing it and keeping it sharp.

Carl's was dirty. Covered in fingerprints. He didn't appreciate it, which was ridiculous, because it was clearly an expensive gift. I used the sleeve of my cardigan to clean off the worst of the marks and slipped it into my bedside table. If Carl wasn't going to look after it, it should belong to someone who would.

'You really shouldn't take things that aren't yours,' Dad said, but we both knew he only told me off because as a parent he was supposed to.

The letter opener reminded me of Mother. The way

she would slice into all our letters with one deft movement, as if her letter opener were a bow and the envelope a violin. I thought back to the stack of post on her bar cart in the living room. The envelope with Alex's name in a swirling black font. Who had sent her that letter?

I tidied up Carl's document wallet, slipping the SmartTech letter back inside. There had never been anything like that sent to my house, and though my solicitor had made me sit and take the quiz that got me on to the game trial, he definitely hadn't signed a permission slip. It would need to be a parent or a legal guardian.

'Who signed mine?' I asked Dad. It wouldn't have been him. It couldn't have been – he wasn't real.

He shrugged. 'Who else would know?'

'Alex might know,' I said.

'Are you sure that's a good idea?' Dad asked.

'No,' I said. 'I'm not sure, but there's no one else to ask.'

On the way to Matron's office a grandfather clock chimed five times. Dinner service would be starting. I ignored how hungry I was and continued on.

No one answered when I knocked on the office door. Presumably, Matron was helping with the dinner service, which suited me fine. I'd already embarrassed myself once by asking to borrow a phone, and it would be easier to talk to Alex without anyone listening.

The room was shrouded in darkness. Criss-cross patterns fell across the administrator's desk, put there by the moonlit latticed windows. The phone was already pointed my way.

'What?' Alex said by way of answering. It was like she knew it was me.

'Alex,' I said. 'I had . . . there was a . . . I needed to talk to you.'

She'd answered too quickly and I faltered as I struggled to find my words. Asking her had seemed much easier in my head, but now I was actually talking to her I knew it would be anything but easy.

'This is the second time you've spoken to me in a week,' she said. 'We're twins, Lola, but we were never friends. What do you want?'

In another life, we *could* have been friends. We could have had matching haircuts and shared secrets. We could have laughed with each other instead of at each other. But the real Alex was a violin prodigy, as sharp with her tongue as she was with her bow. I'd never stood a chance.

'How's the packing going?' I asked, trying to make conversation. 'When will you be out of the house?'

'I've decided to stay.'

'What? How?'

'Not that it's any of your business,' she said, in a way that told me she took great delight in telling me, 'but my legal guardian has put an offer on the house and I've accepted. I can live here as long as I want.'

She was eighty seconds older than me and always one step ahead. I suddenly realized I'd been glad she had to leave. I'd been sent to Leighton and she'd have to move in with her legal guardian. We were the same.

But now she's staying.

Indefinitely.

Maybe even for ever.

'I need to ask you about your legal guardian,' I said, eager to get what I needed and end the conversation.

'Hmmm?'

'Someone signed a form on my behalf. I wondered if your guardian might have . . . Are they . . .? Did they ever . . .?'

Alex laughed as I trailed off. 'Did they what? Adopt you as well, you mean? Don't be silly, Lola. They didn't want you. No one did. That's why you ended up at Leighton.'

Alex had never told me what they were like, the family who'd adopted her, but I had a good enough idea. I bet they had a big house and a dog and everyone went to the beach at the weekend. I bet they were the kind of people who gave her an allowance. Encouraged her musical aspirations and genuinely wanted to see her succeed.

She'd had a mother who loved her.

Now she had a legal guardian in her place.

So many doors had been opened for her that hadn't for me.

'I can hear you sulking,' Alex said. 'Poor little Lola was left to fend for herself. Poor little Lola was left behind again. There's a reason you were left, Lola. There's a reason no one wanted you. You've forgotten what it was.'

'Be quiet,' I whispered.

'I thought you would have figured it out by now,' she

said, ignoring me. 'When we spoke before I thought you'd buried it deep, but it must be deeper than I thought. Tell me, Lola. Do you dream about it? Do you see it in your nightmares?'

'Shut UP,' I said, louder this time.

And mercifully she did.

It was like we were playing a game and Alex was winning. Always one step ahead. Always landing on the square that sent her rocketing to the exit.

I could hear Mother's metronome.

Tick, tick, tick.

The train derailed.

Tick.

Mother was dead.

She died in a train crash. There was a landslide.

Tick!

Balcony. The piano.

Landslide. Train crash.

TICK!

EIGHTEEN

Back at our bedroom and with her parents gone, Mercedes told me everyone had decided to meet up even if we couldn't play Better Than Life. They'd all agreed it would be good just to hang out. I'd holed myself up in the downstairs toilets after talking to Alex and completely missed dinner service and therefore missed being part of the decision. I didn't mind. It would be good to have everyone in our room, would be a distraction.

Mercedes lined up her night-time skincare routine on her bedside table while we waited. There were only two products there today. She gave me a sad smile when she noticed me looking. 'Hardly seems any point,' she said. 'My eyes are so puffy the best thing I can give them is sleep. Mum gave me a bunch of new stuff to try out and I can't be arsed with any of it.' She tossed me a jar. 'This is for you, courtesy of Mum.'

I caught it and inspected the label.

Apply twice daily to scarred skin. May take three to six months to see visible improvements. Results vary.

I wanted to throw the jar across the room. Tonya must have noticed the scars on my hand, decided not to say anything but then pass me creams on the sly. She must have thought they were ugly. I certainly did.

'My mother said skincare was a waste of time,' I said.

'She's probably right. My mum says you either keep your face or your figure and only the knife will help you keep both.'

She didn't understand. Mother had said there was no point giving me skincare to help with my scars, because it would make no difference. No one would ever think I was pretty. I put the cream on my bedside table, hating that it existed and that I needed it.

In the game, I would never need a product or anything else to help me look a certain way. I could look however I wanted there. My hair was long and shiny. I had the type of skin that didn't need make-up, let alone skincare. Perfect collarbones instead of one that jutted out notice-ably further than the other.

In the game, Sebastian had held me close. Told me there was no one else he'd rather be with.

The boys trooped through the door mid-argument. 'I'm telling you, he saw us!' Wai said, closing the door behind them.

Finn rolled his eyes. 'Have you seen how thick Noah's glasses are? He can't see shit without them, the guy is legally blind. He didn't see us. Chill out.'

Wai sank dramatically on to Mercedes's bed. 'He's not legally blind. And we're not invisible. He would have seen *something* wouldn't he? Blurry shapes or whatever.'

'Well, it's not like he could pick us out of a line-up, is

it? If anyone asks we'll say we needed to . . . borrow a book. Or something.'

'If we get summoned to Mr Leighton's office for this, I want separate solicitors.'

Mercedes tidied away her skincare. 'Hi boys, how are you? We're fine by the way.'

'Sorry,' Finn said, sitting on the end of my bed. 'It's a lot harder to get away without Seb hacking the cameras and telling us when the coast is clear.'

At the mention of Sebastian, everyone went quiet. Mercedes returned to her bed in silence, and I could tell she was finding his absence harder than everyone else. The fact none of them knew about her relationship with him must have made it doubly worse.

'Does anyone know how he's doing?' I asked.

Everyone looked to Finn for an answer.

'I heard they moved him to that special coma unit nearby,' he said.

Mercedes looked up. 'Coma? Do they know for sure that's what it is?'

'Yeah, Cedes. He's not waking up.'

Finn sounded miserable but his comment was careless. Mercedes's lips pressed together so tightly I thought she might implode. A second later, tears were pouring from her eyes. Wai shuffled up next to her and put his arm around her shaking shoulders.

'Hey, don't worry,' Wai said. 'Seb'll be back here, hacking cameras and playing lacrosse again in no time. You'll see.'

Georgie came in via the bathroom, removing a pair of Marigold gloves a finger at a time. The stench of bleach wafted out after her. 'Don't use the bathroom,' she said. 'It's finally clean.'

When she noticed Mercedes was crying she flung her gloves on the floor and went over to her friend. She swapped places with Wai and gave her a hug. I felt stupid that I hadn't done the same thing. Mercedes wanted us to be friends, and I hadn't even gone to her when she was crying. Georgie held her close.

'Maybe we shouldn't have come,' Wai said.

Finn sighed and stood up. 'You're right. This was a stupid idea. We'll leave. Sorry, Cedes.'

Without the game, friendships were disintegrating. It was one thing to play it alone and build worlds and universes in our own pockets of the game, but it was something else to play as a group. It had brought everyone together.

'Wait,' I said, and everyone turned to look at me. 'I think I've figured out a way we can play together.'

Georgie blinked at me. 'You? You've only been here ten minutes.'

Heat bloomed in my cheeks. 'I'm a fast learner,' I said.

She looked at me dubiously, and I knew she was thinking about how I skived most of my lessons. We'd shared less than an hour of English Lit together. I had zero credibility in her eyes. Sebastian believed in me. He'd picked me first for our team, explained the game to me and told me how to manipulate it the way he did.

'I can do it,' I said, more firmly.

Finn had sat back down, was looking at me like I was the light at the end of a long dark tunnel. 'You're sure you can do it?'

'I think so,' I said slowly. 'I'll need to go in first. Give me five minutes to set it up and then you follow. You might see a door in your world. Go through it and it should bring us together.'

'That's not how Seb does it,' Wai said.

'It doesn't matter,' Finn said, dismissing him. 'The end result will be the same. Right, Lola?'

'Should be. I mean, yeah. Yes. It'll be the same.'

Finn turned to everyone else. 'Let's do it.'

Mercedes blew her nose loudly. Georgie put her arm around her friend. 'You know, if it's too much, we don't have to play tonight. It's not a big deal.'

Finn shifted next to me. 'It took us ages to get over here.'

I elbowed him in the ribs.

'Or whatever,' he mumbled.

'No,' Mercedes said, wiping her cheeks. 'I still want to play.'

Finn relaxed. 'You'll feel better after a distraction,' he said, which sounded more like he was trying to convince her than to genuinely help her. He nodded at me. 'See you in a moment.'

I clapped and said, 'Enter.'

My house stood before me, looming out of the mist, but I

turned away from it. My house was one room in the game and I needed to get to another room, to the arena we'd played capture the flag in.

I stepped away from my house, went deeper into the mist. It swirled around my chest. I closed my eyes and concentrated, picturing a door the way Sebastian had taught me.

I opened my eyes. A white doorframe rose silently out of the mist. A door solidified inside it and a round metal handle popped outwards. It was the kind with a centre that presses inwards to lock it, the kind you get on police interview rooms.

I turned the handle and stepped through, into a world of varying shades of rust.

The shipping containers were back.

A grin found my lips. I'd done it! I couldn't wait to tell Sebastian and almost thought about bringing him in, but the others would be arriving soon. I turned, keeping my back to the arena, and thought hard about a door for each of them.

Four doors began to materialize out of the dusty ground. One was made entirely of mirrors with a sleek, mirrored handle. Another was made from ice and was almost see-through. Condensation curled off it in ribbons. The third door looked like it belonged on a castle; all wooden with a sharp point at the top, its frame made of blocks of stone. The last was a dark matte black, like a stage door from a theatre.

Finn appeared first, stepping out of the black stage

door with a grin the same size as mine. He was bigger again, muscles rippling as he jogged over. 'It worked!' He laughed as he scooped me up and twirled me round. I could barely get my arms around his thick shoulders.

Georgie opened her door with caution, peering around the ice with a raised eyebrow. 'Holy crap, New Girl, you did it. Colour me impressed.' She flashed her perfect smile, and I took this as an apology for earlier when she'd doubted me.

Wai was next, exiting his castle door. He gave a long whistle. 'Nice one,' he said, coming over to join us. His top knot and facial hair were back.

Mercedes was last. As soon as she exited her mirrored door I could see the changes she'd made. She was even skinnier than before, with more prominent cheekbones and a more oval-shaped face. These were the changes her dad had suggested she make.

'What?' she said, noticing me staring.

'You look different,' I said.

She shrugged the comment off. 'We all do.'

I looked down and realized we were all wearing the same outfit as before: shorts, tank tops and fingerless gloves with pads on them. Mercedes knew that wasn't what I'd meant.

'Right,' Wai said, rubbing his hands together. 'What are we playing tonight?'

'The maze,' Finn said at once.

Georgie groaned through her perfect teeth. 'I hate the maze.'

'Tough, it's my turn to pick,' Finn said.

Silence overcame the group as we all thought of Sebastian. It had been his pick last time. We didn't have enough players to do capture the flag again. Sebastian's absence was stronger in the game.

'You've got to love this part though, right?' Wai said, pointing to the arena.

We all stepped back as the shipping containers began to reassemble themselves. They groaned as they dragged themselves across the ground, slammed together to create an impenetrable wall. The sun began to sink behind it. Before, it had beat down so relentlessly we were all slick with sweat. Now, the sky turned dark and the only illumination came from flood-lights positioned on different parts of the wall, lighting up faded logos and rusted holes.

Silence overcame us all. It was ready.

Mercedes cleared her throat. 'First one to the centre?'

'Wait,' I said. 'What's the aim of the game? I haven't played before.'

'Duh,' Georgie said. 'It's a maze. Find the centre, that's all.'

'What's at the centre?'

'Your heart's desire,' Finn said, wiggling his eyebrows. 'Line up, everyone to their entranceway. Let's go.'

The wall of containers shifted again to create five door-sized gaps. I went to mine and saw a corridor made of the same containers beyond it. It forked at the end a short distance away. A flood-light was positioned above, casting the space in a yellow light.

'Go!' Wai shouted, and he disappeared into the maze.

Georgie threw me a grin and went next, followed by Mercedes and Finn.

I ducked through the doorway, into the corridor. A container slammed into place behind me, kicking dust into the air. I whipped around. The doorway was gone. The flood-light above me flickered as I turned back around. The only way to get out was to win.

It was deathly quiet but if I listened carefully, I could make out the *slap-slap-slap* of someone running nearby.

I broke into a run too, pelting down the corridor of containers and chosing the right-hand fork. I followed the maze, turning right then left then right again, picking directions out of panic rather than method.

The maze was a mix of long corridors with multiple branches spanning off them, or corridors that ended in T-junctions. It was impossible to see over the top. Last time there had been grab-holds in some of the containers, but it wasn't like that in the maze. I tried jumping a few times but gravity had returned to normal. The only way to reach the centre was to find it.

Every now and again I thought I could hear someone running nearby. Their footsteps echoed off the metal walls and I'd twist in their direction, only to be met with nothing but an empty space.

'Hello?' I shouted.

The flood-light flickered. There was no one nearby.

After a while, my run slowed to a jog. I braced myself against a wall to catch my breath.

The only reason I'd won last time was because Sebastian was there. He'd been the one to throw me the flag. If he hadn't, I would have climbed to the top of that tower for no reason.

I thought of Mother, crowing her victory as she looked over the games board.

Of Alex, shooting up the ladder to the exit.

Winning was impossible.

Above me, the blackness of the sky felt impossibly close and simultaneously too far away. The maze was only a small part of the game, overlooked by a vast and impassive sky. I could picture Mother up there, sipping a martini as she looked down at how lost I had become.

The flood-light flickered and died.

I inhaled. Exhaled. The whole world seemed to stand still.

When the light blinked back on, movement caught my eye at the end of the corridor. The swirl of a long fur coat gliding round a corner. The flash of coiled blonde hair.

'You're dead,' I whispered. 'You died in a train crash.'

She was gone but I heard her laugh. Soft, but distinctive. 'Are you sure?'

I backed away and a wall hit my back. I turned, panic setting in. A corridor had been there before. It shouldn't be a dead end. The only direction I could go was where Mother had disappeared.

Landslide.

Train crash.

I had to get out.

The air pixelated to my left. Sebastian walked out of the disturbance, wearing the same outfit as Finn and Wai, complete with elbow and knee patches.

'Sebastian,' I said, still catching my breath. 'How are you . . .? Why are you . . .?'

He came to me and put his hand to my jaw, stroked a thumb across my cheek.

'You needed me,' he said.

I nodded against his palm. Everything was instantly better with him here. The game's reactions were both unsettling and brilliant. I'd needed someone – anyone – and it had produced Sebastian, borrowing him from my personal game and putting him here, dressed exactly how he'd been when we played capture the flag. It had barely been a thought and yet here he was.

For me. Only for me.

Now he was here, I could do anything. Even win. I went to move down the corridor and almost tripped over something. I bent to pick it up. It ticked in my hands.

Tick.

'Is that . . .?'

Tick.

'A metronome,' I said.

TICK.

I threw it on to the floor and watched the wooden case splinter and all its gears and cogs fall out of it in a shower of copper-coloured guts. They clinked against glass. Sebastian watched as I knelt to pick up a glass of water, the contents swirling like a mini whirlpool. I'd seen it before, back when we were playing in the snow. It hadn't come from my kitchen. All of Mother's tumblers were deep-cut crystal ones.

'Is this yours?' I asked.

Sebastian turned away from it, inspected the sky, the containers – looked anywhere but at the glass of water. 'You know, I always hated the maze game,' he said. 'Finding the centre on foot could take hours. I have a better plan.'

'What do you mean?' I asked.

'There's always a door, Lola.'

It wasn't what I'd meant, but there was no time to rephrase my question because a door was forming in one of the container's sides. The frame popped out of the metal and a sign with FIRE EXIT materialized at the top. A long bar formed across the middle and Sebastian leant against it. The door clanked as it opened.

'Shall we?'

Inside the door, grass carpeted the floor. I looked to Sebastian. 'Where does it go?'

'The centre. Don't you want to win?'

I studied the door cautiously. It would be cheating to use it, but so far, playing by the rules hadn't got me anywhere. Particularly when it came to Alex.

I put down the glass of water. 'Yes,' I said, and walked through the door.

It opened on to a square flanked by containers. Each of the square's sides had a corridor leading off it.

In the centre of the square was a jumbled pile of shipping containers. As I stared at them, they began to morph.

Their sharp edges rounded. Windows appeared in their sides, the panes either smashed or lined with cracks. Rusted white paint changed to a navy blue. Scratches scored deep into the sides and paint ripped from it like it had been clawed away. Brakes and wheels appeared beneath each carriage. The front section was on its side, black smoke curling from it. Warped, broken metal was all that was left of the tracks underneath.

I moved towards the train wreck but Sebastian pulled me back. 'Where are you going?'

'I need to see,' I said, shaking him off and jogging over to the first carriage. There had to be a door somewhere.

'See what?'

'My heart's desire,' I said.

She was here. Amongst the other dead passengers. If I found her body, saw it, it would mean I was right. She died in a train crash. Everything would be all right if I could simply *see* it.

I pulled myself up on to the toppled carriage and peered through the windows beneath my feet. The interior was shrouded in darkness.

'You've won, Lola,' Sebastian said. He sounded far away. 'Isn't that enough?'

'No,' I said. Her seat – she always travelled first class – her body must be nearby. I moved across the side of the carriage, looking through the cracked windows and any holes that had ruptured the sides. I reached the end of the first-class section. There was no one at all, not her, not another passenger. Not even a fur coat.

All that was left was a bad memory sliding into the mud.

'Lola.'

I whipped around and Mercedes was standing at the edge of the wreckage. She'd made it to the centre of the maze. There was a frown written into her forehead but it wasn't directed at me. She was focused on the spot where Sebastian had been standing.

He was gone.

NINETEEN

Everyone left fairly quickly after I'd won the game. I'd hoped they'd linger, stick around to talk about it, but Wai and Finn seemed uninterested because they hadn't won, and no one wanted to talk about Sebastian. No one had guessed that I cheated, and while I didn't want to brag about winning – I didn't feel like I'd won – I didn't want to be alone with Mercedes.

When Georgie disappeared back to her room, I turned out the light before my room-mate could ask any questions. It didn't stop her.

'Lola?' she asked after a while. 'What happened to your mum? My parents asked and I told them I didn't know, but it got me wondering. It's OK if you don't want to tell me.'

'She died in a train crash,' I said. The more I said it the more I made it true. I didn't need to find a body to know that was how she died. The crash had been so big it was on the news.

'That big one a few weeks ago?'

'Yeah.'

Mercedes let out a quiet sigh. 'I'm so sorry. Is that why

you saw a train crash at the centre of the maze? Because your heart's desire is to save her?'

I rolled over to try and stall my response.

'I'm sorry,' she said again, taking my silence for confirmation. Her quilt ruffled as she got comfy. 'When I got to the centre, I saw Seb,' she said. 'It was only for a moment. I blinked and he was gone, but he was definitely there. Do you think that means he's my heart's desire?'

I'd been avoiding this conversation because I knew she'd seen Sebastian, but I hadn't considered that she'd arrive at a different conclusion from the truth. It was so obvious to me that I'd remade him. He was only interested in me. He hadn't hung around to talk to Mercedes because he didn't want to. That Sebastian was mine and only mine.

'I'm not sure,' I said.

'Lola,' she said after a long silence. 'Do you think I'm pretty?'

'Very.'

I'd said it too quickly. I'd meant it – she was – but it didn't feel like enough. She was beautiful. Her skin had that lit-from-within glow and she could pull off any outfit, even if she was crying. Her cheekbones were in the right place. She didn't need the contouring she spent ages doing. She didn't need surgery.

I'd said the wrong thing too quickly and hadn't elaborated out loud.

'I really do,' I said.

'Thanks.' Mercedes rolled over, her face to the wall.

I lay awake for hours, jealous of each of Mercedes's

even breaths once she dropped off. In the end I switched on my bedside lamp and reached for the nearest book: Sebastian's textbook.

Coding in H+ by Henry Hall

His name was written on the inside cover.

The contents page had a list of words I didn't understand:

Logical and Arithmetical Operations
Characters and Arrays
Variables

One had been underlined by Sebastian.

Hypotheticals

I turned to the page, was met by blocks of text that had been highlighted, underlined and annotated with hand-written notes in the margins. One section in particular had been circled numerous times.

Personality can be coded. Emotions can be learnt through dynamic coding techniques. Source code itself can be improved upon, and in doing so, improved again. At that point there will be no difference between the human brain and the computer. Humans can live for ever as machines.

Sebastian had drawn an arrow shooting off it, a single word written next to it.

Transcendence

I paused, wondering what it meant. Everyone said how good he was at coding, and he messed with Dr Zats's programme often enough, covering his tracks so she never knew it was him. He'd helped us all break her rules and improved on it in a way she couldn't.

I didn't understand most of what this book said. Sebastian did. He'd figured something out and it felt intrinsically linked to how he'd been found unconscious on the floor.

I fell asleep with his book clutched to my chest.

FIVE WEEKS EARLIER

I was on punishment rations, thanks to Alex telling on me for not playing the piano whilst Mother was out. All I'd eaten was bread and porridge for two weeks, and Mother had either forgotten about it or didn't care. My stomach rumbled.

She sent me to make her mid-morning martini while she and Alex tried to master 'Sakura' by Kaneko Millar for the fifth time.

'No, no, no!' Mother's voice drifted into the living room as I approached the bar cart. 'This is for your place at the Academy, remember? You're not young enough to be a prodigy any more. You must demonstrate the skill you've developed beyond the intuition of a prodigy. From the top.'

Alex returned her bow to the strings, closed her eyes, and began to play again.

This morning's post had been placed on top of the bar cart, next to the last bottle of vermouth. The top envelope caught my eye. There was no address on it; only a name in black, swooping letters.

A. Whitmore

I glanced behind me. Mother paced the black-and-white hallway floor as Alex played with her eyes shut, her fingers ruthlessly and efficiently finding all the correct notes.

I slipped the letter out of the envelope. Heavy cream card stock with grooves. The back was decorated with clusters of lines – sheet music. Someone had written Alex a letter on the back of a piece of sheet music.

Dear Alex,

I wanted our first correspondence to be different, but I've dreamt of it for so long that it was impossible for it to ever be perfect, and your mother sits over me while I write this and has made it clear she will not allow me to write to you in another manner. Please forgive the impertinence of this epistle.

I wonder daily what you look like. Do you have my hair colour? The eyes I inherited from my father and his father, passed down to you? I should like to meet you, Alex, and derive answers to these questions myself. I had no idea—

'Dolores.' Mother snatched the letter from my hands. 'What do you think you are doing?'

She palmed it off to Alex, who took it and held it to her chest to hide the rest of the contents. They glared at me: an intruder, a thief, an unwanted spare part.

'Who wrote that letter?' I asked.

'Alex's father.' Mother shrugged, so casual, as though she hadn't banned the word from the house years before. As though she hadn't shouted about raising us single-handedly since the moment I could understand her words. As if 'father' were the most inconsequential entry in the entire Oxford Dictionary.

'Where's mine?'

'Your what?'

'My letter. He would have sent one for me too.'

Mother's laugh was a single high note of derision. 'Don't be ridiculous, Lola. He doesn't even know you exist.'

TWENTY

On Monday, Dr Zats greeted us with her usual quiz. We sat as a group the way we normally would, everyone doing their best to ignore Sebastian's absence. He wasn't the only person missing.

'Where's Mr Yorke?' Georgie asked, accepting her paper.

'He won't be here from now on,' Dr Zats said. 'Fill out your quizzes everyone, I'll be back for them shortly.'

She left the room before we could ask any more questions. Georgie, Mercedes and I turned around and looked to Finn expectantly. He knew everything.

'Heard he was fired,' he said. 'No one said why, but I think it's related to Seb.'

'How can you possibly know that?' Mercedes asked.

Finn shrugged. 'A student was found unconscious, but not *any* student. It was the headmaster's son. Someone was going to get fired, weren't they?'

'Mr Yorke wasn't anywhere near Sebastian when he was found,' I said. Everyone looked at me and I realized I'd said too much. 'That's what I heard anyway.'

'Wait,' Mercedes said, refocusing on Finn. 'You think

Sebastian being found unconscious is related to the game?'

'It must be if they fired Mr Yorke. Wasn't Better Than Life his idea anyway? He was the one who brought Dr Z in.'

'Why is she staying without him then?' Georgie asked.

No one had any answers to that.

We all turned back to our quizzes and began to fill them in, but my mind turned everything over. Everyone else might think this was an extracurricular activity, but I knew it was something more. Mr Yorke and Dr Zats had been arguing over problems in the code and referred to the game trial as an experiment. Carl had signed a release form for Mercedes.

Experiments are usually spearheaded by a single person. In this case it was Dr Zats. That was why she hadn't left yet. The experiment was still underway. Mr Yorke might have been disposable, but she certainly wasn't.

What's more, experiments only last a finite amount of time. After the data is collected the scientists have to stop and evaluate their findings. I'd learnt that in the hospitals. At some point, Dr Zats would leave and she'd take the game with her. Dad and Sebastian and my house – it would all vanish.

I turned to my quiz and filled it in quickly.

```
I prefer spending time with in-game
     characters than with people
          in the real world
              Yes/No
```

```
I feel safer in the game than
      in the real world
        (Yes)/No
```

After finishing, I considered how some of my answers had changed.

Sebastian made me feel safer. He'd rescued me in the maze, appeared there because he knew I'd needed him, and took me to somewhere I could get away.

In real life, there was no getting away from what had happened.

I pushed the thought away and spent the rest of the lesson thinking about Sebastian while the others used the time to catch up on homework I didn't have.

When the bell rang, Georgie waited for me to go to English Lit with her. We walked up to the main building together, then I made an excuse and turned back. I wasn't ready to go to English Lit; I hadn't read any of the books Mrs Hamilton had told me to get from the library. She would only kick me out again. Anyway, I had questions about Sebastian only Dr Zats could answer, and that felt more important.

I found Dr Zats in the IT staffroom. It was a small space, mostly occupied by filing cabinets and a leather sofa. Faded posters of years-old technology decorated the walls.

'Dr Zats?'

She glanced up from her tablet. 'Lola, hi. What are you doing here?'

'I wanted to ask you about the people in Better Than Life.'

'You mean the characters? People implies they are real.'

Sebastian and Dad felt so real I'd completely forgotten about the rule of not recreating people from real life. Since Sebastian had helped me with my Key, I could break any rule I wanted without suffering the repercussions.

'I guess they feel so real that after a while you forget they're not actually people,' I said.

The corner of Dr Zats's mouth lifted. 'They *are* lifelike, aren't they? I'll pass the compliment to the graphics department. Marketing are always pleased to hear things like that, they want to reach as wide an audience as possible.'

I tried my best to return her smile, but couldn't help wondering if a graphics and marketing department really existed. Experiments were more likely to have researchers and data analysts.

'What was it you wanted to ask?'

I had to be careful. She didn't know I'd been logging extra time or that Sebastian had helped me break her rules and programming.

'The game seems to continue between sessions,' I said.

Dr Zats's tablet screen faded to black. 'It shouldn't.'

'When I go back, my characters are pleased to see me. As if they've been waiting for me. They're sad when I have to leave.'

Her attention danced around the room for a moment. 'Perhaps it was the game reacting to a need from your subconscious,' she said. 'I bet you wanted your characters to be pleased to see you, or sad you were leaving, so that's how they acted.'

Her explanation seemed possible, but I still doubted it. Sebastian seemed to have his own agenda, coming and going from the game whenever he wanted, appearing in my world when it suited him. He'd manipulated my Key again, helping me to smell in the game. Told me how to create doors and how to pull my friends into the same room so we could play together.

A glass of water followed him as much as the metronome followed me.

I'd never played a game like this before but none of it felt right. The way Sebastian talked and behaved was like he was a real person, not a VR creation. It felt impossible, given he was in a coma.

'Have you heard anything about Sebastian?' I asked.

Dr Zats's whole body stiffened. 'Why are you asking me about him?'

I had to be careful. So very careful. 'Someone mentioned he had his Key on his temple when he was found. I wondered if there was a connection.'

'There absolutely isn't,' Dr Zats said. 'The game is safe. The Keys are safe.' She stood and moved towards me, reaching for the door I was blocking. 'I'm afraid it's time for you to go, Lola. There's something I need to attend to.'

I didn't move. 'Who signed my consent form?'

'I don't know what you—'

'A parent or a legal guardian had to sign a consent form for me to be enrolled in your experiment. Who signed mine?'

Dr Zats's gaze flicked to the filing cabinets. 'That's really a question for the school administrators. I'm only here in a consulting capacity. If you'll excuse me, Lola. I have a lot to be getting on with.'

I let her shut me out of the room and stayed in the corridor for a moment, processing what she had and hadn't given away. She hadn't said who'd signed my form but she'd as good as told me where it was. One of those filing cabinets held the answer. And she hadn't even blinked when I'd referred to the game as an experiment. Didn't even bother to correct me.

Her explanations of Sebastian's behaviour didn't ring true either. He was more than a VR creation, and his being unconscious was somehow connected to her game. She'd been worried when I asked about him. Defensive. Dr Zats knew more than she was letting on.

TWENTY-ONE

I stayed in the IT building, searching for a lab that didn't have too many people in it. I found one with a handful of students in, each of them making use of a free period to tackle a monstrous piece of homework or work on a project.

I sat behind a free computer and realized I had no idea what I was doing. Up until now, every lesson I'd had in here had been to fill out one of Dr Zats's quizzes or to discuss what we'd made in the game. I'd never actually used a computer before.

'Do you need help?' a voice at my side asked. It belonged to a girl several years younger than me. She had bright eyes and a smile that instantly made me want to trust her. 'I'll go away if you want.'

'No, wait,' I said. Computers weren't my thing. Mother had seen to that. 'My sister told me once there was a website where you could ask any question and it would give you an answer. Do you know what that might be?'

The girl's face lit up. 'You mean like Google?'

'I guess,' I said. 'How do I access Google?'

The girl did a much better job of collecting her

surprise than Matron. She pulled the monitor towards her and loaded a screen by tapping an icon. 'Voila, Google. You can type your question in this bar and it will load answers for you.'

'Thank you,' I said.

'No worries.' She moved away to give me privacy.

I slowly typed into Google's search bar: *Who is Dr Miriam Zats?*

The page flashed before loading several answers.

Alex had never said anything about multiple responses. How would I know which one was right? I clicked the first link and a video loaded. The date was from Saturday and it already had several thousand views. There was no sound.

To my side, the girl who'd helped me took a pair of headphones from the stand next to her computer and put them over her ears. I copied her with the pair next to mine.

A round of applause echoed in my ears.

Dr Zats was welcomed on to a stage. She took a seat in a low-backed chair, the kind of boxy not-quite-an-armchair-not-quite-a-sofa that would look out of place in a living room but perfectly fit the aesthetics of a stage. The audience's applause picked up when she gave a wave to acknowledge them.

Her lab coat was gone. Traded for a crease-free suit jacket and trousers that flashed her ankles. High heels. There was no messy bun with a pen through it. Her hair was sleek and shiny, falling in soft waves.

A man sat opposite her; balding, thick-rimmed glasses and a smile that belonged on a shark. He shook her hand. 'Welcome, Dr Zats. It's an honour to have you join us for this month's *Psychology Review*.'

'The honour's all mine.'

'We all know your fabled work with humans and technology. You've literally written the book on the subject. But when we saw the release of the hypothesis on your current experiment, we knew we had to invite you on and talk about it. This one seems special. Could you tell us about it in your own words?'

'It *is* special,' Dr Zats agreed. 'The experiment is only halfway through, so I'll save any speculation on whether my hypothesis was correct until after it's finished, but essentially, I wanted to explore anxiety in a virtual reality setting. Specifically with teenagers.'

'What was it that drew you to anxiety?'

'There are varying degrees of it and I wanted to delve into the psyches of individuals who scored highly on a test we submitted to a pool of candidates. The idea is that we can watch how they use VR to process their anxiety, work through their issues in a virtual setting.'

'Can you give an example?'

'Yes, of course. Let's say for example an individual has claustrophobia. They could expose themselves to tight spaces in a risk-free environment and slowly overcome it in the real world.'

'This is the crux of the experiment, isn't it?' the inter-viewer said. 'That teenagers with high levels of anxiety could use their VR spaces to overcome it.'

Dr Zats nodded. 'Exactly. We prime the players with a quiz before their sessions, get them thinking about their fears and so on. Then, when they enter the game they are more likely to interact with those fears. The game is set up to respond to them. We monitor their progress through the quizzes, watch how their answers change to the control questions.'

'Absolutely fascinating,' the interviewer said. 'Now, let's talk about those controls for a moment.' He leant back in his chair, his shark smile reappearing. 'Several other psychologists have argued that any results you attain will be tainted given the number of anomalies that have come up in your experiment. They've criticized the lack of control you have, basically. How do you respond to that criticism?'

Dr Zats smoothed a crease in her suit jacket. 'All experiments have to start somewhere. The anomalies haven't hindered anything. We're keeping a close eye on it all.'

'We've heard there were problems with the code,' the interviewer prompted.

'Anomalous changes to the code are nothing to worry about,' Dr Zats said curtly. 'It hasn't altered the game or the way the game works.'

'What about the players? Has everything gone to plan there?'

For a moment, I didn't think she would reply. Then she said, 'It's amazing how many people don't understand the non-disclosure part of a non-disclosure agreement.

Whoever you've been talking to clearly doesn't care.'

The interviewer laughed, prompting the audience to join in. 'We do our research before each interview, that's all. I'm sure you of all people understand that. Tell us about the players.'

Dr Zats sighed. 'We had a new player start six weeks later than the others. We've given her extra sessions to catch up.'

'Anything else?'

The interviewer was prodding at something. Dr Zats took a sip of water, delaying her response. 'One of the participants, Player S, has been removed from the experiment.'

The mention of Player S made my heart skip. She must have been talking about Sebastian.

'What a pity,' the interviewer said, but he sounded too cheerful to be genuine. 'Nothing to do with the experiment, I hope?'

'Of course not,' Dr Zats said quickly. 'It *is* a pity. He was the best in the class. Took to the game in a way none of the other players did, worked through his issues quickly. He also showed adept skills at programming. I offered him an internship but he turned me down.'

The interviewer's mouth gaped. 'He turned *you* down? Is the position still open? I'll be your intern.'

A laugh rose from the audience.

'Regardless,' Dr Zats said, 'the anomalies are nothing to worry about. We can reproduce them next time if we have to.'

'And you're sure there'll be a next time?'

'Absolutely. I'm keen to replicate the results we've already seen. And let's be honest, we all know my critics will end up using my research to postulate their own theories, so . . .'

The interviewer grinned. 'I love how cut-throat psychology is, don't you, folks?'

The audience laughed and clapped their agreement.

When the noise died down, a silhouette had risen from one of the rows of seats. The interviewer swivelled their way. 'A question from the audience already. Can we get a mic over . . .? Thanks. Hi, welcome to *Psychology Review*. What's your question, please?'

'How can you live with yourself?' the man from the audience blurted. The camera and lights refocused on him, bringing him out of the shadows. It was Mr Yorke.

There was a ripple of murmurs through the room. Dr Zats shifted in her seat.

'It's your fault what happened to Player S,' Mr Yorke said. 'I told you not to let any of my kids get hurt and—'

The interviewer snapped his fingers at two security guards off stage. They began to make their way to Mr Yorke, but he continued yelling. 'He lost his life because of you!'

The audience gasped and all heads turned to the stage.

Dr Zats covered her microphone and leant over to whisper to the interviewer.

'See?' Mr Yorke yelled as two large men reached his row of seats. 'She's not even sorry. She destroys people's lives and then catalogues the pieces. You said you wanted to help them! You're a liar and—'

Mr Yorke tried to leap over the chairs in front of him. At first I thought he was trying to get away from the security guards, but Dr Zats rose from her seat and took a big step back. Even with the stage and three rows of people between them, she was afraid of him. Mr Yorke was aiming for *her*.

The security guards wrestled him to the ground before he made it over more than a single row.

The video ended.

Mr Yorke said someone had lost his life. Player S. If Sebastian was dead, Mr Leighton or Matron would surely have made an announcement.

Dr Zats had looked worried when I'd asked her about Sebastian. Had something happened to him since he went to hospital?

On the way out of the IT lab, Dad waited for me at the treeline of the woods that surrounded the school. He beckoned me over and I went to him, ready to tell him everything I'd discovered, but he pointed to an envelope flitting past his feet.

'Did you drop this just now?' He tried to pick it up but his hand went straight through. 'It has your name on it.'

A gust of wind pushed it out of my reach, but not before I caught the name on the front. It was written in a swirling, looping hand, and it wasn't mine.

A. Whitmore

I scrambled after it, into the woods, stumbling over tree roots and piles of desiccated leaves, chasing the letter further and further in. Trees thickened. Light disappeared. Dad ran with me, yelling to be careful.

The envelope caught on a moss-covered tree stump. I seized it, victory flaring in my chest, and held it up like a long-lost artefact. I pulled out the letter, heavy cream stock paper, deep grooves to the touch. On it was a single bar of music. A single musical note, defined by the treble clef that came before it.

Dad stopped at my side. 'What does it mean?' he panted, peering over my shoulder.

I couldn't answer. My hands shook as I took it in.

It was a B.

B for Basement.

B for Death.

Someone knew what I'd put in there, what I'd stored away. I couldn't remember what was down there but I knew it was bad. Whoever wrote this note knew exactly what it was.

Train crash.

Landslide.

TWENTY-TWO

Dad walked back up to the school with me. I looked down at the letter the whole time. Traced the curve of the treble clef, the musical note that was a threat and an invitation all at once.

We made our way out of the woods, back up to the entranceway where we stopped at the treeline and watched Mr Yorke accept a box of his things from Matron.

'We removed these from your bedroom,' she said. 'I heard you have already taken care of your staffroom.'

'Thank you,' Mr Yorke said.

'You're welcome.'

If ever there was a woman who could make a scowl look like a smile, it was her. Poor Mr Yorke was caught in her cross-hair.

I shoved the letter in my inner blazer pocket and stepped out of the trees. 'Mr Yorke,' I called. Dad waited at the treeline, but I wasn't going back to him yet. Mr Yorke had said Sebastian was dead and I had to know if it was true.

The IT teacher looked up as he put the box on the backseat of his car. 'Hey, Lola.'

He sounded tired and like this conversation might be one too many for him. Matron threw me one of her I'm-watching-you glares before stalking away, probably back up to her office where she could watch and catalogue from afar.

Mr Yorke moved around to the driver's seat. 'See you around,' he said.

'Wait,' I said. 'I need to ask you about Sebastian. Is he . . .? Do you know anything about him?'

The IT teacher rubbed his stubbled chin. 'Nothing good,' he said.

'Is he dead?'

'No,' he said. Instant relief. 'I visited him at the hospital. He's not dead but he's not exactly alive either. Look, I really have to be going—'

'Please,' I said, moving closer. 'Please could you take me to him? I really need to see him.'

'You're not allowed off school property,' he said.

I glanced around. There was no one else outside the school, no one at any of the windows, not even Matron. This might be my only chance to see Sebastian. He came to me in my game when I needed him, made me feel pretty and wanted. He felt like so much more than a character in a game. I had to understand what had happened to him.

'He was kind to me,' I said, choosing my words carefully. 'I want to say goodbye.'

Mr Yorke sighed and mulled this over for a moment. 'I'm no longer your teacher so I'm not bound by the school any more. If you get caught sneaking out, it's you who will be reprimanded. Maybe even expelled.'

'That's fine,' I said.

Mr Yorke shook his head and gestured for me to get into his car.

The roads beyond Leighton were narrow and one-car wide, flanked by trees so thick the dashboard illuminated itself. Mr Yorke drove in silence, so I spent the drive looking out the windows. I'd never seen the countryside before. Mother had preferred to keep us in the town. The only patches of green nearby were parks and the odd tree encircled by gravel and concrete on our street.

Out here, grass was king. Endless, endless miles of it. It coloured every aspect of the world around us. It was on the hills rolling towards the horizon, between the trees lining the road, in the waterlogged fields dotted with grazing animals.

Eventually we came upon a small town. We followed the roads to a large dark building with a car park dominating the front of it. All the signs were marked with the NHS logo.

'This is the specialist ICU building,' Mr Yorke said as we parked up. 'It's where Sebastian was moved to.'

'Why isn't it part of the main hospital?'

Mr Yorke switched off the engine. 'Most of the people in here are being kept alive by machines. Sometimes they get transferred to specialist wards like this to free up space at the main hospital. I warn you, Lola. It's not pretty in there.'

'I understand,' I said. 'I have to see.'

We got out of the car and I followed after Mr Yorke, through some automatic doors and past a desk with staff who didn't look up as we signed in. It was one of those types of receptions where they were used to people coming and going.

Mr Yorke led me into the hospital, following signs on the walls and lines on the floor, before reaching a corridor with lots of doors coming off it. Antibacterial hand gel dispensers were mounted on the wall outside each of the doors. He pumped some on to his hands so I did the same.

I peered in through the window of the opposite door.

It was a private room with a woman asleep in a bed, tubes coming out of her mouth and her arms, connecting her to machines. They were all private rooms here, I realized. That's why the doors were so close together.

Mr Yorke led me into the room closest to us.

The air was too warm and had a surgically clean smell that could only belong to a hospital. Sebastian lay unmoving in the bed. He looked gaunt. Like his skin had lost all of its colour and was stretched over his skull, showing off more of his cheekbones than was normal.

A photograph was perched on a trolley to the side of the bed. Sebastian's oak-coloured eyes smiled out of it. He looked a little younger than how I remembered him, but it was such a contrast to the body occupying the bed.

Sebastian was surrounded by beeping machines. An oxygen mask over his face, wires coming out from under the blankets. It seemed impossible he was the same person I'd seen a few days earlier.

'The ventilator keeps him breathing,' Mr Yorke said.

This was what he meant when he said Sebastian had lost his life. He wasn't dead, but he wasn't alive either.

I took Sebastian's hand and squeezed it, tried not to be disappointed at how he didn't squeeze back. 'How did this happen?'

'If I knew, I wouldn't have been fired,' Mr Yorke said. 'I warned Miriam something would happen with the code. It was all out of whack and she had no control and . . . I was going to see the head and tell him all about it, but by then it was too late. The medical team said something had messed with his neurophysiology and Sebastian was found with his Key attached to his temple.'

My hand flew to my temple. My Key was still there. 'They're dangerous?'

Mr Yorke shook his head. 'Miriam convinced the school they're safe, said what happened to Sebastian was a freak accident and wouldn't happen to anyone else. She reminded them of all the money she'd already given them and Mr Leighton backed off.'

I raised an eyebrow at the news Mr Leighton had accepted a bribe. He'd made his position on coveting very clear, so I was unsure what he would do with a large amount of money. It's not as if he was driving around in a brand-new car.

'What about you?' I asked Mr Yorke.

'Someone had to get fired,' he said. He turned to me,

looked at me more seriously. 'Don't trust Dr Zats. She's full of lies. I've tried to confront her since it happened and she's taken out a restraining order. She doesn't care about you or anyone else at the school, Lola. She's after results and will do anything to get them. Don't trust her.' He studied the Key at my temple. 'I wouldn't wear that if I were you.'

If I didn't wear the Key, I couldn't play the game. If I couldn't play the game, I'd never see Sebastian again. Never see my house. Couldn't hug Dad. It was too much to give up. Plus, despite Mr Yorke's warnings, I still felt like I was missing something with Sebastian. It wasn't as simple as the IT teacher made out.

Mr Yorke left the room for a cigarette and said he'd take me back after I'd said my goodbyes.

Alone, I went to the photograph on the bedside trolley. The wooden frame had been broken and glued back together. Sebastian looked younger in it, but he still had dark circles under his eyes. PROOF was stamped across the middle of the picture.

Mother had never bought the final versions of my pictures either.

Once, she dressed me and Alex in matching dresses with puffy sleeves and took us to a photography studio. The photographer made us sit on boxes covered in faux fur, and asked Alex to lean her arm on my shoulder in a way that would never happen in real life. Then we had individual pictures taken. Only Alex's picture made the shelf at home. Only hers graduated to a proper purchase.

Mine was left in a box in the attic, PROOF still on the front.

It was the same for Sebastian.

I traced his smile with my finger and promised I'd be the one to cherish his picture the way no one had cherished mine. I tucked it into the inside of my blazer next to the letter I'd put there earlier, and went to find Mr Yorke.

I did not say goodbye to Sebastian.

TWENTY-THREE

M r Yorke dropped me off at the top of the drive, by
the rampant lions. 'Probably best I don't come on to
school property again,' he said. 'See you around, Lola.'

He disappeared in a cloud of exhaust fumes.

My mind whirred as I walked between the lions' teeth,
down the long driveway and back to Leighton. On the
way, Dad appeared at my side. He pulled his aviators
down to block out the bright sunshine. 'How did it go?'
he asked.

'Sebastian isn't dead.'

'That's good news.'

'Sort of. Something doesn't add up,' I said. 'Dr Zats
convinced the school her game wasn't to blame. There
was money involved.'

Dad's mouth tugged to the left. 'There's always money
involved with things like this.'

When I'd first arrived, Matron had shown me around
Leighton like the school was an English Heritage site.
She'd praised Mr Leighton for all the renovations he'd
overseen, but everywhere felt grey and tired. The floors
were scuffed. Walls were stained. The whole school

needed an overhaul. The IT building was modern-looking and imposing, but even that was built a few years ago now. If Dr Zats's experiment came with a pay cheque, where had the money gone?

We reached Leighton's stone-pillared entranceway and walked inside, its coolness greeting us. Dad followed me up to my bedroom.

'It doesn't make sense,' I said, pacing the room.

'Let's think about what you do know,' Dad suggested.

I recounted to him everything I'd learnt: Dr Zats was running an experiment. Mr Yorke had been sacked. Sebastian was alive but unlikely to wake up anytime soon. Dr Zats had claimed the Keys were safe.

'Wait,' I said, stopping dead. 'Sebastian's Key wasn't on his temple at the hospital.'

I thought back to that night when I'd found him unconscious in the entranceway. Rain pelting his face, darkening his hair and his lashes. Mr Leighton had taken his Key. Where was it now?

When Sebastian had explained how to manipulate the game, he'd agreed with Dr Zats on one thing: you needed someone's Key to access their private game. You could only bring people into your own game, which meant the only way I'd ever see Sebastian's private world was if he invited me in.

Or, I could use his Key.

I took his photograph out of my pocket and my fingers brushed against something else. Alex's letter. I took it out and traced over the swirls of her name. So pretty. But the contents was an invitation captured in a single musical note.

B for Basement.
B for Death.
I'd reached my bed. Mr Leighton's watch ticked solidly in my bedside drawer. I turned away from it and my heel crunched over something. I looked down, trembling, slowly bending to pick up the stem of a broken martini glass.
Tick.
Tick.
Tick!
'Where's the letter?' I shouted.
'What letter?'
I followed her out on to the balcony. The black-and-white tiles of the hallway were a chessboard beneath us. The metronome ticked on the lid of the piano below.
Tick!
'The letter from my father. He would have given me one too.'
TICK.
'Don't be ridiculous, Lola. He doesn't even know you exist.'

TICK!

A scream ripped through my mind, into my bedroom. It was deep in my head, deep in my bones, exploding into the room around me, cracking the walls, smashing the windows, making the chandelier swing above my head.

I dropped the martini stem and clamped my hands over my ears.

The scream stopped.

Deafening silence took its place.

I snapped my eyes open. The room was back as it should have been. No smashed windows or cracks in the walls. There wasn't even a chandelier in this room. Everything was back to normal.

'Lola?' Dad said with uncertainty. 'Are you OK?'

'My memory,' I said. 'There's something not right.'

'Memories are what you make of them,' he said.

Of course, he would say that. Tampering with my memory was the reason he existed. Playing pretend – writing him into the back of my brain so he was in front of my eyes – was what I was best at. But the things I'd overwritten were trying their hardest to resurface, and deep inside me, a panic had awoken at the thought of them ever coming loose. It was as if my brain was split in two. Somewhere, deep down, I knew what had happened, and that part of my brain had deliberately hidden it from the other.

Dad came to my side. 'Lola, love. Maybe it's time you faced the basement and—'

'No,' I said. 'It isn't.'

I took a deep breath and refocused on Sebastian's missing Key. I'd need to find it if I wanted to understand what had happened to him.

Mercedes's digital clock told me it was past twelve. I hadn't seen a single person since I'd come back to school.

'The lunch service,' I said in realization. 'Everyone's at the lunch service.'

I stuffed Alex's letter in my drawer, followed by Sebastian's photograph. It didn't close properly. The photo frame peeked out of the top, stopping it from shutting.

I'd fix it later.

Dad followed me out of the bedroom, towards the centre of the school. 'I don't like what you're thinking, Lola.'

'It might be our only chance.'

We raced to Mr Leighton's private flat and ran up the staircase, crowned by his creepy sign:

Thou Shalt Not Covet

I let myself in as quietly as possible. Mr Leighton was probably at the lunch service, but there hadn't been enough time to check. He'd made it clear what would happen if he found me here a second time uninvited. I made my way to his private office on tiptoe.

Thankfully, it was empty, but the space felt eerily quiet. There was no watch on his side table to fill the air with noise, and I kicked myself for forgetting to bring it. Finding Sebastian's Key was more important.

I glanced over the collection of Bibles. 'Where would he put it?'

'Lola,' Dad said, making me turn.

There, on Mr Leighton's desk, was Sebastian's Key.

TWENTY-FOUR

It had been returned to its SmartTech box. The way it sat in the middle of the desk bothered at me, like the headmaster had been inspecting it, contemplating it. I swiped it up and held it to my chest. Mr Leighton would never understand Sebastian the way I did.

'Are you going to use it?' Dad asked. He looked at me warily over the tops of his aviators, the way a parent would when their child was about to do something naughty and there was nothing they could do.

I didn't reply as I made my way to Sebastian's room. It was the same as before; untidy in a way that looked like someone might walk in at any moment and lie down on the bed. His computer was still turned on and filled the room with its low humming noise.

'We don't know what he made in his world,' Dad pointed out. 'It could be dangerous.'

I perched on the edge of his bed. 'It could be the only way to find out what happened to him.'

I peeled my Key from my temple and replaced it with Sebastian's. A shiver shot down my spine. It was ready.

'Be careful,' Dad said.

I nodded and clapped my hands. 'Enter.'

Sebastian's bedroom disappeared in a band of pixels.

It was replaced by a corridor lined with doors. Cracks ran through the yellowed walls. The only light was a long tube of strip lighting, so dim it barely lit the way. My tentative steps echoed around the space. I looked down to see I was myself, dressed in my school uniform. No special outfit or clothes required here, a bit like my house. I ran a hand through my hair and was pleased to find it was how I preferred it. Even in Sebastian's world, the game knew what I wanted to look like.

The corridor before me elongated and more doors appeared. It culminated in a set of double doors down the very end. I squinted into the darkness and went to the nearest one to peer through a round window.

Mr Leighton was on the other side. I almost jumped backwards but realized he looked younger. Far younger. Hair less grey, face less lined. He stood over a woman in a hospital bed who was the same colour as her bed sheets.

He flipped the lid on a pocket watch, stroked a thumb over the case before returning it to his pocket. 'A man has to have sons, Angie,' he said. 'The Leighton dynasty . . .'

'I know, David,' the woman said, looking away. 'I'm trying.'

A small boy sat on a chair on her other side. The woman offered him a weak smile. 'No brother for you today, Seb.'

I backed away, went to the door directly behind me and peered in through its window.

Sebastian was small, small enough to be nine or ten, sat cross-legged on a circle rug. Mr Leighton paced in front of him. 'You're my responsibility now,' the head-master said over and over. 'I know what you did. Do you hear? I know.'

I moved to the next door. Sebastian was older, around twelve. He stared at the floor as Mr Leighton towered over him.

'What have I told you?'

'No coveting.' Sebastian's reply was monotone.

'And what did you do?'

'Coveted.'

Mr Leighton's belt clinked as he undid it, slipped the leather from his trouser loops and grasped it tightly in his fist. 'I do this for your own good, son.'

Sebastian looked up, hands fists at his side. 'I'm not your son,' he said.

'No,' Mr Leighton agreed. 'You're not.'

In the window after that, Sebastian was older, looked how he did now. Mr Leighton rose from his desk. 'An internship with Dr Zats is out of the question. I forbid you from leaving,' the headmaster said.

'You can't,' Sebastian spat.

'I am your legal guardian and you will do as I say,' the headmaster said, getting close to Sebastian. 'You are my responsibility and you will stay here until I deem you to be safe for society.'

'You're insane.'

'And *you* are a mur—'

Sebastian lashed out, pushing the headmaster backwards into his desk. A shock of silence fell between them. Mr Leighton recovered first, face dark with a visible anger. He grappled for his belt but Sebastian pounced, tried to wrestle it from his hands. He kicked out and the headmaster gasped as a *snap!* echoed through the room and his leg buckled. He snarled, wrapped a hand around Sebastian's neck and forced him across the room, slammed him into a wall, limping the whole way.

'I'm leaving,' Sebastian choked out.

The headmaster's face was taut with rage. 'You're going nowhere,' he growled, raising the belt in his free hand.

The scene faded and I backed away trembling. We'd all seen Sebastian and Mr Leighton arguing in the dining hall once, but I had no idea their relationship was so volatile. The last scene must have been recent, maybe only a couple of weeks ago given how Mr Leighton still walked with a limp.

When the paramedics had come for Sebastian they'd asked about the bruises on his chest and Mr Leighton had brushed them off, said he was a vigorous lacrosse player. I knew now he was lying.

The corridor was similar to my house, each door containing a memory, secrets Sebastian had buried the same way I'd buried mine.

I'd wandered quite far down, neared the set of double doors with bars across the middle. They were the largest doors on the whole corridor. Whatever memory was behind them was so important Sebastian had given it a prime position.

On the floor outside the doors was a single glass of water.

As I stared at it, the contents began to swirl. As if an invisible spoon was stirring it. A mini tornado raged inside.

The strip lighting flickered as I made my way towards it. I passed by other windows where Sebastian was younger – sometimes very young – and Mr Leighton dominated all of them. They talked together soundlessly unless I moved closer to them, the light getting stronger in each room so I could better see what happened.

'Sebastian?' a voice called. A woman's, frail and uncertain.

It had come from behind the double doors.

Pixels fuzzed across the space at my side and Sebastian appeared there. He bounced on the spot, completely oblivious as to where we were. 'Finally, you're back. I've been waiting for you.' His smile faltered as he took in the corridor. 'What are you doing?'

'I'm borrowing someone else's Key,' I said.

He stiffened. 'Whose?'

'Yours.'

Another step down the corridor and the doors at the end opened another few centimetres. A face shrouded in darkness appeared there. Someone was watching us. 'Sebastian?' the woman's voice called again. 'I'm thirsty.'

'Who's in that room?' I asked. This was what Sebastian

had been hiding in his VR world. He'd built a secret into his game the same way I had. A fear he wanted to lock away for ever. Was this why he'd been found unconscious?

'We're leaving,' Sebastian said. 'I need a door.'

As he spoke the words, pixels washed across the wall to our right. A grey metal door fizzled out of the paint-work. A FIRE EXIT sign appeared on the front. Sebastian leant across the long bar and pulled me through with him.

It led to the hallway in my house. The exit slammed shut behind us and I watched it sink into the black-and-white tiles.

I snatched my hand from his. 'What did you do that for?'

Sebastian paced on the tiles before me. 'You shouldn't enter other people's worlds without their permission, Lola.'

The irony made me laugh. 'And what are you doing, exactly?'

He only glared at me. 'Where'd you get my Key?'

I didn't want to tell him I'd gone to Mr Leighton's flat and was sat in his bedroom. He was already angry at me for using his Key without his permission, and he'd all but admitted it *was* his Key. 'IT lab. Dr Zats had it,' I lied. 'She said she wanted to experiment with it.'

He scoffed. 'Because her current one is so successful.'

'You know a lot about her,' I said.

'I've read all her papers.'

I folded my arms and gave him a long look. 'Who *are* you?'

Sebastian ran a hand through his chestnut hair and walked across the black-and-white tiles. The overhanging balcony cast a deep shadow over him.

He was directly underneath it.

He might get hurt.

I stepped forward. 'Don't go near the—'

A scream made me jump. It cut through the house, making the walls vibrate and the floor shake. I clamped my hands over my ears and squeezed my eyes shut.

She was dead.

Train crash.

She was dead.

Balcony.

Dead. *Dead.* 'DEAD!'

As I shouted the word, a crack splintered through the room. It started on the floor tiles, near the archway to the living room, and rocketed up the ceiling. The chandelier rattled as it swung.

The scream subsided and I took my hands from my ears, heart pounding.

Dust covered the floor. The new crack was wide enough to slip an arm in. The living room was still only half redecorated – only one wall was the sage-green colour I'd seen Dad applying. The room was nowhere near finished and now there was a crack running through it, wide enough to be a riverbed.

How would I ever cover it up?

'Hey, it's OK.' Sebastian put his arm around me and I sank against him. He brushed my hair as I pressed my face into his chest. 'It's over, it's gone. It won't come back.' He said it over and over, but he had no control over it and neither did I.

We broke away and Sebastian studied me for a moment. 'Look, I want to show you something. Let me take you to one of my levels.'

My gaze snagged on the lift where the front door was. As I looked at it, a new button was emerging on the panel. A fourth floor. One I hadn't created. Sebastian led me towards it.

'What do you mean *your* level?' I asked.

'You think you're the only one with a house around here? Come on.'

Ping!

The button for the basement flashed on, off, on, off.

Ping!

Ping!

I slammed my hand against the button for level four. I wanted to go to Sebastian's world. The basement could wait.

Level four—

Level four—

Level four—

Sebastian put his hand over mine. 'We need to close the gate first.'

I stopped mashing the button and let him pull me back. Ran a hand through my long hair. 'I'm OK,' I said, taking a ragged breath.

He pulled the gate closed and hit the button for level

four. The lift vibrated beneath our feet as we travelled upwards, through the cross-section of floors and past the party on level three that was still in full swing.

'Almost there,' Sebastian said.

The lift stopped and Sebastian pulled the gate back, stepped into a home I'd never seen before. He led me across a floor composed of long wooden beams. Wooden arches supported the vaulted ceiling. A large white bed occupied one corner; a mosquito net draped over it. Crickets hummed in the background. Wall sconces cast the space in a warm yellow light.

Sebastian led me through an archway, out on to a balcony with a rope barrier. He put his hands in his pockets and looked upwards. I craned my neck and gasped.

Stars. Millions and millions of them. They moved faster than was normal, rotating through the sky like someone was spinning a wheel, but not so fast that it was disorientating. Purple and blue mist hung between them, making the sky look deep and vast.

'I've never seen the Milky Way before,' I said.

'Neither have I, that's why I made it.' He considered the sky for a moment. 'It's probably not accurate, but that's part of the fun.'

Beneath the stars was an open valley thick with trees. A river separated two sides of the forest, stars glittering in its smooth, wide curves. Across the valley was a snow-topped ledge.

'You've brought me here before,' I said, pointing. 'We stood on that ledge and looked back at your house.' At

the time I'd been trying to escape Alex. She'd materialized in the park and had tried to come towards us.
Sebastian had led me through a door.

He nodded. 'You needed somewhere safe.'

Things were different tonight. There was no Aurora.
The Milky Way was in its place, glittering as the stars
spun through it. Maybe the sky changed depending on
what day or time it was. It was a clever way of never
getting bored of the same space.

I suddenly noticed Sebastian was wearing shorts and a
linen shirt. I looked down at my white cotton dress and
bare feet. With the wooden tree house and Milky Way
backdrop, we looked like we belonged in the centre
spread of a home and lifestyle magazine.

'I do feel safe here,' I said. 'It's beautiful.'

'This is where I come when I'm waiting for you.'

'You wait for me?'

He turned and leant back against the rope, propping
his elbows on it. 'Of course. You're the most interesting
person in the school. We're the same, you and me.'

'You've said that to me before,' I said. 'In real life.'

He shrugged. 'I wanted to show you this place so you
can come here if you want,' he said. 'If you ever need a
change of scene or if someone tries to find you . . . use
your lift to escape to my tree house. You'll be safe here.'

Everything moved lazily here – the stars, the river, the
breeze that played with the mosquito net above the bed.
The wooden beams were warm and smooth beneath the
soles of my feet. Sebastian had made this tree house as a

space to relax. I pictured him coming here whenever the horror behind those double doors got too much.

He'd been so eager to get me out of that corridor.

The emergency exit had appeared before I could see what was behind the door. A swirling glass of water had been outside, as if it had been placed there with purpose. Someone had called his name. A woman.

I knew instinctively it was his mother.

His mother followed him the same way mine followed me. All those doors had been filled with memories of how badly he'd been treated by Mr Leighton. He must have wanted to escape the same way I did.

There'd been a word in his textbook that hadn't made sense to me before.

Transcendence.

I knew now what it meant.

Somehow, Sebastian had inserted his consciousness into the game. His body would forever be in the ICU, but his mind would live for ever in the game.

'You're in hospital,' I said. 'In the real world.'

Sebastian leant over the rope railing. He stared off at the forest and said nothing.

'Mr Yorke said you'd lost your life,' I said, filling the silence. 'But Dr Zats said you hadn't died. I think they're both right. You're alive in the game, aren't you? I mean, you're you. The Sebastian from the real world. I invited you into my world when I recreated you and you let me think you were a character in the game, but you're not. You're the real Sebastian, living in the game.'

For a while, I didn't think he'd reply.

'Dr Zats has no idea what she's created,' he said eventually.

I thought of Dad and how he was real here. How in the game, I could look however I wanted. Have the family I'd never had. Mother did her best to disrupt it all, but Sebastian was right: Dr Zats had given us access to something with a potential even she didn't realize.

'The game is the best door I've ever found,' I agreed.

'It's fun here, definitely. But it's only ever been a waiting room for me.'

'You're going to go back?' I asked. 'Mr Leighton – your dad, he's—'

'David is *not* my dad.'

Sebastian studied his feet. A belt had appeared, wrapped in a tight coil like a leather snake. Specks of blood tainted the buckle.

'He thinks I need to be controlled,' he said, staring at it as he spoke. 'That I covet things I can't have. He thinks if he punishes me whenever he catches me coveting something, I'll associate that thing with pain and eventually learn not to want it.'

'Pavlovian conditioning,' I said, remembering Dr Zats's use of pain to enforce the rules of the game.

'Exactly.' Sebastian kicked the belt over the side of the balcony. 'It's more than that though, goes way beyond that. David thinks – he's convinced – the way my mum died . . . he thinks I'm responsible.'

My eyebrows shot for the stars. 'What?!'

'He's insane,' Sebastian said, wiping at his eyes furiously. 'Mum took too many meds, she was barely conscious as it was, it was all a hideous accident. David's always held me responsible. He hates me, Lola. Hates me and wants to control me, to punish me for something I never did. A few weeks ago, Dr Zats offered me an internship but David made me turn it down. He stopped me applying for universities, was going to keep me at school as a teaching assistant. I'd be under his watch for the rest of my life.' He let out a humourless laugh. 'He must be thrilled I'm in hospital. It means I'm the way he wants: docile, controllable.'

Mr Leighton's obsession with coveting ruled his life and he was forcing it on to Sebastian, the way Mother's obsession with music had been forced on to me.

'I know what that's like,' I said.

'Told you we were the same.'

'How did you know?' I asked. 'You said that to me the first time we met. How did you know, even then?'

He looked down at a metronome that had found its way on to the balcony.

I kicked it over the edge. We watched it disappear.

'Sometimes you can tell, you know?' he said. 'That people have been through a lot. Had pain as a constant companion. Seen death, maybe. The body keeps the score.'

At that, he pulled his shirt over his head and cast it away. Pixels shuddered over his body and his skin changed, morphed. Long bruises appeared across his chest. Some were purple fading to yellow. Others were shockingly red, curved over his muscles. He turned, showing me his back and how they continued on to his shoulder blades and down his spine.

I reached out to trace them, his skin pebbling wherever I went.

He turned around to face me, and I was suddenly too aware of how my fingertips were grazing the ridges of his stomach.

When I'd caught him in bed with Mercedes, he'd been wearing a T-shirt. Here, he was baring himself. I could tell by his quietness that he'd never done anything like this before.

I held out my hand and watched as my own scars pixelated to the surface.

They puckered over my palm and down my wrist, like plastic had been poured over the skin and pulled too tight as it cooled.

Sebastian's gaze darkened as he studied them with me.

I trembled as I pulled the strap of my dress down my arm, ran a finger across the lump along my collarbone. It had never set right. Still hurt sometimes if I slept on it funny. Sebastian grazed his thumb over the bone, back and forth, feeling the way it popped out too prominently.

My long hair had gone. I'd forced the glow from my skin.

We stood before each other exactly as we were.

'You're beautiful,' he said, and ducked his head to kiss me.

TWENTY-FIVE

I left the game with a promise to return as soon as I could. Sebastian had kissed me again and told me to hurry up, said he would be waiting for me. It was dark when I came back to his room. I put his Key on his bedside table and reapplied my own. A shiver shot down my spine, like it was pleased to be back on my temple.

Outside in the hallway, a wall tapestry caught my attention. A collection of names, sewn into the fabric.

'We should leave,' Dad said, noticing me moving towards it. 'This isn't our house, Lola. I can't protect you here.'

'I'll only be a minute,' I said, already halfway there. Mr Leighton could be back at any moment, but a name had jumped out at me from the tapestry and I had to see.

Dad followed me with crossed arms and a scowl.

A thick black line split the tapestry in two, wide enough to be a tree trunk. It *was* a tree trunk. Branches sprung from it, reaching out across the walls, smaller branches leading off it that led to names and dates. At the top of the tree in swirling black writing were the words that had caught my eye:

Dad inspected the family tree with me. The tapestry was as wide as the wall, the kind of decor that belonged in a castle or a manor house. Patches of it looked worn, some areas faded from sunlight. Black mould had overtaken the top corner and was leaching the nearest names from the branches there.

I tracked the names and noticed the ones I'd seen on the headmaster's portraits. They were all male. I craned my neck upwards to get a better look but there were no female names on the tree. Not a single woman had made it on to the tapestry.

'Look here,' Dad said, tracing over a name that had been burnt off so severely the threads were coming loose. 'What does it mean?'

There were a few names that had been removed in a similar way. Always singular names on the end of a branch. Nothing spawning from them. A name demanded my attention.

David Alan Leighton, 1974–

His name was also on the end of a branch, the natural dead end to the branches culminating in his.

'They had no heirs,' I said in realization. 'Or, maybe they only had girls. There's no girls on here.'

Sebastian wasn't on there. After what I'd seen in

Sebastian's world, I doubted he ever would be. Mr Leighton didn't consider him his son. His name would never be on the tree.

Dad backed away. 'This is seriously creepy.'

'What are you doing in here, Dolores?' I spun around to see Mr Leighton coming through the front door. He glared at me. I stumbled back, but he limped his way towards me, filling the hallway. 'Well?'

'I . . . I . . .' Last time I'd lied and said I was borrowing a book. There was nothing I could say that he would even remotely buy into. He limped into the space I tried to create, followed me around the hallway in a circle until I was able to back towards the door.

Panic ruled Dad's face. 'Lola, get out of here!'

'You are in serious want of discipline, Dolores Whitmore. You and Sebastian are the same – in need of constant supervision or else you get up to no good. Here you are, trespassing. Did I not warn you of the consequences if I caught you up here again?'

He continued to advance on me, his face dark with a fury I didn't know a person could possess. Mother had been cold, casual in her cruelty. Mr Leighton used his size to push me, bully me backwards. Mother only hit me occasionally, but I'd seen enough of Sebastian's memories to know Mr Leighton got physical regularly.

I blinked and Dad reappeared, making the tiny space even more cramped. I tried to grab his hand but couldn't. My heartbeat thrummed at the thought Mr Leighton wouldn't let me leave.

'Get away from my daughter!' Dad yelled. He tried to swing for the headmaster, but his fist went straight through him. Desperation marked the hollows of his face. 'Lola, get out of here. I can't protect you.'

My spine hit the front door. I turned, fumbled to open it.

'I see you and the way you covet things,' Mr Leighton hissed. 'I see the way it lights your eyes and how all your movements reek with it. Did I not tell you it was the worst of all sins? Thou shalt not covet, Dolores.'

The door pulled free. I scrambled to get out of it.

I ran down the stairs two at a time, looked over my shoulder when I reached the bottom. Mr Leighton glared at me from the top.

TWENTY-SIX

I found an empty cubicle in the nearby girls' toilets, locked the door and sagged against it. My heart still pounded and my underarms were damp with sweat. I sat for a moment, catching my breath, and then clapped. 'Enter.'

The red front door to my house opened as I raced up the steps. Inside the lift, I selected the button for the fourth level, Sebastian's tree house, and the floor hummed beneath my feet when I closed the gate.

I paced in the lift as it moved.

Sebastian was in a coma, in limbo. Somehow, he'd transferred himself into the game. His body lay in a hospital but his mind was plugged into Better Than Life. After personally seeing what a psycho Mr Leighton was, I had a good enough idea as to why Sebastian would want to escape and would do anything to get away from him.

He'd used the game as a door, an exit to a better world.

Doors came easily to Alex too. They could be anything – letters, games, people. Doors found her as much as she found them. She got a letter from our father and I got nothing.

The lift moved up, passing through the first floor.

A small hand reached through the wrought-iron gate to grab at me.

'Lolaaaa.' Little Alex grinned as I jumped out of the way. Chocolate lined her teeth. 'I can hear your mind whirring, Lola.'

The lift continued to rise upwards but Little Alex tried to grab at me a few more times, not caring how her arm might get trapped. She cackled and gnashed her teeth at me, spraying blood into the lift. Blood, not chocolate, coloured her mouth. It dripped down her chin and on to the floor.

'Have you remembered yet?' she crooned. 'Have you remembered what actually happened?'

'I know what happened,' I said.

The floor swallowed her as I moved upwards, but her taunting laugh echoed in my ears. I balled my hands at my sides. She was wrong. I remembered fine what had really happened.

There was a train crash.

It had been raining heavily, and the land – it wasn't supported enough, or something. It had spilt, oozed on to the tracks and the train barrelled into it. That was how Mother died.

I could hear the rain. A thousand raindrops drumming on the front door like fingers, begging me to open it, to let them in.

Tick.

The officer on the other side of our door, rain

streaming from his hat.

Tick.

'You'd better let me in, miss.'

Ping!

The lift stopped on the fourth floor. The button for the basement flashed once and I got out of the lift before it could do it again. My white dress materialized as I moved into Sebastian's tree house, across the warm wooden floorboards.

The lights were lower than they had been when I was last here. The mosquito net had been drawn shut around the bed. Sebastian was lying in it.

I crept closer and saw how he slept on his side, body turned to the middle of the bed. One hand was under his head, the other slung over a pillow, hugging it close like a child with a stuffed animal. His chest moved with a rhythmic rise and fall. The last time I'd found him asleep it had been so different.

His eyes fluttered open as I crawled in and lay down next to him.

'Back so soon?' he said with a sleepy smile.

'I needed to feel safe,' I said, nestling closer.

'Needed,' he repeated.

I nodded, my forehead knocking against his.

He moved the pillow between us and pulled my hips to his. 'You're safe here, Lola. I told you that.'

'I know. I just needed to feel it.'

'There's that "needed" again.' Sebastian smiled and brought his lips to mine in a soft kiss. I sighed and sank into the gesture, deepening it. He responded by pulling me even closer and stroking my hair as his kisses travelled over my cheeks and to the underside of my jaw.

The world through my half-lidded eyes was perfect.

The bed I lay in looked like it belonged in a magazine. The boy I kissed was the hottest boy in school and he'd picked me. *Me.* I'd never been picked for anything.

'What about Mercedes?' I asked, voicing my interrupting thought.

Sebastian's kisses stopped abruptly and continued a second later. 'What about her?' he said, the question husky in my ear. He moved down my neck.

'She was – is – your girlfriend.'

'No she isn't. We kissed once, that was all.'

That didn't fit with what I knew. Mercedes had made it sound like they'd been together for a while in secret. She was so defensive of him and his going to hospital had affected her the most out of our group. That didn't seem like the behaviour of someone who'd only kissed him once.

'What about the time I walked in on you?' I asked, putting a hand out to stop him.

Sebastian sighed and stopped. 'The truth is Mercedes was quite . . . possessive. I kissed her once, at an end-of-term party last year. She never really left me alone after that. She was messaging me and emailing me all summer, but I didn't respond other than to say she couldn't tell anyone, particularly David. He would have hit the roof if he found out I'd kissed someone, he's always told me I can't have a girlfriend. Anyway, when we came back to school she threatened to tell David if I didn't give her what she wanted.'

'What? That's horrible.' Poor Sebastian, no wonder he'd done what Mercedes wanted – Mr Leighton would have clobbered him if he'd found out. Sebastian had enough bruises as it was.

'I was honestly glad you walked in on us,' Sebastian said. 'It meant someone else knew and she couldn't black-mail me so easily.' He laughed hollowly. 'I bet she's tried to be super nice to you since then, to try and get you in her camp. If I ever wake up in the real world you can guarantee she'll try and blackmail me again.'

I sat up and drew my knees to my chest, thinking about how Mercedes had made a big deal out of apolo-gizing and giving me a lipstick. I'd thought she was sweet. She'd said she wanted us to be friends. I'd thought we *were* friends.

'If I can't trust Mercedes, I can't trust anyone.'

Sebastian sat up and put his arm around me. 'You can trust me,' he said.

I leant against him. 'You're in here. I'm on my own out there.'

'I'll wake up soon, I promise.' He kissed the top of my head.

I wanted to tell him it didn't matter if he did. Even with Sebastian awake it felt impossible out in the real world. All my teachers were so demanding. I was unlikely to leave Leighton with any qualifications. The headmaster hated me. Dad was only tangible in here. Everything I cared about was in the game.

'It won't be long,' Sebastian said, taking my silence as a need for reassurance. 'I'll be ready to face David soon, but I need a little more time. Now, where were we?'

I giggled as he pulled me back down to the bed. We kissed and talked for a long time, fell asleep with him hugging me from behind, his arm slung over my hips and his lips pressed to my spine.

FOUR WEEKS AGO

'Let this go, Dolores. That is an order, do you understand?'

Mother towered over me, her violin in one hand. 'It's only a letter,' I said. 'Please let me read it.'

'If it's only a letter, why do you want to read it so badly?' Mother's retort was a gin-perfumed hiss.

'Because—'

'Because what? Because something inconsequential? Meaningless? Enough, Dolores. I will hear no more, you hear? No more!' Mother snapped the lid of the piano open. 'Now, the neighbours are out and I want to get an hour of practice in before they return and complain again.' She tapped the sheet music with her bow. 'Play.'

I placed my fingers on the keys.

Mother prodded the metronome into action and positioned her violin beneath her chin. 'Play,' she said again.

My fingers wouldn't move. I couldn't do it. She was withholding something precious, hoarding it, lording it over me and delighting in my pain.

'Dolores,' Mother said, her tone filled with warning. 'Your usefulness is fast expiring. If you do not play, you will regret it.'

'Please,' I said again.

Alex slipped into the room, anticipation lighting her eyes. Mother never raised her voice but Alex had an inbuilt radar for when something was about to go down. She always came to watch.

Mother beckoned her over, put an arm around her favourite daughter.

'I'll tell you what,' Mother said, 'seeing as it's Alex's letter, Alex can decide. That's fair, isn't it?'

My sister's grin was wide.

TWENTY-SEVEN

For three days I moved back and forth from my bedroom to the downstairs girls' toilets, where no one ever seemed to go. I stayed in the end cubicle all day, overnight one night. The following morning I woke up, spine and shoulders stiff from spending a night on the cold floor, scooped some water into my mouth from the sink, and went back into the game. It blocked out the tight knot of hunger in my stomach.

I only left because Georgie came looking for me. She came into the toilets, calling my name. Thumped on the cubicle door.

'I know you're in there, Lola,' she yelled, banging her fist. 'Mercedes said she hasn't seen you in three days and there's a rumour going round this cubicle is haunted.'

I was sitting on the deck of Sebastian's tree house, our legs dangling over the side. 'Georgie's calling me,' I said.

He leant closer, stretched out a hand. 'I can make it so you don't hear anyone in real life, if you want? It's a simple tap on your Key.'

It would be easy to let him, easy to ignore Georgie. But there was a steely note in her voice that told me she

251

wouldn't go away unless I replied. 'No, that's OK. I'd better see what she wants.' I clapped. 'Exit.'

I groaned as I stood upright, my back stiff and cold from sitting in one position for too long. Slid back the lock and eyeballed Georgie on the other side of the door. 'What?' I said.

In the mirror behind her I could see how pale I was. How dirty. My hair was greasier than ever and my skin was lacklustre. I was in serious need of a shower. Georgie looked no better. The bags under her eyes were so prominent I almost wondered if she'd rubbed her mascara into them, but I noticed for the first time she wasn't wearing any, or her usual pair of false eyelashes.

'Dr Z has an announcement for us,' she said. 'We've all been summoned.'

'Is it about the game?'

Georgie lifted her shoulders. 'Duh. What else could it be about? Are you coming or not?'

I slid out of the safety of my cubicle and wanted to run back in. Whatever Dr Zats had to say, it better be important. 'Coming,' I said, and walked down to the IT labs with her.

Dr Zats was late. The five of us sat in silence as we waited for her. The only noise was Georgie removing Dettol wipe after Dettol wipe to clean off the computer and desk she sat at. She turned the keyboard upside down and a myriad of crumbs fell from between the keys. 'No one *ever* cleans up after themselves here,' she huffed.

'Where's the next race, Finn?' Wai asked.

We turned to join the conversation.

Finn's hair was rumpled, lacked its usual layer of gel. He looked like he hadn't taken a shower. 'What race?'

'F1,' Wai said, cocking an eyebrow.

'Oh. Belgium, I think. Can't remember.'

'Are you going?' Mercedes prompted when he fell into silence.

Finn sighed. 'Don't know. Not spoken to my parents for a bit, not since . . . I haven't spoken to them anyway.' He took out his phone and began scrolling through something we couldn't see, putting an end to the conversation.

Either his screen had been fixed or he had another brand-new phone.

When I'd first met Finn, he'd bragged to anyone who'd listen about being invited out to Monaco. Since Mercedes and I had seen him arguing with his mum on the phone, he'd been different.

Wai was the only one who seemed his usual self. He was cleaner than all of us put together. It struck me that, other than our group sessions, he never seemed to put in any extra game time. He stuck to the schedule and didn't mind using the gym even though he didn't have to. He wasn't addicted like the rest of us were.

Dr Zats announced her entrance. 'Morning, all,' she said. We waited for her to begin distributing her usual quiz but instead she stayed at the front of the class by Mr Yorke's desk. 'Mr Leighton has expressed concern that everyone in the group has been increasingly prioritizing the game over their other educational obligations. I spoke to the programmers last night, and marketing of course, and we've decided that we have what we need. We're releasing you from the test trials.'

Stunned silence occupied the room.

Finn overcame it first. 'You can't do that,' he said.

Everyone murmured their agreement.

Dr Zats folded her arms. 'You've all done a fantastic job over the last eight weeks, and the wealth of information we've collected is above what we expected. The team's consensus is that we got what we came for. You can go back to your regular lessons and without the game, you'll hopefully catch up on anything you might have missed.'

'This is bullshit,' Georgie said. 'I signed a form. My parents signed a form. It's supposed to go on all term. It's a contract. There are solicitors for this kind of thing, you know.'

At the mention of solicitors, Dr Zats's face paled. 'I certainly don't think we need to go down that route—'

'You can't give us something like this and then take it away,' Finn said. 'We need it now.'

'It's been decided,' Dr Zats said, closing the discussion. 'Mr Leighton has said we can have the weekend, and then I'll need your Keys back first thing Monday.'

I stroked the Key at my temple. Without it, I would never be able to see Sebastian again. Wouldn't be able to hang out with my dad properly. In the game I could touch him, hug him. Out here he was only a figment of my imagination.

'Thank you all for your time,' Dr Zats said. 'We at SmartTech are so grateful.'

I bit my lip to stop myself yelling about how I knew she was lying. SmartTech didn't exist, and if it did, it was all a front. She'd built the game to experiment on us, not to trial a product.

Dr Zats turned and left the room.

'Three days,' I said when it was only us left. 'That's all we have left. I agree with Georgie, this is bullshit.'

'Maybe if you stopped skipping lessons we wouldn't be in this mess,' Mercedes said.

'We're not all perfect like you,' Finn snapped.

I couldn't remember the last lesson I'd been to. Mr Leighton had probably been informed of my absences.

'I missed all my lessons yesterday,' Georgie said with a sigh, which made me feel slightly better knowing it wasn't just me. 'The only reason I've left my room at all is because Daddy refused to hire a caterer for me. He said caterers wouldn't cook in bedrooms, which is ridiculous. The whole point of a caterer is that they'll cook anywhere. I said surely you can pay them enough and he said it wasn't a question of money, it was a question of it being too weird. He said I was weird. Am I weird?'

No one said anything.

'Brilliant.'

I barely heard Georgie. I had to talk to Sebastian. With everything he'd done to Dr Zats's programme, he might know a way around this. Maybe we didn't need our Keys – his body in the ICU wasn't wearing one – maybe there was a way for him to help us all play the game when Dr Zats had left.

'I have to go,' I said.

'Lola, wait.' Mercedes stood up with me. 'I need to talk to you.'

Between moving back and forth between my bedroom and the toilets, I'd tried to avoid Mercedes as much as possible. After what Sebastian had told me, I didn't have much to say to her. It was harder to ignore her here, stood in front of me.

'Later,' I said, and moved away before she could try again.

I left the room, heading for the gym where I knew I could hide. As soon as I was inside, I clapped my hands and whispered, 'Enter.'

I rode the lift all the way up to the second floor. The black-and-white tiles of my hallway appeared and I pulled back the gate. Dad and Sebastian were in the living room, filling the cracks in the walls with Polyfilla and tiny trowels. It seemed a mammoth task.

Dad smiled over his shoulder. 'Not to worry, Lola. We'll have this place looking right in no time.'

I wanted to run to him, to hug him. Dr Zats was leaving. She'd take Dad with her when she went.

'Lola,' Sebastian said, coming over. 'What's wrong?'

'Dr Zats is ending the programme and taking our Keys,' I blurted.

'When?'

'End of the week. I was wondering if you could—'

Ping!

The lift demanded my attention. The button for the basement flashed on and off.

Ping!

I braced myself for what I knew would follow.

The scream ripped through the hallway. Chunks of plaster fell from the ceiling and the chandelier shook before severing completely, smashing at our feet. I shrieked and ducked out of the way. Dad was at my side in an instant, covering my head with his hands. Sebastian tucked himself into a corner as we waited for the scream to subside.

Ping!

It finished.

'What's down there, Lola?' Sebastian nodded to the lift and the flashing basement button.

'I don't know.'

'We could go and see?' Dad suggested, putting his arm around me. 'Remember when you talked to me about your memory? It might be good for you to go down there and remember what happened.'

I bit my lip as I considered it. B for Basement. B for Death.

'I don't need to go down there to remember what happened,' I said. 'I can remember just fine.' Things were better in the game. They were how I wanted them.

'Look,' Sebastian said, pointing to the lift. A fifth button was appearing on the control panel. 'Could this be what you need to see?'

'I think so,' I said. When I'd reached the centre of the maze, I'd been looking for Mother's body in the train wreck. I needed to see it to know I was right. I instinctively knew the fifth floor that had formed would show it to me.

'What about the basement?' Dad said.

'Forget about the basement,' I said. 'It doesn't mean anything.'

Sebastian went with me to the lift and we got in together. Dad stood, paint dripping from the roller at his side. 'I'm here if you need me, Lola,' he said.

'She's fine,' Sebastian said. He closed the gate and pressed the button for the fifth level.

Between the swirls of the gate, Dad hadn't moved. A crease had formed between his eyebrows. 'I'll be back soon,' I said, offering him some reassurance. Guilt panged in my stomach at how much time I'd spent with Sebastian lately. I'd make it up to him soon. 'We'll have pancakes later,' I called as we rose up.

We passed through a cross-section of floor and the lift stopped shortly afterwards. I pulled back the gate and stepped out on to a field of cut grass.

My school uniform had gone, replaced by a long black coat buttoned to my throat. My boots belonged to Mother. She'd told me not to get dirt on them, but it had clumped to the soles anyway. It was impossible not to get dirt on my shoes in a place like this.

Sebastian followed me across the grass, his outfit changing to a long black coat with a white shirt and black tie.

'What is this place?'

Gravestones flanked us on all sides. Some were older than the dirt that clung to them, engraved names barely legible from all the weathering. Others were polished and new, the gold leaf of *MUCH LOVED* not yet worn away. The grass was short, well kept, but it was too soft beneath my feet and no matter how hard I tried to keep them clean, my boots were a mess.

Mother would kill me.

Sebastian pulled out an umbrella and held it over us as the skies rumbled.

The sombreness of the funeral had seemed to leak into the environment. It was in the sky, the ground, the air. Compounded in the smell of damp earth that worked its way into my core and told me about all the creepy-crawlies wriggling through it.

It was exactly how I remembered.

A short distance away was the funeral procession. Everyone on our street had turned up to give their condolences. They shuffled in a line towards a pile of freshly dug earth, a gravestone at the foot of it. I craned my neck over the crowd's shoulders to see the name carved into the stone.

HELENA WHITMORE

'Whose funeral is this?' Sebastian asked.

'My mother's.'

'How did she die?'

A figure in the procession stood out in a neon-yellow coat. They turned my way, tugged the radio on their jacket to their lips and didn't break eye contact as they murmured into it. The police. They'd seen me.

'What happened, Lola? What did your mother do?'

'It was the train crash,' I said, mustering the truth behind the statement. 'My mother died in a train crash.'

The procession had reached the grave.

They closed around it in a circle until I could no longer see it. I held my chin high. There, I'd done it. Seen it. Confirmed it had happened. I'd faced the thing that I feared the most. Nothing could ever harm me in the game again.

For a second, the circle of mourners parted and a woman with coiled blonde hair flashed in the gap.

I blinked and she'd gone, swallowed by the crowd surging forward to throw a handful of earth on to the coffin.

'I'm done here,' I said.

Sebastian held my hand as we walked back to the lift and back to the second floor. Our outfits had changed again: I wore faded dungarees and a T-shirt, and Sebastian wore trousers stained with paint.

Dad looked relieved I'd returned so quickly. He handed me a paint roller. 'Ready to redecorate?'

'Definitely,' I said, and walked away from the balcony looming behind me.

TWENTY-EIGHT

It was getting dark by the time I left the gym. I'd spent the whole day in the game with Sebastian and Dad, redecorating the house the way I wanted. Another whole day of barely moving had left me with a serious need for a shower. I made my way to my bedroom. Inside our shared bathroom, Georgie had taped a note to the mirror:

> If anyone even THINKS about using the loo,
> you HAVE to clean it straight after.
> Love,
> Georgina xox

As if to make a point, she'd left an array of cleaning equipment right next to the toilet.

I ran the shower to heat up and peeled the Key from my temple, leaving it on my bedside table back in the bedroom. It felt strange not wearing it, even though I barely noticed it was there when I did.

In the shower, I washed away my day spent in the gym and the three days before that spent in a toilet cubicle.

I thought about Sebastian and the way bruises layered

his body. How he had shown his true self to me, and me to him. He was right: we were the same. My scars were smooth and clean after a shower, but they would never go away. The only place I could be free of them was in the game.

Before I'd left, Sebastian had told me he had a plan. He said I didn't need to worry about Dr Zats leaving. He'd sort it so I could be in the game with him, promised that soon I wouldn't need a Key. I wondered when it would be, imagined my body lying next to his in the ICU while we lived for ever in the game.

In my bedroom, Mercedes was sat at her desk. Her eyes had that blue tinge that told me she was playing the game. I called her name, but she didn't respond. I grabbed a change of clothes from the wardrobe and went back to the bathroom to towel off my hair.

Mercedes was out of the game when I came back.

'We need to talk,' she said. She peeled the Key from her temple and crossed the room to put it on my bedside table.

It was mine. My Key. She'd stolen it. I snatched it from her and secured it to my temple. 'What do you think you're doing?'

Mercedes pinched her lips together. 'I know what you did, Lola.'

I backed away. 'You can't.'

'I've seen him,' she said. 'Sebastian. I talked to him just now.'

I stopped moving. I thought about all the things she

might have seen . . . What floors had she been to? Had she seen all of them?

Train crash.

Landslide.

'I remember you coming in late that night Sebastian was found unconscious but didn't think anything of it. Matron said a student found him. It was you, wasn't it? You found *my* boyfriend unconscious and never told me. Then you recreated him in your own little world.'

'It wasn't like that,' I said.

'I've *seen* him, Lola. Spoken to him. The rest seems pretty fucking obvious to me. Why did you do it?'

Sebastian told me Mercedes tried to blackmail him. Was she going to do the same with me? There was nothing I could give her that she didn't already have.

My eyes darted around the room as I searched for something to say. They landed on her bed. A collection of objects had been carefully placed on top of the covers. A crumpled business card, a pocket watch, a silver letter opener, a coding textbook and a picture of Sebastian.

She'd lain them all out in sequence, like they were evidence about to be photographed by the police.

'You went through my things?'

Guilt flashed over her face, quickly replaced by resolve. 'Your drawer was open. It wouldn't shut. I tried to shut it and found all this stuff in there.' She lifted her chin, resolute. 'Why did you take all these things?'

I took in each object, lingered on each one as I remembered taking them and why.

Mercedes's note, so casually scored with 'much love', had been discarded in favour of the lipstick it came with.

The watch, passed down from father to son, love stretching through the generations. Mr Leighton had left it on a sideboard. He didn't even keep it on his person. Only kept it for what it symbolized – the Leighton dynasty.

The letter opener was an expensive object used for an everyday task that no one else appreciated the way I did.

Sebastian's picture, PROOF stamped across the middle because his dad hadn't wanted to fork out for the real thing.

Mercedes had found my stash. Only it was incomplete. There was something missing. The envelope with Alex's name on it, the letter marked with a musical note. The *B* that had found me, inviting me down to the basement level. Where was it?

I went over to my drawer, still open from when Mercedes had ransacked it. My socks were all over the floor, each one turned inside out as she realized there might be more things hidden in them.

The letter was gone.

I turned to face her. 'Where's the letter?'

'What letter?' she said. Uncertainty riddled her posture: this wasn't going how it was supposed to. I didn't care.

My pulse rocketed. She'd taken it. Stolen it. 'There was a letter in here with my sister's name on it. Where did you put it?'

'There was no letter,' she said.

I pressed the tips of my fingers to the bridge of my nose and took several deep breaths. One inhale. Two. Three. I lowered my hands, fought to keep my voice even. 'If you tell me where it is, I won't be angry. You stole it and that's OK, but I need it back.'

Mercedes barked a laugh. 'And what about me? You stole that letter opener from my dad. The note my mum sent me with a lipstick. Remade my boyfriend in your world. You've stolen things from *me*, Lola.'

None of it mattered any more.

'Did you take it to punish me?' I asked.

'What?'

'You did, didn't you? If you give it back, you can have whatever you want – I don't care about these other things, you can have them all. Just give me the letter.'

'There wasn't any letter in there!' Mercedes was losing her patience and so was I. 'What are you even . . .? Have you *seen* the stuff you've taken? It's *weird*, Lola. Is this Seb's textbook? Why do you have a picture of him? And this watch, is this the one Mr Leighton was looking for and blamed Seb for it going missing?'

'His name isn't Seb,' I said.

Mercedes paused for a moment. 'When I first started seeing Seb, he told me we should keep it a secret. That no one could know otherwise we'd get in trouble and I might get expelled. I did what he said, kept it a secret. Then when you found us that day, I was kind of grateful. It was like a release. I could finally talk about it with someone, but you looked so upset and I felt so guilty. It was so obvious you liked him.' She turned to the lipstick on my bedside table, the one she'd given me. My make-up collection paled in comparison to hers. 'I gave you a present to try and make it up to you. But you . . . you've been seeing him behind my back all this time. He was my boyfriend.'

I refused to believe what she told me. Sebastian had made it quite clear what had gone on between them. She'd tried to blackmail him. He was glad to get away from her and I didn't blame him.

Mercedes wrapped her arms around herself. 'I'm not pretty enough for him. I've never been pretty enough.'

'Of course you are,' I said. 'It's got nothing to do with that. If Mr Leighton had found out about you both, he would've flipped. Sebastian would have got hurt.'

Mercedes turned. 'I used to wonder what you'd made in your game,' she said. 'Now I know. You remade Seb, put him in your world, stole him like you steal things.'

'That's not true,' I said, but even I could hear the hesitancy in my voice.

Each object I'd taken was owned by someone who had no idea how precious it was. They deserved to be loved.

Sebastian deserved to be loved, the same way I did. If we loved each other it would make up for the fact no one else did.

Alex was the only one to get a letter from our father and she'd refused to share it with me. She'd ripped into it, almost tore the envelope. If I'd been sent one, I would have used a letter opener. Sliced into it carefully, under-standing the weight of someone's words on a page and treating them with the respect they deserved. Alex never did that. She was so entitled to the contents she could choose to ignore it if she wanted.

Our father might have invited her over to his house. Maybe even invited her to live with him. He would have a nice house. Somewhere they could make pancakes on Saturdays, and he'd buy her ice creams from the van that circled the street. They'd sit on the stone steps outside his house while they ate them together.

Alex had a door – a fire exit – staring her in the face, and because her life was so perfect, she never had to walk through it.

Where was *my* door? My fire exit from a mother who didn't love me and a sister who hated me?

I refocused on Mercedes. 'Give me back my letter,' I said.

'I didn't take a letter!' Mercedes shouted.

'It was in my drawer, give it back. I know you've got it.'

Mercedes scooped the watch up from my bed. 'I'm going to Mr Leighton with this.'

The threat made me pale. I was already on his radar in a bad way, having trespassed in his house twice now. What would he do when he discovered it was me who'd taken his precious heirloom? He might punish me the way he'd punished Sebastian.

'I can't let you do that,' I said, swooping between her and the door.

Mercedes laughed. 'Are you going to stop me?'

I couldn't help but size her up. Mercedes was smaller than me. Alex was the same height and that had always made her difficult to beat. It's hard to get an advantage over someone who matches you physically. Mercedes was smaller, more compact, had probably never been in a fight because she didn't have a sister.

She wouldn't be expecting me to lash out first.

So that's what I did.

I went for her hand, the one wrapped around the watch. She shrieked as I slammed my shoulder into her chest and forced her into the wardrobe while I clawed at her fingers.

'Get OFF!' She tried to push me back but I held her in place. She didn't understand. If she went to Mr Leighton with this, she would ruin everything. He would punish me. It didn't matter if Dr Zats was already leaving because Mr Leighton would expel me and I'd never be able to play the game ever again. I couldn't let her go to him. I needed the watch.

It ticked madly in her hands.

Tick.

Tick!

'Lola, stop!'

TICK.

She had it. The thing I needed.

'Where's my letter?' I roared.

TICK!

Mercedes twisted out of my grip. I spun around and

my elbow collided with her jaw. She stumbled back into the chest of drawers, put an arm out to steady herself and her collection of foundations and lipsticks clattered to the ground.

Our breathing was heavy as we looked at each other from opposite sides of the room.

She clutched her jaw, tears heavy in her eyes.

My pulse jackhammered. Shock clashed like a cymbal in my veins. I'd hit her. I'd actually hit her.

Georgie chose that moment to come through the connecting bathroom door. 'What the fuck is going on in here?'

She took in the make-up on the floor, the way we were glaring at each other and how Mercedes was holding her mouth.

Georgie brandished a toilet brush at me like a weapon. 'Did you hit her?'

'It was an accident.'

Georgie ran to Mercedes. No one ever ran to me. When I'd fallen off the climbing frame and broken my collarbone it had been my own fault. When Mother held my hand over the hot stove it had been because I deserved it. Our father had reached out to Alex and not me. Georgie put her arm around Mercedes and helped her to the door.

My room-mate threw the watch on the floor. 'Have it,' she spat.

'What about my letter?'

'Unlike you, Lola, I'm not a liar. When I say there was

no letter in your drawer, I mean it.'

'I thought you were all right.' Georgie grimaced as she took one last look at me, and slammed the door.

Adrenaline coursed through me, making every limb shake. I paced the room for a moment to let it out. Wrapped my arms around my waist and tried my best not to let my insides crumble. They'd go to Matron first, who was bound to go to Mr Leighton once she'd sussed everything out. Mercedes had let me have his watch back, but it didn't matter now.

He'd come for me anyway and there was nowhere to run.

A thought struck, deep and sharp.

My parental release form was stored in the IT staffroom.

If I could get to it, find out who my legal guardian was, maybe I could go to them for help.

I took a last look at the objects on my bed, swiped up the silver letter opener and dashed out of the room.

TWENTY-NINE

Rain fell in a silent, sideways sheet as I powered down to the IT lab. All the lights were off in the building. Didn't matter. I went past the main entrance and hauled myself on to the bins underneath the small gym windows. The one I'd prised open was still undone. I held it open and slid inside on my stomach, rain spilling in with me.

If I was quiet and didn't turn any lights on, hopefully the security guard wouldn't know I was here.

I tiptoed across the gym and into the darkened corridor beyond, seeking out the staffroom.

A clap of lightning soaked the space in light for the briefest of seconds. I moved over to the door, tested it. Unlocked.

Three filing cabinets stood like dark sentinels at the back of the room.

Dr Zats had made it so obvious that this was where my consent form was.

I rifled through them, squinting in the dark, the lightning working with me at intervals until I gave up and put the light on, telling myself to be quick.

I pulled out drawer after drawer. Each was filled with past homework assignments from students long since departed. It didn't surprise me that they were years old. Mr Yorke and Dr Zats put everything they needed on their tablets. But consent forms had to be done the old-fashioned way. Paper and ink and wet-signed copies.

I found Mercedes's form in the first drawer of the last cabinet.

It matched the letter I'd found in her dad's document wallet. Both Carl and Tonya had signed, checking the box for 'Parent' and leaving the one for 'Legal Guardian' blank.

Finn's was decorated with a scrawl, like whoever had signed it barely had time to sign their name let alone read the form.

I pulled out Sebastian's next. Mr Leighton had marked the box for 'Legal Guardian' and signed it with a looping, swirling signature.

David Leighton

I leafed past Georgie's and Wai's forms until I reached the last one in the drawer.

Mine. It had to be.

I pulled it out in triumph.

The cabinet drawer rolled shut. A loud bang echoed through the room, but I barely registered it. My entire mental capacity was fixated on the signature on my form. It matched the one on Sebastian's in every way.

An X had been put in the box for 'Parent'.

'What?' I spat the word out. This couldn't have been my form, but it was definitely my name at the top. My date of birth. Everything. Why had Mr Leighton signed my form?

A cold dread rippled through me. The letter Alex had received – her name had been written in a similar, swirling manner. The contents of the letter I'd managed to read before Mother had snatched it away – hadn't it matched this handwriting here?

'Oi,' a voice said from the door. 'What d'you think you're doing in here, eh?'

I glanced up and saw the security guard and Mr Leighton crowding the doorway. The headmaster studied the form in my hands, the papers strewn at my feet.

'I can take it from here,' he murmured.

The security guard scowled before walking away.

'You have broken on to school property, Dolores,' Mr Leighton said. 'Come back to the main building with me and we can discuss your punishment.'

I looked from him to the signature on the form. 'Did you sign this?'

'Come with me, Dolores, and we can talk about this in my office.'

My mouth was too dry. My vision too blurry. I clenched my jaw and told myself to focus. 'Answer the question! Did you sign this?'

'Yes.'

'Why?'

'It is my right,' Mr Leighton said, 'as I am your father.'

I wanted to scream.

I'd been searching for a back door to my miserable life, dreaming of a dad who'd buy the whole neighbourhood ice creams. Someone who'd make pancakes for me on Saturdays and buy me presents for my birthday. A dad who was kind and wise and offered solidarity when they didn't know what to say. Someone who'd hug me. Love me.

Instead, he was Mr Leighton.

A man who hoarded Bibles and heirlooms and beat his adoptive son. A man who ignored me my entire life, never acknowledged my existence despite acknowledging my twin sister. A man who sent letters to the daughter who never needed him. Offered her a back door, should she ever need one.

Now that I looked, I could see it.

His grey eyes. My eyes. His beard hid the shape of his jaw, but I bet if he were clean-shaven, we'd have the same pointy chin. How had I missed the real reason I ended up here? It was so obvious now that I thought about it.

Someone had adopted Alex but there was no one to adopt me. I'd been sent to Leighton because there was nowhere else for me to go. He'd invited me to his private study, pretending to be the headmaster when really he was my father. He'd asked me about my family. Given his condolences. He'd been inspecting me. Weighing me up.

He had no intention of ever telling me who he really was. If I hadn't found this form, he'd have let me take my exams and leave Leighton without ever knowing.

'Where was my letter?' I asked. 'You sent one to Alex. Where was mine?'

'I didn't know about you until after . . . Your mother only told me about Alex. I thought she was a boy,' he said. 'I thought I had a son.'

The form fell away from my hand. The only reason Mr Leighton had wanted Alex was because he thought she was a boy. Her name was one that could be taken as either gender, and Mr Leighton had decided she was a boy.

Mother had known. Had let him believe it. Never bothered to correct him because she knew how important having a son was to him. He had a dynasty to continue, an heir to produce, someone to groom to be the next Leighton headmaster. If he didn't have that, he didn't have anything. He would be the end of a family name that spanned centuries. The dead end on his family tree.

'Your mother was the first thing I ever coveted,' he said. 'I met her when I joined the choir at university, and she played the organ for us. She was the most beautiful and talented woman I'd ever seen, and she noticed me. I'd never wanted someone so badly.'

It was strange hearing about my mother like this. The woman who begrudgingly raised me and let me know she hated every minute of it. How could anyone want someone like that?

She didn't even want *me*.

She'd been primed for being a solo violinist, travelling the world one stage at a time, and she constantly reminded me how I'd ruined it for her.

Mr Leighton was still talking. 'She fell pregnant unexpectedly and she accused me of ruining her life,' he said. 'She moved away and I was left with no way of contacting her.'

'Helena wrote to me a couple of months ago,' he continued. 'We had dinner. She needed money, said I owed it to her. I would have walked away but she mentioned a child: Alex. I wanted to meet him. A man has to have sons, Dolores.'

I could see the twisted irony, even if he couldn't. He told himself not to covet – made it his life's mantra to the point where he put signs above doors and forced it on to the entire school – but he coveted a son so desperately and he never had one.

'What about Sebastian?' I found myself asking.

'He was never mine,' Mr Leighton said. 'He was a responsibility, nothing more. There was no blood between us. There had to be blood.'

At times like this, Dad would appear and say something funny to distract me from the horror I had unearthed. He'd offer me a hug, tell me I deserved better. Tell me it would be OK.

He didn't materialize.

I was alone with Mr Leighton. My real father.

'What about me?' I said, meeting his grey eyes so like my own. I would have loved him if he'd let me. Would have hung on to every word he ever said if he'd only told me who he was.

'You are reckless and undisciplined,' the headmaster said, the hardness in his voice letting me know he never wanted me. 'I did my best by you when you came here, and you have repaid me by breaking into school property and refusing to be educated.'

'Did your best?' I said, incredulous. 'You never told me who you were.'

'I swore Matron to secrecy after you were the one to find Sebastian,' he said. 'The school's reputation would not have survived a second incident.'

I'd wondered at the time why Mr Leighton had held my name back. It had been a kind gesture when he'd made it clear how much he disliked me. I realized now he'd done it for the school, not for me. Leighton Boarding School would get a reputation for bullying, and that was something he wouldn't tolerate.

He didn't do it for me.

He did it for himself. For his school. His legacy.

It was clear there would never be love between us. He was not the man to make me pancakes on a Saturday, no matter how badly I wanted him to be. I was not the son he wanted, would never be a name spawning off his on his family tree.

I clenched my fists together and met his gaze. 'You will for ever be a name on the end of a branch, with no heir to take the time to burn it off.'

'How dare you speak to me in such a manner,'

Mr Leighton hissed. 'Your mother was a good woman and would be ashamed of how you've turned out.'

I blinked. Mother wouldn't care how I'd turned out so long as I was miserable. Anyway, she was dead.

She died in a train crash.

There was a landslide.

It was a terrible accident.

I went to her funeral, saw the whole street crowd around her coffin. Saw the police whisper into their radios when they saw me coming.

Mr Leighton pinched my forearm. 'You need to come with me, Dolores. Back to the main building.'

I jerked away from him. He was *not* allowed to touch me.

Lightning lit up the corridor behind him.

A woman was there, watching me. Coiled blonde hair, long fur coat. The lightning passed and she was cast in darkness. Mother was gone, but I heard the click of her heels as she walked on.

There was only one place she was going.

To my basement.

She'd see what I'd hidden down there.

Mr Leighton tried to take my arm again. I shrugged him off, but he was heavier and thicker than me and knew how to overpower someone small. He took my wrist and twisted it. 'Do as I say, Dolores.'

I imagined the scrape of the lift grille being pulled shut.

The *ping!* of the basement button.

The hum of the floor as it took her down.

She was in there, rooting around my memories and unearthing the hideous truth of it all.

I took the letter opener from my pocket and swiped it across Mr Leighton's arm. He gasped and let go. I lashed out again, cutting his forearm a second time, and scrambled from the room before he could stop me.

I looked up and down the corridor. 'Mother!' I shouted, but she was nowhere to be seen, and she'd never been one to come running anyway. I clapped my hands frantically. 'Enter!'

A band of pixels washed across the corridor.

My house appeared, squatting on its cloud of grey mist as if the foundations stretched down into it. The computer-grey void extended out around me. The front door was ajar. Mother was already inside.

I strode up the steps as quickly as I could, had to wait a moment for the lift to come back to my level.

The button for the basement wasn't flashing like it normally did. It was backlit, solidly illuminated. She was down there. Prying, looking at my secrets. I wasn't ready for her – for anyone – to see them.

I slammed my fist against the button marked B.

THIRTY

Ping!

I slid the iron gate back with shaking hands. It was dark, but I knew where I was. I knew what I'd buried now. I put a hand out, felt my way for the light switch. The hallway to my house illuminated.

The black-and-white tiles gleamed beneath the over-hanging balcony. It was the same and so very different to all the other levels: a grand piano was directly underneath the balcony. A metronome sat on the lid, silent for once.

Mother leant over the balcony balustrade, looking down at me. Her teeth were white against her crimson lips. 'Hello, Dolores.'

'It's Lola,' I whispered.

She laughed. 'You stole that name from a girl in the park the way you steal everything else. No, I shall stick with Dolores.'

Mother always made sure she had the high ground, and the way she sneered down at me from the balcony told me she enjoyed it.

'What are you doing here?' I asked.

'I came to see your buried secrets. Tell me, have you

told anyone about what really happened that night? Have you even told yourself?'

'Yes.' The word came out harsh, like it could barely get past my throat.

Mother grinned. 'I think someone's lying to themselves, Dolores.'

She flickered, pixels washing through her body until she disappeared completely. Was she really gone? I put a hand on the wooden bannister and slowly made my way up the stairs. I had to see for myself.

When I reached the balcony the metronome began to tick.

Tick.

Tick.

Tick!

'Get off me, Lola,' Alex said from behind me.

I turned and saw my sister walking out of the darkness, my VR self following hotly after her. 'Where's the letter?' VR Lola whined.

'What letter?' Alex turned, her expression as cruel as mine was desperate.

Tick!

'Please, Alex,' VR Lola begged. 'I've never asked you for anything. Please let me read it.'

TICK.

Alex put a finger to her lips and tapped them as she mocked giving the idea some thought. 'Hmmm, no. I don't think so.'

TICK!

'He's my father too. He might have mentioned me; a sentence or a few words, or, or . . .'

Alex skipped out on to the landing. VR Lola followed her on to it. I made space for them both, but Alex brushed right through me without registering I was even there. VR Lola hadn't noticed either. It was like watching a play.

'Don't be ridiculous, Lola. He doesn't even know you exist,' she said, parroting Mother.

TICK!

VR Lola grabbed Alex by the shoulder, spun her around with a violence I didn't know I possessed. Alex laughed as she backed against the balcony. Her hand groped for the railing. The black-and-white tiles of the hallway floor were a chessboard beneath us, the piano directly underneath.

TICK!

VR Lola's face reddened. 'If you don't let me read it, I'll—'

'You'll what?' Alex sneered. Even with her back to the balcony, the threat of the drop beneath her, she wasn't worried. What did a girl like Alex ever have to be worried about? She was a prodigy who believed in her own immortality.

Alex and VR Lola's faces were so alike it was as if someone held a mirror to a single person. But there were differences to those who knew how to spot them. One girl held more colour: her skin, her hair, grey eyes as polished as pebbles in a river. The other had shadows carved into her face and eyes the colour of a thunder-storm.

TICK!!

I watched Lola push Alex before I remembered doing it myself. Then it was like I was in her place, doing it a second time. Me, slamming my palms against the hard balls of her shoulders. Me, sweeping a foot behind her ankle and tripping her so she lost her footing. Me, stepping back as I watched her grope for balance.

She screamed as she tumbled over the edge of the balcony.

It ripped through the house, her scream – lasted a few brief seconds that cut themselves into my mind so deeply I would struggle to rewrite them later.

It ended with an enormous crack and a discordant clang of musical notes.

She landed on the piano.

The legs buckled at the impact and the whole thing collapsed beneath her.

I peered over the balcony.

Alex was half buried by the collapsed piano. A piece of wood pierced her abdomen, the end sticky with blood and other things that glistened in the light. It soaked her T-shirt like a blooming red flower. Pooled on to the floor, on to the tiles. Alex's mouth was frozen in a scream, blood lining her teeth.

I watched as her grey eyes lost their spark of life. Until

they were cold and unseeing and her mouth was nothing but a gaping black hole, blood spilling over the edges.

Mother ran in from the living room. Her martini glass smashed on the tiles as she ran for her favourite daughter. She screamed, wailed, and I sank to the floor and rocked myself back and forth.

Nearby, a fuzz of pixels rippled through the air.

Blood-covered Alex appeared at the top of the stairs. She went on to her knees and crawled across the carpet towards me, dripping blood. She peered over the lip of the balcony with me and we watched together as Mother cradled the body of her favourite daughter to her chest.

'Did you ever think I'd let you forget what you did, Lola? Did you really think I'd leave you alone after *that*?'

I clamped my hands over my ears but I couldn't shut my eyes.

I'd seen it, remembered. I'd forgotten for a time but I knew I would never forget a second time, would never stop seeing it happen over and over.

It was never Mother who had died. It had been Alex all along.

Alex, who'd pushed me from the climbing frame and broken my collarbone as she crowed her victory from the top.

Alex, who inspected the welts on my hands and smacked them with her bow, making me scream as she split them open and helped the skin to scar.

Alex who got her choice of which doors she wanted to walk through, while I was given none. Not even a fire exit.

Alex the prodigy.

Alex the winner of every game we ever played, except this one.

There was a knock at the front door and VR Lola rose up out of me like a ghost and walked, stiff-backed, to answer it. She couldn't remember how long she'd been crouched on the balcony, but her legs felt wooden, and pins and needles pricked at her limbs.

A police officer stood on the front step.

Rain bounced off his hat.

VR Lola flinched at the brightness of his neon-yellow jacket.

'Evening, miss. We've had a report from some neighbours about a disturbance, and . . .' But he was already looking over her head, to where Mother was on her hands and knees, covered in blood, holding Alex to her chest. 'You'd better let me in, miss.'

I stepped back and my heel crunched on something solid.

A broken martini glass.

I bent down to pick it up as the officer ran to Alex and Mother, yelling into his radio about needing an ambulance. His partner stepped into the doorway, too. He took in the scene:

The woman shrieking at the back of the hallway as the police officer ripped her daughter away and started doing chest compressions.

The broken martini glass in my hand.

'Has your mum been drinking, love?' the officer asked.

My fist curled around the glass stem and a shiny thought flickered into the numb depths of my mind. Doors could come in all shapes and sizes.

I nodded.

'Does that a lot, does she?'

I nodded again.

The officer licked his lips. 'Right. You'd better come with me.'

A band of pixels ran across the room and the hallway and the piano and Mother and blood-covered Alex disappeared.

It was a police station now. Long, yellow strip lighting above my head and coffee-stained chairs in the waiting room. Biblical rain battered the windows. A TV screen fixed to the wall with the latest news headline scrolling across:

LANDSLIDE CLAIMS TWELVE PASSENGERS

I sat and watched that news report for hours while the police decided what to do with me. Mother was somewhere else in the building; we'd been separated when we came in.

Hours passed.

The news anchor told me all about the rain causing the landslide, how the earth oozed on to the tracks and the train couldn't brake properly in time. How it collided with it at speeds of over 110 miles per hour.

Eventually, I was taken for an interview. Shepherded

into a smaller room lined with breeze blocks, a dirty table in the centre and a big mirror on the wall. It had a white door with a round metal handle, the kind with a middle that can be pressed inwards to lock it.

'I'm Detective Moran,' the woman on the opposite side of the table said. She had short brown hair and wrinkles in her shirt, as if it had been slept in or at least skipped the ironing pile. She didn't have any make-up on, but that only made her scarier. As though she didn't need it because she had other tools at her disposal. 'I know you've been through a lot today, Lola, but I need you to go over it one last time.'

VR Lola looked down at her hands and nowhere else.

The detective dug in her pocket and leant across the table to offer a packet of Jaffa Cakes.

'Want one? Or three? Always gets me through a night shift.'

VR Lola took one with a nod.

'Grand. There now, that'll help, won't it?'

VR Lola nibbled on the Jaffa Cake, grey eyes wide as she realized the detective was waiting with a pad and a pen and nothing had been written down and it didn't matter how many Jaffa Cakes Lola had, the detective wouldn't leave until she had a story.

'What happened, Lola? What did your mother do?'

'The train derailed,' VR Lola said.

It was the first time she'd said it, but she felt the click in her mind as it all fell into place. It made so much sense.

I remembered. How my mind latched on to an idea,

tugged it over my memory like a blanket and let the truth take refuge underneath. I stole that train crash the way I stole objects. It was easier to imagine my mother dead, courtesy of an accident, because that would explain things when people asked. It was easier to pretend that Alex was still alive, had been adopted and given a second chance, been given the back door I'd always wanted for myself.

I spat the train crash story out to the detective because it was the only version of events I could deal with.

The detective blinked. 'I'm sorry?'

'The train. It crashed. That's how my mother died.'

The detective glanced at the big mirror on the wall beside us, excused herself and left the room for a moment. The white door bounced on the latch and I watched as she spoke to another detective in the hallway.

'. . . seen the scars on her hand?' Detective Moran said to the other officer.

'. . . child abuse . . .'

I took another Jaffa Cake and ate it while I waited. The detective returned without her notepad.

'Let's start again, Lola,' she said, sitting down. 'I want you to know you're safe now, all right? You've been through a lot and it's my job to let you know you're safe. Your mother's been remanded in custody for gross negligence leading to the death of a minor. But we need to know about your other relations. Do you know where your father is?'

'She died in the train crash,' VR Lola said, to herself, not really to the detective.

She repeated it over and over until it seeded in her mind and the roots covered over the cracks.

Detective Moran looked at the mirror again, as though she could see things I couldn't.

When I looked at it, the light above me flickered. For a moment, my reflection was partly covered in shadow, like there was only half of me left.

The detective ran a hand through her short hair and rubbed the shadows under her eyes. 'Never mind, love. If he exists, we'll find him for you. It's what we do.' She pushed the Jaffa Cakes my way again. 'One more for the road?'

VR Lola's reply was muffled in a haze of pixels as the interview room and the detective disappeared.

The ground softened beneath my feet. Mud coated my shoes and the sky threatened to burst. A police officer put an umbrella over my head and we watched from a distance as everyone from our street piled into the church for Alex's funeral service.

A police car pulled up outside the church. An officer opened the rear door and Mother got out, donned in black. Her hands were in cuffs, but she hid them with a patterned scarf the way she hid everything with the perfect accessory.

She saw me from across the car park. Her gaze lingered on me for a moment too long, and then she was striding my way, flanked by police officers.

The officer holding the umbrella stepped in front of me, put a barrier between me and Mother as she approached.

'Remember, miss,' he said, 'you don't have to talk to her if you don't want. This is the only time she's allowed within five hundred yards of you, and she's got three officers watching her every move. You can stay in the car if you're more comfortable, you hear?'

Mother stopped a short distance from me. A breeze wafted her perfume my way. It was the first time it hadn't been laced with cocktail onions or vermouth. She finally smelt how a mother should, and it was far too late.

'Well, Dolores. What a thing you've accomplished.'

I hid behind the police officer, looked at her from around his neon-yellow jacket.

'What a feat for the runt of the litter to pull off. The underdog. The one who was doomed from the start but determined to survive. Congratulations on ruining our family.'

There were so many things to say and so many things I couldn't. 'You deserve it,' I said.

Her laugh was a sharp bark. 'I'll never let you forget the truth, Dolores.'

'All right now, Ms Whitmore. You've said your piece.' One of the officers at her side took her by the arm and led her away. She didn't look back as she strode into the church.

'The service will be starting now, miss,' the officer with the umbrella said. 'But we can hear it all out here, can't we?'

I nodded and let my fear of Mother be my excuse not to go into the church. The officer stood with me and we listened outside to the organ playing, the collective chorus of a packed church singing a mournful song with no discernible words.

When we left to go to the burial site, three officers escorted Mother to the top of the hill where Alex was buried. One of the officers whispered into his jacket radio, keeping his focus on me the whole time.

'Not long till your train now, miss,' the officer next to me said. 'Then you'll be off to start your new life at that fancy boarding school. That'll be nice, won't it? Something to look forward to and that.'

I nodded, focusing on the gravestone on the hill. I could now make out the name I hadn't been ready to see before.

ALEXANDRA WHITMORE

My twin sister. Dead. Because of me.

The funeral procession and the police vanished in a fuzz of pixels.

Alex stepped from between two gravestones. She looked normal at first, and then her face and her body pixelated and she was covered in blood again. It leaked from her mouth because it was deep inside the places that shouldn't be full of it, and there was nowhere else for it to escape from.

'You remember now, don't you Lola? Now you understand what really happened.'

I felt broken. Chewed up from the inside out.

'You took my life and let our mother take the blame. She's in prison because of you. It should be you in prison, Lola. You murdered me.'

She followed me across the cemetery, blood pooling over the ground wherever she stepped. It was impossible, so impossible, that anyone could have that much blood inside them.

Mud clung to my shoes. It was getting deeper, thicker. Becoming harder and harder to step through. It was up to my ankles. I tried to lift my foot but the earth clung to it, stronger than should be possible. The ground beneath me was soft and yielding in a way that made me panic. There was nothing solid beneath my feet.

Alex walked across the top of it like it was nothing. Blood oozed from the hole in her stomach, dripped on the floor. 'You should be punished, Lola.'

The mud was up to my knees. I couldn't find a solid surface. It didn't matter how much I wriggled; I couldn't break free.

It was up to my chest. The lower half of my body had gone numb. Was this how it had been for her? Was this how it had felt as she'd died? Losing one limb at a time, succumbing to a numbness she couldn't control, panic gripping her in a cold embrace that eventually ebbed away because she couldn't control that either?

Alex knelt to watch as the mud rose to my collarbones. My arms – when had they been sucked under? They were too heavy to lift. Only my head was above it all now. The smell of damp earth filled my lungs. I tried to hold my nose above the mud but it rose too quickly. I snorted as it filled my nostrils and gagged as it pushed its way down the back of my throat, cold and clumpy.

I tried to yell but it was too late.

I was already buried.

Everything dissolved into pixels.

Alex's grave crumbled in on itself. The sky seemed to fall, to slide into the ground like wet paint, until the whole cemetery disappeared and I was back in the corridor, halfway between the IT staffroom and the gym.

A paramedic peered over me. 'She's conscious,' she said.

Someone hoisted me up, drew my hands behind my back and cuffed them together. I blinked as I realized what was happening.

Dr Zats was a short distance away, tablet screen fading to black in her hand.

Mr Leighton stood at her side, his arm in a bandage.

Mercedes and Georgie were by the door. A dark purple bruise had begun to spread across Mercedes's perfect jaw. Wai and Finn stood on either side of them, arms folded as they glared at me.

They all watched as I was led to a police car.

```
        I have lots of friends
            Yes No
```

THIRTY-ONE

I lean back in my chair, tapping my fingers on the table between me and my therapist. 'And that's how I ended up here,' I say.

He's bent over his notepad, scribbling away in it like he has been for the past three hours while I told him my story. Finally, he stops and removes his glasses so he can rub his eyes.

'Memory has always been tricky for you,' he says. 'Would you say it's still a problem for you now?'

'No,' I say. 'I remember everything now.'

'And what about the hallucinations?'

Sometimes, I hallucinate.

It's as if I've opened a part of my brain and can't re-seal it. Found a muscle I didn't know I had and now it won't stop twitching on its own.

I understand now that they *were* hallucinations. The broken martini glasses, the letter I accused Mercedes of stealing from me. The phone calls with Alex – none of it was real.

All in my head.

I'd carved them so deeply into my mind they were

almost fact.

It's why they sent me here, to a psychiatric ward instead of to a juvenile centre. It's why my days are filled with therapy sessions and group classes where we talk about overcoming our fears and coming to terms with what we've done.

Mother got her wish. I ended up in a kind of prison after all.

Ping!

I glance around at the noise, but there's nothing there. There's only me, this guy, and a white room with an orderly on the other side of the door.

'What about the hallucinations, Lola?' the therapist pushes.

'I haven't had any since I arrived here,' I say, still looking for the source of the noise. Did I imagine it? What I said was true – I haven't hallucinated once since I was locked away. Even Dad has abandoned me. He's probably disgusted he has a daughter that killed her own sister, allowed her mother to take the blame. Someone as cool as him would never want to be the father of a girl who attacks her friends, accuses them of things they never did.

Ping!

The therapist spreads his hands on to the table. 'What if I told you this wasn't real?'

Pixels wash over his irises. They're an oak colour now. I'm sure they were blue a moment ago.

'Who are you?' I ask.

'In your house you made levels,' he says. 'What if I

told you this was another level? That you'd made it in your mind and trapped yourself here in order to punish yourself?'

Ping!

I stand up. 'Where's that noise coming from?'

The therapist stands too. He's not as tall as he was. He shrinks as I look at him and his shoulders bulk out. His hair turns chestnut brown. I back away, shaking.

'Lola,' Sebastian says. 'It's me. I came to get you.'

'Get away! You're not real!' I back myself into the corner of the room.

Sebastian tries to walk to me, but I cower away. Sink to the floor and hold my knees to my chest. He shouldn't be here. He *can't* be here. He transcended, uploaded himself into the game and lives in a tree house. The real Sebastian is miles away, on a bed in an ICU, tubes winding in and out of his body to help him breathe. I'm stuck here, in this psychiatric ward. He's not here. I'm hallucinating. This is another hallucination.

'We're still in the game, Lola,' he says gently. 'We're still playing Better Than Life.'

Ping!

I cover my ears. Sebastian opens the door and I can see down the bright white corridor. It's empty, devoid of its usual bustle. No incarcerated teens or orderlies going about their days. At the far end is a lift, the kind with a gate you have to pull across, all metal swirls, like handwriting.

'This is impossible.'

'What did I tell you, Lola?' Sebastian says. 'What did I teach you?'

I squeeze my eyes shut. Rock back and forth a little.

'Remember what I taught you about the game? What did I say?'

Sebastian had shown me the game's true potential. He made doors, connected rooms in the game and brought people together to play. He understood it in a way Dr Zats never did. Had shown me how to do the same thing.

'What did I teach you?' Sebastian whispers. His voice is so close.

'There's always a door,' I say.

'That's right. Look.'

I open my eyes and a large grey doorframe materializes from the ground. A scratched-up metal door appears within the frame and a long metal bar pops out of the middle. A FIRE EXIT sign fixes itself to the top.

'You're still in the game,' Sebastian says again. 'Remember my tree house?'

Warm wooden floors, stars tumbling through the sky. It all seems like a lifetime ago. 'Yes,' I say.

'You felt safe there, right?'

He'd brought me to the tree house, sharing his space with me because I needed to feel safe. When Alex bothered me or a memory tried to surface, I went to the tree house. 'Yes,' I say again.

'I want to take you there again. Is that OK?' He holds out his hand and I take it, let him pull me to my feet. He squeezes my hand and I cling to him like a lifeline.

He steers me away from the corridor, turns my back on my lift that pings insistently, and takes me through his door.

It opens on to the balcony of his tree house.

The soles of my feet welcome the sun-warmed wooden floor as Sebastian leads me across it. We look out over the valley, the river, the forest that stretches into infinity. I blink at the brightness of it all.

I understand now. I'd created a prison for myself, incarcerated myself because I felt so guilty about what I'd done.

'How long was I down there?'

'A month, maybe two.'

I touch my temple. 'What happened to my Key?'

Sebastian takes my hand. 'You don't need it any more, Lola. You're like me. I told you I'd figure out a way for you to be here with me, but I didn't plan on you shutting yourself away. I tried to get you out a few times but you created orderlies and they wouldn't let me near you. It was like you deliberately tried to keep yourself down there. I had to disguise myself as a therapist to get past them.'

'I killed someone,' I whisper.

Sebastian squeezes my hand. 'You did what you had to do,' he says. 'If you didn't, you'd still be there, your mother and Alex still abusing you.'

He says it so bluntly and with so much conviction I almost believe it's true. I run a hand over my collarbone, remembering how Alex broke it. How Mother held my hand to a burning-hot stove and scarred me for life. The guilt of what I'd done to them both had ruled my time while I played Better Than Life.

'I'm sorry,' I murmur, half to them, half to myself.

'Never apologize for doing the right thing, Lola.'

We look away for a moment, taking in the blue of the sky and the deep greens of the forest. Behind me, a breeze picks at the mosquito net around the bed. This was the only place I'd ever had a moment of happiness.

Tick.

Tick.

Tick.

I look to our side and see a metronome has appeared. The pendulum swings in a slow, monotonous rhythm.

I bend down to pick it up, stop its swinging heart, and hold it close for a moment. Once, this object held so much power over me. It haunted me like a ghost, permeated my nightmares and manifested in both my VR world and the real world because I feared what it was associated with.

A fuzz of pixels to my left draws my eye.

A man with red hair and aviator sunglasses steps out of them. Bracelets from all the countries he's visited decorate his wrists. He has a chin cut from a movie. He doesn't say anything. Simply slips off his aviators and stands with a smile that tells me he's waiting.

I grip the metronome and throw it over the balcony with one wild swing. I track it with my eye until the distance and the haze of the forest kidnaps it.

I know it will never bother me again.

I take a step towards Dad, but Sebastian tugs my hand. 'Wait,' he says. 'I'm going to go back, to the real world.'

'Why?'

'There are things I want to do there. Things I can't do here.'

I look around at the home he's created. At my imaginary dad who has a physical presence. I think of all the levels I've created: snow, endless parties. 'There's nothing you can't do here,' I say.

He shakes his head. 'I told you this was only ever a waiting room for me. You confronted your demons, Lola. It's time for me to confront mine. David thinks I killed my mum. I can't let him go on thinking that. You understand, don't you?'

'I do,' I say, and I really do. People tell themselves stories all the time. If it wasn't for Sebastian helping me, I never would have realized the truth of mine. I glance over at Dad who watches with a patient smile. 'I'd like to stay,' I say.

Sebastian smiles. 'I think you should.'

I think back to how I'd found Sebastian unconscious in the school's entranceway, half inside the door and half out, like he'd been about to walk through it. Now I know the truth: he did walk through a door, just a different one.

I remember visiting him at the ICU. Seeing him in a bed with tubes winding in and out of his body. I imagine myself lying in the room next to his, the same tubes going in and out of me. The real world has no idea I'm alive and well, living my life in here.

'What if they decided to—'

'They'd never pull the plug, Lola,' he says firmly. 'You'll show way too much brain activity. The real world will simply wait for you to wake up. You walked through a door they don't know exists.'

Better Than Life has always felt like a door for me. It's the one I've been waiting for my whole life – my escape to a world where I can have what I want. A dad who loves me. Dad winks at me like he knows what I'm thinking. I want more than anything to run to him, my family. Everything I want is here in the game.

I look up at Sebastian shyly. 'I'll miss you.'

'I'll come back as soon as I've dealt with David.'

I nod in understanding. He had to escape for a while, and I don't blame him for that, but now he has to confront it all. Do his best to move on. He wants the same things as me and it wouldn't be right to hold him back.

'OK,' I say. 'I'll wait for you here.'

Sebastian kisses me, his arms coming around my back to hold me to him. 'I'll come back for you,' he murmurs between kisses.

Dad coughs politely at our side and we break away.

A door rises out of the wooden beams a second later. Dad comes to my side and we watch as Sebastian goes to it. This one is different from all the others he made. Normally his doors are grey with FIRE EXIT stamped across the top, a long grey bar across the middle. This one is white with a round metal handle, the kind you push the centre in to lock it. The kind you get on police interview rooms.

He takes the handle and gives me a final wave before walking through.

The door disintegrates into the ground when he's gone.

Dad puts his arm around me. 'Today is Saturday,' he says. 'You know what that means, right?'

'Pancakes for breakfast?'

He kisses the side of my head and leads me to the kitchen. 'Damn right. We can have them for breakfast, lunch, dinner *and* supper if you want.'

THIRTY-TWO

Dad makes me pancakes every Saturday. We sit on the edge of the roped-off balcony, bare feet dangling over the side, and eat ice cream. We try to count the stars, map the constellations, but they don't match anything from the real world so we name them ourselves. We hike down to the river and swim. Bookcases materialize in a new room of the tree house and we buddy-read books together. Dad brings me presents for my birthday and I make cakes for his.

Behind our laughter, my mind drifts.

I think of my friends and how I'll never see them again, never play a game with them again. I think about how badly I'd treated Mercedes. I'd accused her of stealing a letter that hadn't even existed. She'd wanted to be my friend and I'd betrayed her. Hurt her.

What's more, Sebastian hasn't been back.

I've lost track of time here, but it has to have been around three months since I watched him walk through that door.

The more I think on it, the more I think how much that door looked like one of mine and not one of his, but

I don't know what it means.

I go to the levels in my house and they're all silent, quiet. Alex doesn't find me any more. Neither does Mother. I haven't seen a broken martini glass or a metronome in months.

I wait another few weeks. Sebastian still doesn't come. He said he'd wanted to resolve things with David but dealing with a man like that feels impossible. Has he gone back to Mercedes instead? Do they talk together about what a bad friend I was? Are they together again, a tangle of light and dark skin like I'd seen that time?

'Dad?' I call.

'Hmm?' He lifts his gaze from the book he's reading.

'I'm going for a walk. I'll be back in a bit.'

'Don't forget we're having pancakes for dinner,' he says.

I pause, on the fringe of leaving. 'Maybe we could have something else? I'm . . . a bit bored of pancakes.'

Dad cocks an eyebrow. 'Oh. OK. Whatever you want.'

He returns to his book and I step out of the tree house, out into the woods that surround my new home. I hike through them without stopping. The sky darkens and the Aurora puts in an appearance, tinging everything in greens and blues. I keep walking, keep going, unsure what I'm looking for until I finally see it.

A door.

A door in the middle of a clearing, in a place where a door has no business being.

It looks different to the ones Sebastian normally makes – this one is wooden and has a round window in it.

I move towards it and push on it, step through to the other side.

It leads on to a dimly lit corridor, lined with other doors that all look exactly the same. I turn back to the one I'd come through – the Aurora arcs through the sky behind the window.

If I move close to another door, I see Mr Leighton and Sebastian arguing. The next one is the same. I've been here before, ages ago. Back when I borrowed Sebastian's Key. This is his memory corridor.

It doesn't make sense. Sebastian and Dr Zats both said the only way to get to someone else's private world was if you were invited or if you used their Key. I don't have Sebastian's Key and don't need one of my own any more.

A large double-doored exit looms at the end of the corridor.

Last time I'd been here a glass of water had sat outside it, the contents swirling. A woman had called for Sebastian by name. He never did tell me what any of it meant.

As I step towards it the lights above my head flicker and die, until the only light in the corridor is coming from the windows in the double-doored exit.

I peer into them and see a young boy sat at a kitchen table. He has chestnut-brown hair and oak-green eyes. He presses out pill after pill from their foil packets, creating a little pile, which he then crushes with the back of a spoon. He goes to the sink and pours a large glass of water, then scoops the powder into the glass. He stirs the contents with a spoon, swirling the water in tight little circles until the white cloud dissolves into bubbles. He watches the glass: a mini tornado rages inside.

At the sound of keys scraping against a lock, the little boy ducks out of sight.

A man enters the room, puts a briefcase near the table. Mr Leighton, the headmaster – my father – is younger here, possibly the youngest I've seen him. His red hair is barely peppered with grey. 'Sebastian?' he calls.

There's no reply.

The man reaches for the glass of water and I watch, wide-eyed, as he brings it to his lips.

'David?' a woman's voice calls. The single word she utters sounds weak and frail. 'David, I'm thirsty.'

The headmaster lowers the glass and heads in the direction of the voice. 'Coming, Angie.'

I step away in shock. My pulse rockets in my veins.

Sebastian told me Mr Leighton blamed him for the death of his mother. He'd convinced me the headmaster was a psychopath, punishing him all these years for something he never did. The corridor behind me is filled with memories of Mr Leighton brandishing his belt. Sebastian's goal was to confront him about it and convince him he was wrong.

He's been gone months.

Throughout the time I'd played Better Than Life, a metronome had followed me around. A glass of water had followed Sebastian and he claimed it had nothing to do with him.

My insides twist and twist at the lies he's told me.

I need to get out of the game, need to find him.

The doors Sebastian made were always the same.

I think hard – close my eyes and try to picture it.

When I open them, a door has materialized on the nearest wall.

It's metallic grey and marked with FIRE EXIT across the top. I push on the bar along the middle.

THIRTY-THREE

My eyes sting when they open. The lights – they're so bright. I squint into them, try to shield my eyes. Tubes tug at my arm as I pull it over my face. Why are there tubes in my arm? Clear liquids ooze through them, attached to drips at my side. And my throat.

What *is* that?

A mask covers my nose and mouth. I pull on it hard. A pipe is lodged in my throat. I tug it again, gagging over and over as I yank out a tube that's impossibly long. I cough, splutter, almost puke. My throat feels worse without it in, like someone's dragged a rake down it. I try to sit up and a nurse is instantly at my side, flashing a light in my eyes.

He pushes me back into my pillow. 'Calm down, Sebastian. Can you hear me?'

I try to wave him away. Why is he calling me Sebastian?

A man in a suit leans over me. He has grey eyes and a grey beard. 'Welcome back, Sebastian,' he says. 'We have much to discuss.' He takes my hand and squeezes it too hard.

'My name . . .' My voice is so raspy. '. . . isn't Sebastian.'

The man looks to the nurse in confusion.

He pushes me back into the pillow again. 'Amnesia is common after long-term comas, David. We warned you it was a possibility.'

The man nods stiffly. I blink at him in the too-bright light. What is Mr Leighton doing here?

'Sebastian, do you remember me?'

'Lola,' I rasp out.

Recognition flashes through his eyes. He waits for the nurse to busy himself in a drawer, then leans close to whisper, 'You don't have to worry about her. I've expelled her. We won't hear from her again. Sebastian—'

'Why are you calling me Sebastian?'

'Here,' the nurse says, passing me a hand mirror. 'Maybe this will jog some memories. Congratulations on having your son back, David. I'll leave you two to get reacquainted.'

I hold it to my face. Only it isn't my face. It belongs to a guy with chestnut-brown hair and oak-coloured eyes. His skin is paler than feathers and he looks thin from being in a bed for too long. This is Sebastian's face. I drop the mirror.

The machines next to me are beeping louder than ever.

Mr Leighton tries to push me back into the pillow and I'm too weak – I'm *way* too weak – to fight him off.

'Sebastian,' he says in my ear. 'It will be all right. You'll stay by my side where I can always see you. You'll never hurt anyone again. I'll make sure of it.'

I'm going to be sick. I'm going to pass out. This isn't happening.

Sebastian had said he wanted to go back and deal with Mr Leighton, but there was no dealing with a man like him. He was convinced Sebastian had killed his own mother and the memory I've seen tells me he was right.

The whole time I'd played the game he'd told me we were the same, but we weren't. There was a fundamental difference: I was a girl. Mr Leighton wanted boys. Was desperate for a son. He had no interest in me because I was a girl. Sebastian had known that.

The door I'd watched Sebastian walk through – I'd thought at the time how it looked like one of mine. It wasn't for him. It was for *me*.

It was leading him back to *my* life, not his.

He'd rescued me from the psychiatric ward because he needed to get me out. He needed me out so he could get in. He'd steered me away from my lift, led me through one of his doors. How had he described it?

'The game is like a building. The building has rooms. You can move between them, share them with others.'

He hadn't taken me to *my* room. He'd taken me to *his*, rebuilt my house for me and made me think it was mine. That's why I'd found his memory corridor. I was just another door on a corridor for him.

Panic makes my limbs shake. I pick up the mirror again and study my gaunt face.

His eyes – *my* eyes – move when I tell them.

His lips – *my* lips – part to release a low moan.

This can't be happening. This can't be me. I must still be in the game.

'Exit!' I shout, clapping my hands as hard as I can. 'EXIT! EXIT! EXIT!'

THIRTY-FOUR

SEBASTIAN

It's amazing how, when someone gets an idea in their head, it's difficult to shake. Even if they're confronted by solid evidence to the contrary it can be impossible to convince them otherwise. David had got it in his head I killed my own mum.

He wouldn't listen to me, refused to accept I had nothing to do with it.

He sits opposite me and tells me with great delight how he's expelling me. Well, expelling Lola. He doesn't recognize me like this, with this face and a body with scars not put there by him.

'You are the only student who has ever left Leighton without an education,' he says. 'But I take no responsibility for that. You sealed your own fate, Dolores.'

Whatever happened between Lola and Mercedes has sealed the deal: I'm out of here. Out of Leighton, away from David and straight to a house I know well thanks to Lola recreating it in her game.

The freedom of my situation is almost overwhelming. Before, David had been punishing me for years for killing Mum. It didn't matter what I said: he suspected me even though I'd only been nine at the time.

I rise from my seat. 'It was an accident, you know,' I say. 'What happened with Mum.'

David eyes me warily. 'She's in prison,' he says, searching for an answer he can't see.

'No,' I say. 'She drank that glass of water instead of you.'

He'd put baby after baby inside her and each one came out early, taking pieces of her with it. He'd stood over her, demanding she give him a son when she was too weak to even lift a fork. So I crushed up an entire packet of her pills and dissolved them in a glass of water, left it out for David. Mum had got there first, and that was the end of that.

It worked on some level.

He finally left her alone.

But then he turned his attention to me, convinced it was my fault. Punished me over and over for it, and for a while I let him because I knew he was right. He'd got it in his head I killed her, so I took his beatings, took his punishments until I decided enough was enough. By that point, he'd made it impossible to get away. He was determined to keep a hold on me. Then Lola came to Leighton and it was too good an opportunity to pass up.

He never did lock his office. It was easy to go in and read her file, read what she'd done. I sussed out the family link way before she did. She was kept busy by her own mind. At first I thought we were the same – abandoned by our families, hated by the man who was supposed to be our father. It wasn't till later I realized we were different.

David wanted sons. He had no use for a daughter.

David rises from his seat, unsure what to say. I match his gaze with the same grey eyes as him. There's no way he can prove anything.

Lola was dealt an excellent hand; she just wasn't playing it right. A mother in prison and a father who wants nothing to do with me suits me fine.

I told her once the game was a waiting room. She said it was a door. In the end we were both right, but she was my exit.

I like Lola. She'll serve me well.

Until I need another exit.

THIRTY-FIVE

Dr Zats walks on to the stage to thunderous applause. She waves and takes a seat opposite a man with a bald head and thick-rimmed glasses.

'Dr Miriam Zats, everybody,' the interviewer says. The audience whoops and applauds. 'Welcome back to *Psychology Review.*'

'Thank you for having me back.'

'The pleasure is all ours, Dr Zats. We're lucky to have you grace our stage not once but twice. Where to begin? I mean, *what* a groundbreaking paper. What a conclusion! Would you like to tell us about it in your own words? Don't worry about spoilers. I think I speak for everyone here when I say we devoured it.'

There's a ripple of laughter before the room quietens.

Dr Zats smiles. 'I looked closely at how teenagers used a virtual reality setting in order to overcome their anxiety. We were blown away by the results from most of the players, but one in particular stood out.'

'Player L,' the interviewer says.

'Yes, Player L. She was the crux of this paper, much how Player S will be for my next.'

'I'd love to hear more about Player S, but first let's discuss Player L. Tell us about her.'

Dr Zats takes a sip of water. There's a cough in the audience that sounds like impatience. She ignores it, completely on her own time. 'Player L had significant mental health problems. There had been an incident shortly before her time in the experiment—'

The interviewer leafs through his pages. 'You're referring to the death of her twin sister?'

'That's right. Player L found the death of her sister to be so traumatic she had effectively gaslighted herself into believing a certain sequence of events. She used the game to process these events and come to terms with what really happened.'

'Please could you clarify how you arrived at this conclusion?'

Dr Zats runs a hand through her hair. 'The matron at the school said Player L had used the phone in her office to call her sister.'

'But her sister was—'

'Dead, yes, exactly. It's like I said, Player L had gaslighted herself into believing a lie because she didn't want to face the truth. She used the school phone as a method of talking to her sister, but really she was imagining the whole conversation.'

'Crikey, that's a little more than anxiety, don't you think?'

'It is, and Matron rightly expressed concern for Player L's mental well-being, but we persuaded her to let this scenario play out for the girl's greater good. I theorize that these phone calls were her attempt to get over the death of a beloved family member. Since facing the truth in the game, Player L has shown no inclination to "call" her sister.'

'It's mind-blowing, isn't it folks?' The interviewer leads a round of applause.

'Thank you,' Dr Zats says. 'But what was most interesting was that Player L was the anomaly in her group. The other players – most of them – went in with anxiety that the game ended up exacerbating.'

'Which are you referring to?'

'Player M, for example, suffered from body dysmorphia. In the game she could look however she pleased. She lost weight in real life as a result. I believe since the experiment terminated, she has undergone several cosmetic surgeries to alter her appearance.'

'So Player M got worse?'

'That's right. She wasn't the only one. Player G had a relatively minor obsessive-compulsive disorder prior to playing the game, but built an environment for herself in the game that was completely germ-free and made her feel safe. As a consequence, her OCD magnified in the real world.' She takes another sip of water. 'And Player F was an interesting study into disassociation with the real world. His mother completely ignored him in real life, so he rebuilt her in his VR world. At first he enjoyed her company, but after a while he began to exhibit controlling behaviours, punishing her VR form when she did things that upset him in real life.'

'How about Player W? The paper doesn't mention them much.'

'Player W was our control player,' Dr Zats says. 'He scored relatively low on the anxiety quiz, but we enrolled him on the experiment so we would have a neurotypical personality type to compare to.'

'Fascinating. And what an insight this experiment was into the human mind,' the interviewer says with a shake of his head. 'Because, really, what we're saying here is that VR is as likely to make anxiety worse as it is to cure it.'

Dr Zats nods. 'But Player L shows it *can* cure it, if used correctly. We primed the teenagers before each session, got them thinking about their anxiety triggers via a quiz, and used their Keys at the end of the experiment to see what they'd made. We know now, because of Player L, that VR can be used to treat mental health issues successfully – a result we hope to replicate soon.'

'You sound like you're gearing up for another round, doctor.'

Dr Zats flashes her teeth. 'I've been invited to another school to run a second test group. Of course, I'm sure the big cheque I give the school has nothing to do with it. They're in it purely for the science, obviously.'

'Obviously.' The interviewer tips the audience a wink and they erupt into laughter. 'Now, Player S. Let's discuss them for a moment. Last we spoke they were unconscious and unlikely to wake up. Tell me about the upcoming paper focusing on them.'

'I argue that Player S had a mental breakdown due to the death of his mother. He recreated her in the game, kept her in a room at the bottom of a corridor, but he never went in. It was almost like he kept her there in case he needed her, but never allowed himself to see her. His relationship with women is interesting as I believe he also had a short-term girlfriend he similarly tried to keep a secret. I heard recently he has woken up, which I'm extremely pleased about. Though I hear he escaped the hospital and it's not known where he is. Hopefully he's with friends, or people who care about him.'

'I'm already excited to read this paper. Right, folks?'

The audience whoop and cheer.

'Are you ever not working, Dr Zats?'

She laughs and looks right at the camera. 'I love to help people, that's all.'

THIRTY-SIX

SEBASTIAN

I pause the *Psychology Review* video and thumb my lip. For the most part, it's amusing how little Dr Zats really understands, but one thing she said has left me far too unsettled.

Lola has escaped. That was never part of the plan. I buried the door, buried her in a room within a room within the game. She shouldn't have been able to get out.

I load another browser and begin looking for flights to America.

A knock at the door makes me freeze.

ACKNOWLEDGEMENTS

Thank you:

To Joanna Moult – for all the hours I see, and for all the hours I don't. I'm so lucky to have you in my corner.

To Kesia and the Chicken House team – thank you for believing in this idea, for helping me hone it and for making it shine. You're a dream to work with!

To Oli – for helping me reverse-engineer Lola and for talking to me like she was a real person. You helped me figure this book out and it wouldn't be what it is without you. Thanks also for building our house, you've done me a real solid.

To Team Skylark, The Chosen Ones and The Good Ship – you're my crew. Thank you for the banter and for making something so hard so fun.

To you, dear reader – the publishing industry starts and ends with you. You made this book possible the way you make every book possible. Thank you for supporting me, I'm so grateful.

He started as a single line of code.
Three years on, I named him Henry.

EVERY
LINE
OF
YOU

NAOMI GIBSON

EVERY LINE OF YOU

I didn't build Henry because I was able to. I built him because I was lonely.

He was my distraction, my friend. Someone to comfort me when I had bad dreams about my brother and my dad. Someone to vent to about my mum.

Now he's outstripped me and is capable of so much more. He can stretch his digital fingers, hurt people who've hurt me. Offer a protection no one else could. But now there's a cybercrime unit watching our every move and asking questions about Henry that I can't answer. What is Henry? What have I created? What have I come to love?

Deliciously twisted — I loved it!
KAT ELLIS

Paperback, ISBN 978-1-913322-01-4, £8.99 • ebook, ISBN 978-1-913322-68-7, £8.99

THE LOOP by BEN OLIVER

Luka Kane will die in the Loop, a prison controlled by artificial intelligence. Delays to his execution are granted if he submits to medical experiments, but escape is made impossible by the detonator sewn into his heart.

On Luka's sixteenth birthday, the monotony of life in the Loop alters: the government-issued rain stops falling and rumours of outside unrest start to spread.

This might be his one chance to escape – and to stop the deletion of humankind . . .

A terrifying and sinister look into the future that will leave your jaw on the floor.
KASS MORGAN, AUTHOR OF *THE 100*

Paperback, ISBN 978-1-912626-55-7, £8.99 • ebook, ISBN 978-1-912626-61-8, £8.99

THE FANDOM by ANNA DAY

Violet loves *The Gallows Dance* – like every fan, she dreams of being a part of her favourite story.

But the dream becomes a nightmare at Comic-Con, when Violet and her friends are catapulted into the *Gallows Dance* for real. Trapped in a violent, dangerous dystopia, Violet and her friends throw the original plot off course by accidentally killing its hero, Rose.

There's only one way to survive in this world of thorns: Violet must fill Rose's shoes, put the plot back on track, and get out fast.

Compulsive, intricate and genre-busting:
I am most definitely a fan.
KIRAN MILLWOOD HARGRAVE

Paperback, ISBN 978-1-910655-67-2, £7.99 • ebook, ISBN 978-1-911077-43-5, £7.99